# The Do-Over

A Second Chance Romance Novel

# Julie A. Richman

*Jullie A. Richman*

Julie A. Richman
Text copyright © 2016 Julie A. Richman

This book is a work of fiction. All names, characters, locations and incidents are products of the author's imagination. Any resemblance to actual persons, living or dead, locales or events is entirely coincidental.

The Do-Over
Photo: Wander Aguiar
Model: Forrest Harrison
Cover Design: Jena Brignola
Book & eBook Design: Deena Rae @ e-BookBuilders

**ISBNs:**
 **ePub** - 978-1-942215-51-6
 **Mobi** - 978-1-942215-52-3
 **Paperback** - 978-942215-53-0

*Jullie A. Richman*

# Contents

# Other Books by Julie

*Jullie A. Richman*

For Jean and all the warriors
who have fallen... and their families
And for those who are still
fighting... and their families

*Jullie A. Richman*

"You never know when you're making a memory, they will wish that they were here together again…someday."

~ Rickie Lee Jones
Young Blood

*Jullie A. Richman*

Twenty-
Something...

*Jullie A. Richman*

# Chapter 1

To say I needed to get away would be a freaking understatement. It had been twelve months since my last vacation, and the friend I had traveled with on that trip had been so depressed about her break-up with her loser '*I don't wanna work, why don't you work, babe*' ex-boyfriend, that she refused to leave our hotel room. For seven days, she read the same copy of *People Magazine,* over and over. My vacation definitely did not end up being a holiday. So, I really was in need of this one.

As I leaned my back against the ship's railing, enjoying people watching and scouting for eligible, unattached men, my attention was drawn to him. I might have been a little more than slightly drunk, but I was mesmerized watching him and couldn't pull my eyes away.

With every step, the drink spilled all over his bare feet, soaking the frayed hem of his worn jeans. Step. Splash. Step. Splash. Step. Splash.

Coursing through my bloodstream, a third rum and something was making me feel a bit bolder than usual as I laughed at him and his inability to keep the alcohol in the plastic cup while he attempted to make his way across the windjammer's polished teak deck.

Hearing my laugh, he turned to me, and the look on his face was great, like he was trying hard to give me an angry, dirty look, but didn't quite pull it off, because he was immediately disarmed by my amused smile and slightly drunk giggle.

Instead, he ended up smiling back at me. And oh my God, it was a stop me dead in my tracks smile. And what was even more surprising, was my reaction to it. To him. I could feel the blood rush in my veins and my sharp intake of air created a small gasp. And *that* was a rare occurrence. That never happened to me.

"I'm guessing waiter is probably not in your future," I quipped.

*Laughing, "You're probably right." His voice was deep and melodious and my first thought was,* Damn, I'd love to have phone sex with him, *followed by,* three drinks and some sea air and look at you, you've turned into a perv, Tara!

His icy drink splashed all over my feet, and I could see the laughter in his eyes, saying, "Serves you right. Pun intended."

He was sexy in a non-traditional way. Not your classic good looking guy, but he had charisma, the 'It' factor. He didn't have to try hard to be cool. He was cool. The man was a chick magnet, of that, I was sure. There was something very rock 'n roll about him. A mane of wild dark curls framed his long thin face, and although he was attractive now in his 20's, this was a guy who was going to grow into his rough-hewn looks, and be his hottest in his thirties, forties, and maybe even fifties, especially if he kept his hair. Momentarily, I felt sorry for the woman in his life, who undoubtedly had to deal with her man constantly being hit on by other women.

Finding an open chaise lounge by the pool, I set my rum and whatever down on a little metal table and took a load off as I eased onto the thick blue pad. Looking up at the pitch-black sky, the taut white sails were hypnotizing, their clean lines forming perfect arcs, feeding on Pac-Man-like chunks of the night. Inhaling a deep breath of the damp sea air, I let the oxygen relax me, as my eyes acclimated to the constellations that were happily making themselves known.

Mr. Wet Feet was across the pool handing a drink to a dark-haired girl stretched out on a chaise. His girlfriend, I assumed. He didn't sit down and her body language was screaming her displeasure with him. Viewing this made me so happy that I was traveling alone. There was only one person I had to worry about – me.

And now, after three flights, a delay and nearly twenty-three hours of travel, I was finally on vacation. Sailing on an amazing 148-passenger vessel that was a hybrid between a beautifully appointed cruise ship and a grand, old tall ship. And right now, we were cutting our way through the late-night waters aided by the power of billowing sails on this windy night.

The destination, in this case, was what made the journey. Obscure little islands that the large cruise ships couldn't get to were our ports of call, and the only thing to worry about for the next week was how far my chaise lounge was from the nearest bar. Sighing, I closed my eyes as I approached that state of exhaustion where my body was screaming, *let me sleep, you evil wench,* but my mind was barreling out of control, ready for the adventure to begin.

I could hear the creak as someone sat on the chaise to my right, but didn't open my eyes to acknowledge their presence. My eyelids were just so comfortable in their current closed position.

"I don't think I've ever seen so many stars." It was that melodious voice.

Although my eyes were still closed, I could not stifle my smile. It was his pronunciation of stars that caught me off-guard. *Stahz.* This guy was from one of New York City's five boroughs. And if he continued to talk (tawk), I knew that I just might be able to pinpoint exactly where he was from – Brooklyn, Queens, The Bronx.

"You're right, you probably haven't, the light pollution on the east coast obliterates them," I responded.

"I don't live on the east coast." There was a challenge in his tone.

"No?" I finally opened my eyes and turned my head to look at him.

"No. I live in L.A.," he corrected my assumption.

Smiling, "But you're not *from* L.A.," I paused. "Queens?" Voicing my guess.

That gasp-worthy smile slowly spread across his face. "Very good."

"Okay, keep talking. Let me see if I can figure out where in Queens." I could feel my own smile matching his.

"What do you want to talk about?"

"What's your name?" I asked.

"Wes."

"Hi Wes, I'm Tara. How long have you lived in California?"

"Three years." He was succinct.

"Oh, you are going to make me work for this, aren't you?"

He nodded, but didn't utter a word.

"Favorite beach."

"Venice." The one and two-word answers were not giving me a lot to go off of.

"Is that where you live?"

He nodded and took a sip of his drink.

"Why did you move out there?"

"Business."

Sitting up in my chair, I grabbed my drink. "You'd be a great Mad Libs partner."

Looking at me over the lip of his glass, I could see the tug at the corners of his mouth and I was already aching to see that smile again.

"What kind of business are you in?"

"Apparel." Another one-word answer.

"Ah, a Garmento gone west coast rogue." I nodded and took another sip of my drink.

Caught off-guard by my usage of the popular nickname for execs and workers in New York's fashion and garment industry, Wes started to laugh at my comment, as his own sip of tropical happy juice was already headed down his throat. Abruptly, he sat up straight, coughing. Without thinking, I reached across giving him a few hearty slaps on the back.

"You really are very amusing," he coughed out the words.

"I absolutely can be, but my intent was not to kill you with laughter. Cutting the trip short would probably piss off your girlfriend."

"My girlfriend?" Wes looked startled. And then it dawned on him. "That's not my girlfriend that I'm here with. That's my sister."

"Your sister?"

"Yeah," he paused, rolling his eyes. "She booked this trip with her boyfriend, had laid out all the money and the jerk-off ditched her like two weeks ago for one of her best friends."

"Shitty boyfriend and an even shittier friend."

"Yeah, this chick is a real piece of work and he's a total loser. So, she called me and asked if I wanted to go. And even though it was last minute, this was a hard one to say no to."

"Totally. But I feel for your sister. Poor thing. She got screwed twice."

Wes laughed, "Now she has a legit reason to be a moody bitch versus just being the brat she usually is."

"Seriously, the poor girl. Cut her some slack, big bro."

He looked at me out of the corner of his eye, as if giving me a dirty look, but I knew a smile and smartass comment were on the horizon.

"Sharing a tiny cabin with a depressed chick is not my optimal idea of vacation fun," he confided and I thought, *Oh, I know that story too well.* "You're going to be seeing a lot of me on deck."

I wanted to tell him that I hoped so, but being forward with a guy I was even slightly attracted to, was way beyond my comfort zone. Had there been no attraction on my part, well, then I could have said anything. But with this guy, I could feel the spark.

"So, is that what you are doing out here tonight? Avoiding being confined in close quarters with your bummed-out sister."

Wes squinted at me. "No, silly. I'm out here so I can talk to you."

I know I blushed, even though I tried to act cool and was just glad the stiff night breeze was most likely calming the heat in my face. Momentarily, I looked away from his stare, my heart pounding. *Was I ever going to not freeze up when a guy I was attracted to flirted with me?*

"Me?" I forced a laugh, then a joke. "Good answer."

Holding out his drink to clink with mine, our glasses met halfway.

And with a smile, out of my mouth I blurted, "Forest Hills." Then, "How close am I?"

His laugh was immediate, his eyes squinting into a warm smile. "Close enough to get invited to my mother's house for dinner."

"Damn, I'm good." Smiling, I took a swig of my drink. Okay, so Wes was a Forest Hills boy.

"Let me get you another." He popped up from his seat upon hearing my *oh-so-not-ladylike* slurp at the bottom of my cup.

Watching him walk away, it was impossible not to admire his ass. While he was only of medium-tall height, he had that slim runner's build usually seen in much taller men, the kind of body that screamed adrenaline junkie. I had been trying to decide as we talked whether or not he was cute, and as I watched him getting our drinks at the bar, I realized there was no doubt the man was hot, in an unconventional kind of way. Definitely not your standard good looking or a pretty boy by any means, but the charisma and personality made him even more attractive than the hot-and-I-know-it types. And those lips. Oh, those lips. Full, with a slight sneer that killed me each time he burst into his arresting smile. I was mesmerized by them and I could feel an obsession coming on, needing to know what they tasted like, felt like against mine.

Handing me my next cold drink, I could feel my head waffle and buzz just sitting up to take the glass from him. Between exhaustion, alcohol and the energy I was feeling off Wes, I was totally intoxicated as we settled back into our chaises and the conversation took off at high speed.

*"Seriously, you were at that concert? I was there, too!"*

*"No way that is your favorite movie. Oh my God, I've seen it like forty times."*

*"You went to that camp? Do you know my cousins?"*

*"Stop! I was at the opening Mets game, too."*

*"Which weekends did you have a West Hampton share?"*

*"I was at Limelight the night Pearl Jam played. That was one of the best concerts ever."*

*"Oh I totally agree; Low is such an underrated album. I can't believe it's your favorite, too!"*

*"Get outta here. I used to work in that neighborhood, too."*

*"You seriously did not just use an obscure Bowie lyric on me."*

*"Oh my God, nobody knows that restaurant. I totally love that place. I think it's the best Tiramisu in the city."*

*"Me too, I'm following the SETI project, too. There's got to be other life in the universe."*

*"Stop! That is totally my fantasy you're describing. Get out of my head!"*

As the hours drew on, the conversation continued to gain momentum, the similarity in our lifestyles, the times we were in the exact same places and our paths could have crossed, but never did, kept mounting. It was almost miraculous that it had taken us this long to meet. Our common interests, likes and dislikes, and senses of humor were so in sync. There was never a lull in the conversation. Never a moment where I thought, "Okay, so what am I going to talk to this guy about?"

"You know we have been like one-degree of separation people our whole lives." Wes was amazed. "How did I not know you? And how is it I'm just meeting you because I filled in for some asshole on this trip?"

"This is crazy," I laughed. "We have this parallel universe thing going."

"That sounds very *Dark Shadows.*"

"Nabbed. I stole it from *Dark Shadows.*" We both laughed.

As the sun began to lighten the eastern horizon and the stars silently took their final bows, I was riding high on an energy burst. I quickly tried to search my mind for another time in my life, another conversation that had flowed like the past six hours. I came up blank. Wes and I had just shared a night, under the cover of darkness, where our energies merged. It was as if I had just met my oldest friend for the first time and we immediately had a lifetime to catch up on to bring us up to speed.

Sometimes you just click with people and become fast friends. This was similar, but much more intense, as it was laced with that unspoken male/female tension. I wasn't sure if he just took it as, *great conversation with a nice girl* or if the energy he felt matched mine. *Could a person go on this magic carpet ride alone with the individual sitting next to them experiencing a non-spellbinding, mundane experience*, I wondered? *Or was this the norm for him?* Maybe this was just how he related to people. And while I had no problem making friends and talking to people, and in most cases (except for when I really liked a guy) was very outgoing, what had just happened, was different.

Or at least it had been for me.

Getting up from his chair, Wes reached out a hand to me, leading me to the ship's railing. Side-by-side we leaned on the rail, watching the first colors of morning make their show. I could feel the heat from his body next to me and the clean scent of detergent on his tee-shirt. I wanted to bury my nose in it, letting my senses of touch and smell fill with him.

I caught Wes just looking at me. "What?" I asked. "Do I have raccoon mascara tracks or something."

He shook his head, smiling. "No. I'm just kind of tripping out about meeting you. I mean we have been in the same place at the same time like a gazillion times."

I laughed. "I know. It's crazy. And it doesn't feel like I just met you. You know?"

Bumping me with his shoulder. "Yeah, totally. That's the thing. This has kinda been like when you hear from an old friend from high school or college and you haven't talked to them in a few years and you end up talking for like two hours on the phone and it's like no time has passed."

"Yup. Exactly. I mean, it doesn't feel like I just met you."

Wes was still leaning into me and I rested my head against his shoulder as the low clouds hanging just above the horizon began their metamorphosis from ruby to pink to orange and then yellow before the sun broke the horizon. He didn't move away and we stayed like that for some time. *I don't want to be like a high school friend,* I was thinking.

After watching the sunrise, as we sailed toward some

raised dots in the distance, we walked back toward our cabins, reaching his corridor first. The moment felt rife with awkwardness. I wanted to hug him or kiss him goodbye or invite him back with me. Something. Anything. The night had been so intimate, although we'd barely physically touched. But we'd shared so many aspects of our lives, that I actually felt I'd shared more with him in our six or so hours, than I'd shared after a night of hot, crazy sex with someone.

But we didn't touch. We just said goodnight, although night was long gone, and I made my way back to my cabin, alone.

As I stretched out on the cool crisp sheets, trying to get the pillows just right and stop my mind from its high-speed voyage, I kept wondering what feelings he had just come away with, what was he thinking when his head hit the pillow in those moments before finally surrendering.

I know what I was thinking.

I liked him.

I *really, really* liked this guy.

# Chapter 2

It was nearly noon, and we were tendered off the island of Nevis, when I finally emerged from my cabin, ready to face the day, despite my rip-roaring-lack-of-proper-sleep-and-too-much-alcohol headache. The dining room, with its panoramic ocean-view windows, could only be accessed via the deck, so I had to brave the blaring sunlight to be rewarded with a seriously needed caffeine fix.

My sunglasses didn't feel dark enough or big enough the moment I stepped out onto the deck. Heavy with humidity, the sea air immediately began wreaking havoc on my irreverent freshly-washed curly hair, which gleefully frizzed with each step I took toward my first cup of Joe. I could feel the panic of bad hair settling around me like a dark cloud, ready to rob me of all my self-confidence. Face it, when your hair looks like crap, you feel like crap. I was going to need to learn to get over it quickly - at least for a week - or make my way over to the gift kiosk pronto for a baseball cap.

Breakfast was long over and the dining room was mostly empty, save for a few occupants. I assumed most guests were off the ship exploring or dining at the toney Nisbet Plantation,

one of the island's famed historical landmarks. I perused the scant self-serve pre-lunch choices trying to decide which were the least offensive.

Seating myself in a dark corner where I hoped the dim light wouldn't reveal that I looked as bad as I felt, I sat down with a steaming mug of coffee and a plate of crackers, cheese and fresh fruit, hoping to enjoy them in solitude, while I reviewed everything I'd previously highlighted in my Nevis guidebook. I had already purchased a ticket for a mid-afternoon bike tour around Charlestown, the capital, that included visiting Alexander Hamilton's birthplace and the Admiral Nelson Museum. If I caught the next tender to shore, I'd have plenty of time to walk around town on my own first.

Slam. My coffee actually sloshed in its cup, waves slamming against the porcelain shore and cresting onto the tablecloth. Looking up, I was surprised to see Wes' sister, and assumed her own coffee mug must have slipped out of her hand, causing it to land on my table with such a crash.

"Hi." I smiled at her. "You're Wes' sister."

"I know who I am." She looked at me like I was an idiot.

Trying to maintain my smile at her odd response, "Well, I'm Tara."

"You know, Wes has a girlfriend."

It was at that moment that I realized, from the glare in her squinted eyes and the thin line of her mouth, that her coffee cup probably had not slipped.

Shrugging my shoulders, my palms flipped up in the air and I know the look on my face was very clearly stating, *what the fuck?*

She went on. "He has a girlfriend in California. She's an actress. She's tall and blonde. She looks like Sharon Stone with long, straight hair. And he's crazy about her." She spit out her speech in a staccato delivery as if she'd been practicing her lines in front of the bathroom mirror until he returned at dawn. "Like totally crazy in love with her. So just stay away from my brother, because he'd never leave his girlfriend for *you*. Ever." And with that, she picked up her coffee mug and strolled across the dining room to a table clear on the other side.

*Well, alrighty then.* I took a careful sip of what remained in my coffee cup. *What the hell was that? Actress girlfriend? Sharon Stone? He'd never leave her for you. Seriously? I had just spent one night talking to the man. Ugh and Sharon Stone. Yeah, that one hurt. I was maybe Meg Ryan on a good day, cute and a little goofy. But a sex goddess. Ummm. No.*

The lack of sleep and the assault slammed me and suddenly, I had to fight back tears. But they were tears of anger. Intense anger at being assaulted for no reason. Grabbing my sunglasses off the table, I quickly covered my stinging eyes. My appetite was suddenly gone. Pushing the cheese away, I grabbed my guidebook and slipped the highlighter into the book's metal coil spine. I did not want to be in a room with this bitch and her hostile energy.

Just as I was about to get up, he walked in. His unruly curls were still wet from the shower. A faded Ramones tee-shirt clung to his chest and I closed my eyes for a moment behind my sunglasses, just knowing from the night before the scent of his laundry detergent. His beautiful full lips slowly spread into that magnificent smile that I longed to taste, and for a moment his sister's ugliness dissipated, and all felt right. This was the guy my energy soared with last night. And from the look on his face, seeing me again was a good thing. A very good thing.

And then I heard her voice, "Wes, over here." His head snapped in her direction, stopping him in his tracks, he gave me a quick wave and another smile that said, *the queen beckons,* before pivoting and heading toward her table. She moved her seat as he approached so that he had to take the chair where his back would be to me. *What a bitch.*

I sat for another moment, took a deep breath and reminded myself of the reason that I came alone – to worry about my own enjoyment and not have to worry about anyone else. This woman was a stranger to me and I was going to be damned if she was going to ruin my fantasy cruise through the Leeward and Windward Islands.

And as far as her brother, I would've loved to have every single night of the trip be a night like I had just shared with him, getting to know him and seeing where this thing could go. But if he was already involved with someone, and from his sister's missive, it was serious, then I probably didn't want to have a fling with this guy. Because to this one, I was going to get attached. I liked him. We clicked. And obviously, devil-sister had seen that. I wondered if he had said anything to her.

*Oh well, it wasn't meant to be.* I tried being philosophical, but the disappointment was welling up. The vacation had started with such a stellar first night, but by the light of day, the feel-good was rapidly dissipating and I was beginning to feel like a fool. A romantic little fool who still believed in soulmates and happy endings.

*Pffft.*

And with that, I left without a backward glance, gathered my daypack from my stateroom and took off to discover Nevis.

He was a Marine and he was big, adorable and very southern. I just wanted to touch his arm muscles. Seeing him working out in the ship's health club in the mornings was a sight to behold. It appeared that the single women on the ship had figured out his schedule and the gym became overly crowded during his workouts. Between those delectable arm muscles and a true six-pack stomach, the man was causing quite a stir. Pile on some southern charm, mix in those sweet gentleman manners, add the word Marine to that and this guy had quickly become very popular.

I'd found myself on multiple sightseeing tours with him all week long. Every time I turned around, the Marine was there, and it was a most pleasant sight, one that was helping to distract me from looking for Wes (who seemed to have disappeared) and wanting back the energy we shared the first night.

"You've gotta stop following me," the Marine teased when I was standing behind him in line at the bar.

"The view from behind is really good," I kidded back.

Why I was able to flirt with guys I wasn't into was an absolute mystery to me. Yes, the Marine was handsome and hot, but he was from rural Alabama and I was a Brooklyn girl. I had absolutely nothing in common with him. Not a single freaking thing. And yet, I could kid around and flirt with him without getting all shy and weird like I did around guys I liked.

Craning around to look at his own ass, he agreed, "Yeah, that does look pretty good."

Slapping him playfully on the biceps, "Narcissist!"

"Don't be using those big words on me, Tara. You know us rednecks don't go beyond two syllables." He smiled a dimpled smile, his blue eyes sparkling in the late afternoon sun. "What can I get you to drink?"

"I'll have whatever you're having."

A moment later he turned from the bar, handing me a plastic cup filled with what looked like a pale green Slurpee. "Margarita?" I asked and received a nod and another dimpled smile. *Oh shit, tequila,* I thought. *I'm in trouble. Deep, deep trouble.*

Taking my cup, I made my way over to a chaise, with Hunter, the Marine, following closely behind and parking on the chair next to mine. Across the deck, facing us were Wes and his evil sister, Stacy. She hadn't left his side the entire trip, except to tell me yet another time that he had a girlfriend and wasn't interested in me. And from him, I hadn't gotten much past a brief hello without her literally inserting her body between us. Baby sis possessed some serious cock-blocking skills.

A table away at dinner the night before, she talked loudly about how her brother had been pining all week for his girlfriend, the gorgeous Hollywood actress, and couldn't wait to get home to her and what a lovesick drag he was being.

After having spent a few nights hanging out on deck hoping he'd ditch his sister and show up for a reprise of the first night, I gave up. What seemed so special to me had apparently just been a pleasant conversation for him. I'd probably just made more of it in my head than it actually was – such a chick thing. With only a few days left of the trip, I felt kind of pathetic. I had one great night of conversation with some guy and there I was thinking it was *something*. Seriously pathetic. It truly was time to forget about the guy who was pining over his girlfriend and just enjoy the rest of the trip.

With only a few days left, and having thoroughly surveyed the male opportunities, I definitely knew I wasn't going to find love on this trip, which left me with only one option, some good old, mindless, hot vacation sex, which was clearly the next best thing. And there was a big, handsome Marine who appeared to be more than willing to make that aspect of my vacation a reality.

Three margaritas later, I was numb. Literally.

"I can't feel my fingertips," I shared with Hunter, shock registering on my face. We both descended into drunken laughter.

Grabbing my hand, he began to poke the end of my fingers with his nails. "Can you feel that?"

"A little, but it kind of feels like you are touching them through fabric."

His dimpled smile took on a wolfish cast, "I'd rather be touching you without fabric."

I clenched my thighs, feeling his words rather than hearing them.

"I've got to go pee," was my drunken proclamation in response. And then I laughed, "That wasn't very ladylike, was it?"

He shook his head, feigning seriousness and then whispered, "But right now I don't want to see you being ladylike at all."

With wide eyes and a giggle, I slowly stood, trying so very hard to act a whole lot less drunk than I was and announced again, "I really have to pee."

Sailing under a swift early evening breeze, the sway of the deck was making it impossible to walk straight and I continued to giggle aloud as I made my way down a stairwell. Taking a turn, I found myself in a corridor lined with cabins, but no public restrooms.

"Shit," I muttered and stopped, leaning against a wall while I tried to get my bearings.

I felt his hot breath on the back of my neck and strong arms encircle me from behind. "Lost, Little Bo Peep?" he whispered into my ear, his voice husky.

"I made a wrong turn." We both laughed.

"Hey, don't close that," he called to a cabin steward just exiting a stateroom and heading back to his towel cart.

Grabbing my hand, Hunter pulled me down the hall and into the open cabin. Pointing his hand toward the bathroom, I accepted the invitation with a nod and went flying in there.

Emerging a few minutes later, a smug-smiling Hunter was leaning against the doorframe.

"Thank you." I smiled, still trying not to act as trashed as I was feeling.

Putting his arms around me, he backed me into the bathroom and up against the wall in the open shower. His lips were on mine with a rough kiss, before I could even ask what he was doing. My first thought was how salty he tasted, as I opened my mouth for his tongue, which wasn't as aggressive as the rest of his large, muscular body that now had me pinned to the wall. His kiss was deep and surprisingly tender.

Leaving his muscular biceps, my hands slowly traced up his shoulders, enjoying the solid curvature of his muscles. It had been a total turn-on to see this guy pump some iron in the mornings. As my hands rose, his fell to the sides of my bathing suit cover-up, tugging at it and lifting it off over my head, tossing it out of the shower and onto the bathroom floor. With one hand, he reached behind his neck, yanking off his tee-shirt and baring his incredible chest. We were both now down to our bathing suits and I correctly guessed we wouldn't be in them for very long when he reached behind my neck and pulled the string, freeing my bikini top, my breasts now pressed up against the warmth of his chest.

Hunter groaned, and pinned me to the wall harder with his hips, his erection pressing into me as he ducked his head and sucked a nipple into his mouth while twisting the other nipple between his thumb and forefinger. His sounds, like gruff growls, were turning me on and I found myself panting. Leaning my head back against the wall, my sounds began to mingle with his as I lost myself to the pleasurable pain of his lips and teeth on my nipple and the pressure of one of his thighs between my legs. When he pulled his head away, I thought I was going to implode from the sudden lack of sensation and I groaned even louder.

"What do you want?" he asked with a slow smile, all sweet southern drawl.

"I want you to fuck me," My breath was coming so fast I could barely breathe the words, but I got them out, as if on a mission.

"Happy to oblige."

His bathing suit was off in a single swipe. The man definitely had moves and clearly a lot of practice perfecting them. Lifting me, he wrapped my legs around his waist and with a very smug grin lowered me, without any preamble, onto his thick, waiting cock.

"Feels good, doesn't it?" He closed his eyes and I knew he wasn't actually asking me a question.

"Oh God, yes." *Foreplay is so overrated,* was all I could think.

And then he surprised me, instead of starting to pound into me relentlessly, which is what I expected, and what I needed, he reached to the wall behind me and turned on the shower. As water started streaming over our heads, first a cold blast before turning warm, he leaned his face into mine and began to once again kiss me, but this time I was impaled on his cock.

"Are you ever going to fuck me?" I asked, biting his bottom lip.

"What do you think?"

I laughed, "It might be a pretty hard situation to get yourself out of."

And he drove up into me, slamming me into the wall with his first thrust, "Why would I ever want to?"

"I can't think of a single reason." And our lips met again under the spray of warm water as he filled me again and again, deeply pounding into me.

Hanging onto his broad shoulders, I surrendered my focus to the pleasure that was building with every thrust. This was a man who knew how to use his cock, for his pleasure and for mine, and at that moment, the only thing I cared about was coming and coming hard.

"Harder," I implored and he was all too happy to accommodate me.

"Oh yeah," was all he could say as I held on tight, my shoulders slamming the wall with each thrust.

As he was about to come, his fingers sunk into my ass cheeks, pulling them apart as he forcefully rammed me down onto him. I gasped from the depth of his penetration and sunk my teeth into his shoulder to muffle my scream.

*Holy fuck.*

With the wall literally holding us up, we stood still for a few minutes, just letting the warm flow rain over our tensed muscles. *Damn, that just made my vacation,* I thought.

Grabbing the clean towels the room steward had just left behind, we dried off. I raked my fingers through my soaking wet hair, attempting to gain some control over what resembled a dripping rat's nest in my attempt to exit the cabin without such a blatant *you've been fucked* look. I then slipped on my bathing suit cover-up and wrapped my wet bathing suit in a towel.

"I owe you a towel," I told Hunter as we readied to leave the room.

"You don't owe *me* a towel," he laughed.

"No?" I looked confused. Unlike the big cruise lines, the cabins on the windjammer did not come stocked with many towels, so they were always at a premium.

"Not my towel." He shrugged, his smile and dimples taking on a roguish appeal.

"Isn't this your cabin?"

Shaking his head slowly, I could see he was amused as my eyes widened and the situation began to dawn on me.

"We just had sex in someone else's shower?"

And we both burst out laughing.

"Oh my God, no way." I literally had tears streaming

down my cheeks; I was laughing so hard. I fucked a handsome Marine in a stranger's cabin. The story was getting better and better. My girlfriends back home were going to *love* this! This just may have been the sluttiest thing I'd ever done in my entire life. And it was hot! So freaking hot and so not me!

Hand-in-hand, we left the cabin still laughing. The steward was still in the hall servicing rooms, and Hunter dipped his head into the open cabin, "Hey chief, can we get a few more towels three cabins down in 219." At least we'd be replacing the cabin occupant's used towels with fresh ones.

Turning back into the hall, Wes was about five steps away, coming toward us. My instinctual reaction, coming straight from my heart, without the interference of my brain, was to smile. I could see the edges of his mouth twitch in response, but go no further when he saw my hand lost within Hunter's. His eyes took on a distance I knew I would not have the opportunity to traverse.

"Hi." It was out of my mouth before I could even assess the damage.

He nodded in acknowledgment, fitting of his cool, hipster-like persona, but did not speak.

And my heart just cracked. In that very instant, the joy of the shower was gone, because I knew I would have given anything and everything to have changed a meaningless hot fuck with the Marine for the chance to make love, just once, with Wes and see if our amazing connection soared physically, the way our chemistry clicked in other aspects.

When he was beyond us, I turned, praying he would walk past cabin 219 on his way back to his room. *Keep walking, Wes. Keep walking.* I said a silent prayer for him not to walk into the cabin with the wet towels strewn about the bathroom floor.

No such luck.

I had just fucked the Marine in Wes' shower.

*Jullie A. Richman*

# Chapter 3

Over the next few days, I tried making eye contact with Wes in the dining room. I didn't know why, but I felt like I owed him an apology. I attempted to catch his eye on deck. I stood behind him on line as we disembarked on Dominica. Wes was having no part of me. I'd become invisible to the guy, with the exception of a head nod here and there, and it was really bothering me. He had a girlfriend, so why should he care about who I was messing around with, right?

The Marine was off on a diving excursion and I was signed up for a day tour of Dominica that included an open-air Jeep ride, ziplining, a visit to the famed Ti Tou Gorge and finally ending at the Bubble Beach Spa, a small red rocky beach, with a spectacular view, where the water is warmed by an underground sulphur hot spring bubbling up on the shores of the Caribbean island.

There were only sixteen of us on the tour, so avoiding Wes and Stacy was difficult at best. I found myself sneaking looks at him throughout the day. He was nowhere near as handsome as the Marine and his slim frame seemed downright scrawny in comparison, but as he sat there, hidden behind his Ray-Bans, curls a luscious mess, it was his oh-so-cool attitude and pouty lips that made him so attractive to me. That, and the personality that I knew I clicked with, before it was swept away in that first morning's glare.

I wanted to be near Wes, to sit next to him in the jeep sharing the sights of the beautiful island, have him waiting as I approached the end of the zip line course. I ached for him to be standing there waiting to catch me. I wanted to fall into his arms, laughing with glee. I wanted to fuck him in his shower.

And I hated that one night, one magical night of conversation; clicking with this guy had made it impossible for me to live in the moment and just totally give myself over to the now and enjoy hot vacation sex with Hunter. What the hell was my problem? I hated that I wanted what I couldn't have. It sucked. Sitting in the back of the Jeep, I sent imaginary daggers into Stacy's nasty head. I had a hard time separating my dislike for her and my anger at myself.

Bubble Beach Spa was the last stop for the day and frankly, I just couldn't wait to get back to the boat. I'd had enough of being on this small, intimate tour with a man who was purposely ignoring me and his sister who had perfected giving me dirty looks.

Walking over to the small bar shack, I stood in line, focusing on the hanging nets and conch shells. From the corner of my eye, I noticed Stacy and another woman from the tour enter a picturesque old church across the road. Wes was not with her.

Quickly looking around, I spied him carefully walking along the large rocks that separated a small lagoon-like area from the rest of the bay. He got out to the farthest point, before stepping off the rocks and partially submerging into the water.

"Two Margaritas with salt," I told the warm-smiled

bartender, praying that he would make them fast. I needed to be in the water with those drinks before Stacy emerged from the church. *Maybe she'll stay in there for a while praying for the return of her asshole boyfriend and an STD for her former best friend.*

With drinks in hand, I made my way across the sand, leaving my flip-flops on the shore as I waded out into the lagoon. Warm bubbles from under the sand's surface tickled my feet as I made my way across to Wes. His back was to me as he stood looking across the bay toward the striking beauty of the Scott's Head peninsula, a lush, mountainous outcrop rising from the sea. Standing next to him, I held out the drink without speaking. He took it, never looking down, his Ray-Ban covered eyes still pointed in the direction of the bay.

We stood there in silence. What had happened to our instantaneous connection and our amazing flowing conversation? I willed him to say something before Stacy found us. My brain was pulling a blank and my mouth was also rendering itself useless.

"Where's your boyfriend?" he finally spoke.

"I don't have a boyfriend."

Turning to me, he lifted his sunglasses and raised his eyebrows as if to say, *really?*

"But I understand that you have a girlfriend."

"Yes. I do." He took a sip of his drink.

*What the hell is going on here?* I wondered. I didn't want it to be like this.

"Wes, I had such a great time talking to you the first night."

He nodded, a wry smile appearing on his face. "I did, too."

I wanted to tell him that I wished we'd spent more time together, that I wanted to get to know him better. I was mustering up the nerve to just put it out there, when Stacy sliced the moment to shreds.

"Can you move over." It wasn't a question, it was a demand, and it was directed at me. "Wes, I want to get a picture of you with Scott's Head behind you for Alicia."

Al-ee-see-a. Well, the girlfriend had a name. His Sharon Stone clone girlfriend was Al-ee-see-a. Ugh. Now all I could picture was the uber-adorable Alicia Silverstone from *Clueless*.

I couldn't stay in the lagoon and listen to anymore of Stacy's antics, which I knew would be put on solely for my benefit, so I headed for the shore, without even saying goodbye to Wes, leaving our conversation unfinished and me with that terrible feeling you get when things are left unresolved.

Back at the dock, there were makeshift booths set up selling crafts, jewelry, wood carvings and fresh juice drinks. As I waited for the tender to take us back to the boat, I busied myself by checking out the trinkets. Anything not to look at Wes and Stacy. She wasn't leaving his side for fear that I might get near him again.

"Lady, I have what you need." Waving her hand to draw me over, the older woman gave me a toothless smile.

"I don't know about that," I laughed.

"Your aura is silver and red. You are both sad and angry."

Yes, yes I was. But I certainly didn't want to admit that to her. "How can I be sad and angry in such a beautiful place?" I asked, rhetorically.

She shook her head. "You need to learn to communicate and forgive. It will lighten your color. Let go of the darkness. You are holding onto it."

Pulling a large plastic bag out from under the table, she rummaged through until she found what she was looking for. Before me she placed three small, colorful cloth dolls: a man, a woman and an infant.

"You will need these." She was very matter-of-fact and it was starting to creep me out.

"Do they come with pins?" I joked, trying to lighten

the moment.

Smiling her toothless grin, she shook her head. "No, you have to use your own."

Okay, now I was totally flipped out. I had been freaking kidding.

Waving my hand, "No thank you. I don't think those are for me."

"Yes, they have been waiting for you," she insisted and began loading them into a brown paper bag.

"No, really," I again began to protest.

She handed the bag to me, insisting I take it. Fumbling for my wallet, there was no way this woman was going to let me walk away without these creepy dolls.

Holding up her hand to stop me. "No. No money. They are yours. They have waited a long time for you to come." And she turned to the people who'd just stepped up to the booth, greeted them and began to show them jewelry.

Looking at the brown paper bag in my hand, I wondered if it was bad luck to throw them away, or if there was something special I needed to do to dispose of them. The last thing I wanted was bad juju following me around.

Except for a small carry-on bag, everything was packed and out in the hall, waiting to be collected by the room stewards for tomorrow morning's debarkation. Negotiating past everyone's luggage, I climbed the stairwell and walked out onto the deck. My eye immediately caught the crisp white sails billowing as they stood out in relief against the black night sky. Smiling, I couldn't help but think about watching them take on the wind on that very first night, a night that seemed liked it was a lifetime ago, not a mere seven evenings.

I had been soaring that night. High on rum and the endless possibilities presented by the adventure that lay before me as Wes and I filled hour after hour riding on the power of our converging energy, fueled by the spontaneity of our conversation and laughter and the rich, unspoken sexual tension.

Taking a moment, I now stood at the rail, watching the ship cut through the water, thinking how much I was going to miss being out on the open sea and what a crazy, emotional week it had been.

"I owed you a drink."

I jumped at the melodious sound of Wes' voice. I had been so mesmerized by the water, that I had not heard him approach.

"Thank you." I smiled and took the plastic cup. "Did you have a good trip?" I finally asked.

Leaning with his forearms on the railing, he was standing so close to me, that his arm was touching mine, and all I could focus on was the heat where our skin touched. Leaning into him slightly, I was being greedy for the contact. Why was I so obsessed with this guy? He didn't move away and my heart immediately felt lighter.

Shrugging, "I had an okay trip. My sister was truly miserable and miserable to be around." And there it was, those full, pouty lips broke into a smile, a smile I had waited days to see again.

Laughing, "I'm sorry. That's certainly no fun." Taking a sip of my drink for courage. "Your sister didn't want me near you."

He didn't look at me, his eyes remained focused on the boat's wake. Nodding, "Yeah, I know. I'm sorry, but don't take it personally. I think she invited me to help nurse her broken heart. She wanted her big brother to take care of her. So, she wasn't too keen on sharing me with anyone. And it's my sister, I owe it to her and she did pay for the trip."

His words made me feel somewhat better, but still sad that we weren't able to build upon the promise of that first night. "You're a good brother."

Maybe it was the motion of the boat, maybe it was Wes, but I thought I felt him lean into me just a little bit more and I wanted to stay like that, even though it was just a small portion of our bodies touching, I could feel the connection. The spark. And I wanted to focus on it, just a little longer. But tomorrow he would go back to L.A. and to Alicia, the actress, and although our lives seemed to be running parallel, chances were I'd never, ever see him again.

He didn't move away from me and we stood like that, leaning into one another, as if we were sharing our energy through the skin on our arms. The more I pressed into him, the more he reciprocated.

Wes Bergman was going to go down in my life as a great big what-if. And now, I'd be using our first night together as a benchmark at how comfortable and attuned to a person I wanted to be. And so I told myself, as we leaned on the railing that final night, that the reason I met Wes was to show me how I could click with a guy, and to look for that in future relationships.

Our moment, just like our first evening, was to be short lived. It wasn't long before Stacy made it out onto deck and a half-tanked, very handsy Hunter – who I had successfully avoided the rest of the week until now, came up from behind, and planted his lips on my neck. Moving away immediately, without speaking a single word, Wes never gave me another glance the rest of the evening.

I pounded on Hunter's door when he no-showed at

breakfast, we were already in port and they were about to start debarkation. He'd been so trashed the night before, that I walked him back to his room, removed his shoes and socks and placed a trash can next to the bed. He'd actually passed out several times on the walk to his cabin and now I was worried that maybe he shouldn't have been left alone.

"Hunter, open up. We've got to get off the ship soon." But there was no response from inside the cabin. "Hunter!" I banged again, but still no answer.

After getting him safely in bed, I had walked out giggling, thinking guys can sleep anywhere, but now I was a little worried about him. Maybe he wasn't okay. Putting my ear to his door, I stood very still, listening.

After a few moments, I could hear his snores and breathed a sigh of relief. I guessed when the cleaning staff came along to service his cabin, they would wake him up.

Now that I knew he was okay, I could breathe easy and get to what I had been thinking about, stressing over all morning. Saying goodbye to Wes.

The debarkation process had already begun by the time I got back on deck. Scanning the crowd, I hoped that Wes hadn't left yet. As I stood on my toes to see over people's shoulders, I tried to catch a glimpse of the front of the line, but I didn't spot Wes or Stacy anywhere. The disappointment and heaviness in my heart was startling. I wanted to say goodbye, see his magnificent smile one last time and end things on a note that left us each with the glowing memory that honored that first night.

Getting out of the departure line, I started to walk toward the front of the crowd. With each step, I began to get more and more agitated, fearing that I'd missed Wes while I was off banging on Hunter's door to make sure that he was all right.

As I reached the very front, I could see the back of his head, his dark curls and slim jean-clad body already off the ship and almost all the way down the gangway.

"Wes," I called out, but over the din of departing passengers between us, my voice was drowned out by the crowd. "Wes," I tried to yell louder, but he and Stacy were entering the port terminal. Defeated, I stood there for a few moments, fighting back tears, before getting back in line.

Fifteen minutes later I was in the terminal, but Wes and Stacy were long gone.

Just one week before, I had boarded the ship, ready for a great adventure, as I explored a group of islands I had yet to visit. One week later, I made my way back to the airport, my heart feeling oddly empty. It had been a strange trip indeed, a week where I lost my heart to one man and gave my body to another, and then left totally alone.

My flight home provided no relief, I wanted to sleep to escape the melancholy that had latched on tightly, but all I could do was look out the window.

As I blindly stared at the view above the clouds, I became distraught at the realization that I would never know what Wes' lips tasted like, and the infinite sadness I felt because of that, overwhelmed me.

Wes Bergman would always be my big *What If.*

And I wanted a do-over.

*Jullie A. Richman*

# Still Can Claim 30's... (and I'm sticking to it)

*Jullie A. Richman*

# Chapter 4

"How the hell can one person accumulate so much stuff? You really should consider facing the fact that you might be a hoarder and get some help for this." After pulling out a third salad shooter from my kitchen cabinets, Laynie Campbell's expression was somewhere between amused and a little scared.

"Well, it wasn't just one person. It was three of us. And we had more than a slight QVC addiction." I attempted to explain, but just hearing myself verbalize that, sounded really weird, even to me.

She just shook her head. "Traveling light makes for a faster getaway. It would do you good to remember that, my friend. Do you need this shit?" She pulled out an unopened box containing a vacuum plastic bag sealer.

"No, put that in with the garage sale stuff. The kitchen in the condo has half the cabinet space I have here." I looked around my spacious gourmet kitchen with the long granite countertops, custom cabinets and walk-in pantry and wondered how I was going to fit all my pots and pans into my new, beautiful, but somewhat abbreviated, condominium space.

"What do they say, the three events that can drive people to a nervous breakdown are moving, getting a divorce and changing jobs? And look at you, T, you've got one under your belt and another one in the works. Feeling crazed yet?"

Laughing, "I promise not to do the third. No changing jobs here. I love my job. I swear I would have gone insane without it this past year. And without you," I added. Pulling more late night television purchases from the cabinets, I shook my head. "Moving is seriously harder than divorce. Someday, you are going to have to drag me out of that condo kicking and screaming because I swear I'm not going to do this again. At least not until Scarlett moves me into an old age home."

"That child is going to need to take care of the two of us." *'Aunt'* Laynie was like a second, and much cooler, mother to my fourteen-year-old daughter. With her long, unnaturally red hair and slightly perverse tattoos, I'd heard from my daughter on more than one occasion, "Ugh, Mom. Why can't you be more like Aunt Laynie." That was generally followed by the perfected teen mannerisms of eye roll and hair fling.

Making her way across the kitchen to the built-in desk, she asked, "Do you need these drawers packed up, too."

"Yup. All files go into that box in the corner." I pointed at a carton.

"You are definitely a hoarder," Laynie was shaking her head as she made her way through the desk's center drawer. "Or you have some weird keychain fetish."

Laughing, "Don't throw them away. Scarlett collects keychains on all our trips." And we had traveled a lot.

"Oh great, you're turning her into a Hoarder-in-Training," she muttered, begrudgingly loading the keychains into a small box, before beginning on one of the desk's side drawers. "What the fuck are these, Tara?"

Looking up to see what she was talking about, I was surprised to see the horrified look on Laynie's pretty face. With wide eyes and a look of confusion pressing her brows into near straight lines, she repeated the question, "What the fuck are these, Tara?"

"They're poppets."

"Poppets? What the heck are poppets?" She dropped them on the desk as if they were scorching her fingers.

I laughed at her reaction.

"Please don't tell me when I go back into that drawer that I'm going to find a box of pins."

Without looking up from the cabinet I was clearing, "Then you probably don't want to go back in there."

"You're just screwing with me." Laynie went back into the drawer. "Son of a bitch. Tara, what the hell are you doing, you sicko?"

"Ooooo oooo," I began to make spooky sounds.

"Where did you get those things?" As usual, Laynie wasn't going to let it go.

"I got them years and years ago when I was in the Caribbean. Remember when I did that windjammer vacation?"

"Wow. Why did you get them and do you use them?"

Closing the cabinet, I walked over to the desk and looked down at the colorful dolls. Dominica. I had gotten them on Dominica. I remembered the old, toothless woman insisting I take them.

"No, I don't use them. But I could." I smiled. "This one could be Frank." I picked up the male doll. It did kind of resemble the ex, with its light brown hair. "And this," I picked up the baby poppet, "this could be CB."

We both laughed. CB was the nickname I'd given to the ex's new wife, Crystal. It stood for Child Bride, as she had recently turned twenty-five, nineteen years younger than the ex and less than eleven years older than our daughter,

Scarlett.

Laynie picked up the doll, "CB, I like it." She opened the plastic container with the pins.

"Oh no, what are you going to do?" The hair on the back of my neck stood up.

Laughing, "Relax Tara, I'm not going to mortally wound her or that idiot ex will be back here in a heartbeat crying on your shoulder and wanting you to make him feel better." With an evil grin, Laynie stuck the pin into the front edge of the baby doll's left foot.

"Ouch," I winced. "I think she just fell off her four-inch wedge boots." Shaking my head, I laughed and said, "And you called me a sicko."

"So, who's the third doll?" She picked up the female doll with the dark hair.

"I don't know yet." I shrugged my shoulders. "You're lucky your hair is red." She sneered at me. "Okay, back to packing. Movers will be here in a week. And if you think this is bad, wait until you see my bedroom. I swear I still have that outfit in my closet that I wore to the Green Day concert at the Garden."

Laynie "I travel light" Caldwell looked at me with pure disgust. "That was 1994, Tara." I swear I could smell the acrid taste in her mouth as she verbalized that. "If I find that in your closet, I'm taking it out to the backyard and burning it."

And she did.

"Hi Mom." Scarlett bounded into the house. "Wow, you and Aunt Laynie got a lot done today." She looked at the boxes lining the dining room wall.

"No teenage distractions," I kidded my way-too-wise

for her years fourteen-year-old. "Where's your father?" My ex, Frank, usually came in so we could at least discuss Scarlett's schedule.

"Oh, he wants you to come out to the car." She was already checking her phone for messages that might have arrived in the last nanosecond while she walked from the car to the house.

"He wants me to go out there?" I asked questioningly.

"Yeah, Crystal hurt her foot and he didn't want to leave her alone in the car." She didn't look up from her phone.

"Afraid she might get kidnapped," I muttered, the emphasis on the kid in kidnapped.

Walking out to the curb, the darkened front passenger window of Frank's S500e Mercedes slowly rolled down.

"You were hurt?" I asked his twenty-five-and-a-half-year old wife. Yes, she was still counting the halves that those of us out of our twenties strive to consciously forget. "What happened?"

"My foot just slipped out from under me and I stubbed my big toe. It was bleeding and everything." CB's dramatic delivery was almost cute. Almost. But I was too freaked out to enjoy it, thinking about Laynie stabbing the baby poppet's foot.

We'd been called bitches before, but witches would be a new one.

"Frank, don't forget you have the father/daughter dance at her school on June 16th," I reminded him yet again. I didn't feel like I could remind him enough after he blew her off on the father/daughter holiday dance, ending up with CB in Aspen and an "Oh sweetie, I totally forgot. I'll make it up to you" excuse.

We were still waiting for that make-it-up-to-you and although she tried to act like it was 'no big deal', I could tell that Scarlett was already preparing herself for the disappointment of Frank standing her up on an event that was still months away.

"Geez Tara, that's months and months away. Are you going to bring it up every single time I see you?" He had the nerve to act annoyed.

"Yes, Frank. Every single time. So, get used to it." Smiling I turned to CB, my curiosity had gotten the best of me, "So Crystal, what kind of shoes were you wearing when you stubbed your toe?"

"My new wedge boots, the ones with the open toes."

Oh my God. *I hoped she hadn't heard my gasp.* We really couldn't have done that, could we? Not for real, right?

Yes, witches we were.

# Chapter 5

At home in my new living room, even more so than I was, Laynie stretched out her long legs on the new chaise couch and took a sip of her rosé. "Are you ever going to start dating again?"

"I haven't really thought much about it," I lied. Actually, I thought about it every night when I went to bed, alone.

"Well, you should start. You are through with the move. Unpacked. There's no big stress things looming before you to stop you."

"Come on, Laynie, you, of all people, know how much I hated it and how bad I was at it in my twenties." I shuddered remembering how shy I was with guys I was attracted to. I was terrible at flirting. And if a guy I was attracted to flirted with me, I would totally clam up. "I can't even imagine it now. The available pool is smaller and sure to be even creepier."

For fifteen years, Laynie had been involved with Nils, a man twenty years older than her who lived in San Francisco. They saw one another twice a month, like clockwork, and it worked for them. Skype was their friend. "It's like he's here, except I don't have to clean up after him. There's no pee on the bathroom floor, the toilet seat is never up and he doesn't make me go to sushi restaurants I hate, three nights a week." She referenced my ex-Frank's near obsession with being seen at trendy sushi joints. "Tara, it's time. You're still young and really attractive. The younger ones are going to love you."

I had to laugh, "Yeah, that's good because the ones my age want trophy wives."

"Well fuck those Viagra-popping fools. You need a man who can satisfy you and go all night without chemicals." Pouring herself another glass of wine, she looked around my new living room, "I really like this place. These are awesome divorce-settlement digs."

And that, they were. In a new construction high-rise building in our north shore town, I was able to downsize to a beautiful condo. This new home would not be stealing any of my weekend time with yard work and Scarlett could stay in the same school, which for a fourteen-year-old girl, was the only thing that mattered. The building, one of two towers within the complex, had a full gym and a pool on the twenty-first floor and a restaurant, gourmet grocery and a liquor store located at street level. What else could anyone need?

As with many new buildings, the management company regularly hosted themed get-togethers so that residents could mingle and meet their new neighbors. It was one of many nice perks. The social aspects of the complex were really a bonus when beginning a new life.

Laynie, being Laynie, wasn't going to let it go. "Have you thought about checking out one of the singles' nights they have here? I saw a flyer posted near the elevator bank. That might be a good way to start checking out the dating scene. If they can afford to live here, then you know they at least make a good living and can keep you satiated with sushi." I smiled at her free ping at my sushi-loving ex.

"Yeah, but it's a little close for comfort," I protested.

"If it doesn't work out you still have to see that person at the mailboxes and in the pool and on really slow, torturous elevator rides."

"I'll go to the mixer with you," she offered. "If it's horrible and the men are hideous, we'll just leave and go out someplace fabulous for dinner. C'mon, Tara," she pleaded, "you really need to get back out there. You deserve a life. A happy life. And a big quaking orgasm." She smirked at her afterthought, "You know, one where there's actually someone else in the room with you."

*Bitch.* While I knew she was right, the thought of dating in my late thirties made me sick to my stomach. I could already feel the rejection and I had yet to put myself out there to be rejected. It was like bad high school fears surfacing, and at this point in my life, I really didn't want to deal with it. But Laynie was not going to let up and on some level, I knew she was right. I wanted someone in my life. Someone who gave me everything Frank never could.

A week later, with plans to meet Laynie at the Friday night aptly named *Social Singles Social,* I stood before my bedroom mirror, my seventh outfit of the night on par with one through six. Nothing looked good. My butt looked huge in all seven outfits. Size 10 was becoming snug. That's what a divorce will do to you, I rationalized. *Fuck you, Frank.* I was getting crabbier with each outfit change and the ex was as good a person as any to blame for my surly mood as my anxiety about going to the social escalated.

Going back into my beautiful new closet with the built-in dressers, my new favorite room in the house, I had the epiphany I should have had before I'd even tried on outfit #1. *Wear black.* Black skirt, black blouse, black pumps – the perfect uniform for New York chic, mourning or hiding ten pounds.

The entertainment facilities in the condo complex was the perfect space to host a small-intimate get-together in the pub rooms or a full-scale affair in the 300-person capacity ballroom. Taking over the pub and several of the salon rooms, I was shocked to see the number of singles attending the event; many of whom were new faces I hadn't previously seen on the elevators or in the gym. As the social was for residents from both towers that made up the complex, I realized the pickings might not be as slim as I had originally anticipated.

What was quite surprising was running into people I actually did know. "I had no clue you lived here." It had been a while since I had seen Scarlett's third grade teacher, Jill Presley.

"Part of my divorce settlement," she confided and I wondered how many of us there were in that very same boat.

The group's demographics were all over the place. There was a significant sixty-plus population, both male and female, who I suspected were retirees and then there was a surprisingly large group of twenty-somethings who must've had parents with big wallets or were tech industry wizards. The thirty-to-forty age group was a little sparser, but consisted of mostly females, and I felt a flash of fear as I silently prayed that this was not the place divorcees were sent to wither into sex-starved spinsters. Standing back, I assessed the room, and immediately I felt more hopeless than ever. These women were gorgeous with their perfect long tresses and trainer sculpted size 4 bodies. They all looked airbrushed, like retouched photos, with plump lips, perky boobs, spray tans and perfect, straight noses.

Yes, I was intimidated. I didn't want to be dating again and I didn't look like these women. What was wrong with just focusing on raising my wonderful teenage daughter and concentrating on a career I loved? Did I really need a man to make my life complete? No. But truth be told, in my most honest moments, when I actually let myself dream, I wanted to share my life with someone who just *got* me, someone who I could laugh with, someone who would hold me when

I cried, someone who would show up with a bunch of blue hydrangeas just because, someone who making love with was hot, passionate and yes, meaningful. Someone who knew how to get me off.

But as I looked around this room at the *retouched* beauties, the chances of ever finding someone seemed more and more like a distant little girl fantasy. And I wanted to run from this room that was feeling increasingly claustrophobic. I just wanted to run.

*Where was Laynie?* It had to already be time to leave for dinner. *Shit.* Jill was deep in a conversation with a woman she knew from yoga and I just stood there, red wine in hand, in a room full of hot cougars sipping white wine.

"Hello, Tara. Good to see you." I jumped as I hadn't seen the man approaching from behind. He looked vaguely familiar and clearly I knew him, since he knew my name.

"Hi." I smiled brightly, trying desperately to hide my *who the fuck are you* look. "I didn't know you lived here."

"I'm over in the other tower." He too was drinking white wine.

*Who the heck is he?* An inch or so shorter than me with a receding hairline and glasses, I would describe the man as being non-descript. The only thing that stood out was that he was very well-dressed. I recognized the shirt, having bought the same one for Frank for his birthday prior to the divorce. It was an Armani and this guy did not buy it from TJ Maxx. And he was wearing a gold Tag Heuer watch. *Okay, so who was he?* I culled my brain. It was right there, on the tip of my tongue, like trying to place an actor, when you know they've been on another show you've watched, but you can't figure out what character it is. I knew this guy, but I couldn't place him. *Who was he?*

Sensing my inability to recognize him, he leaned in, his Armani Gio cologne making my nose tingle with its mild and pleasant scent. "Dr. Rentsler," he whispered in my ear.

"Dr. Rentsler!" That's who he was! My dentist! "I didn't recognize you when you're not in my mouth." *Oh God, I didn't just say that to the man, did I?*

His smile was slow and predatory. "Well, we can fix that."

Sputtering, I choked on my wine. *Make a joke,* I screamed at myself. But my mind drew a blank.

Her bright red hair caught my eye and I waved, praying her long legs would lead her across the room quickly.

"Finally," she sighed. "Crosstown traffic was hideous tonight."

Saved! Dr. Rentsler's height was perfectly synchronized for him to have a direct eye-view of Laynie's braless breasts on full display under a colorful sheer blouse. And like a puppy easily distracted, the man moved on to the next possibility.

"Tara, are you not going to introduce me to your beautiful friend?"

*No, pervert, I'm not* was my first thought. "Laynie, meet my dentist, Dr. Rentsler."

"Phillip, call me Phillip," he warmly addressed her breasts.

Smiling, what I know is her fake closed-mouth smile, I couldn't tell if she was just grossed out by this boob talker or merely didn't want him to see her teeth for fear that he'd try to persuade her to let him into her mouth.

"I need a drink," she announced, leaving me alone with my lecherous dentist.

"And I need to find the ladies' room, excuse me." I turned from Dr. Rentsler before he could start talking to my chest, too.

The first restroom I reached was the private one designated for families. Finding it unlocked, I slipped inside. Turning to lock the door behind me, I let out a surprised and alarmed, "Ahhh," that wasn't loud enough to be a scream. Dr. Rentsler was in there with me and he was locking the door.

"What are you doing in here?" My anger overtook my fear, mainly because I was probably stronger than him.

"I've come to show you my favorite probe," he offered with a smug smirk.

"Are you freaking kidding me?"

His hand was on his zipper, "It's not like I haven't been in your mouth before, Tara."

That was it. The jerk may have thought he was being amusing, or even sexy, but I was beyond pissed. He had crossed a boundary. With my face just inches from his, I let loose. "Pull that zipper down and you'll be singing in the Vienna Boys' Choir, doc."

His eyes widened and his pupils dilated. I couldn't tell if it was fear or if he was turned on by my full-blown rant. I prayed it wasn't the latter.

I wasn't done with him. "And to top that off, now I have to find a new dentist and you know, I have extreme dental phobia from being drilled without Novocain as a child." I was more pissed about that than anything else. "Now move out of my way."

He stepped away from the door without uttering another word.

As I was walking through the door, I stopped, then turned around. Pointing a finger at the man, I hissed, "And don't you come walking out of here in two seconds to make it look like we had sex in the bathroom. You stay in there for ten minutes." I had just put my former dentist in timeout.

Laynie was approaching as I pulled the bathroom door shut behind me and cocked her head to the side with a questioning look.

"Don't ask." I practically growled at her. "You made me come to this thing and now you owe me dinner. A really, good dinner. One that ends in chocolate and has lots of red wine."

Quickly, I looked around for Jill to see if she'd like to

join us, but she had apparently already left. As we walked out of the salon room, I was still muttering. "I can't believe I have to find a new dentist now."

My post-divorce dating life had officially begun.

# Chapter 6

The only positive to come out of the condo's social was seeing all my gorgeous, fit neighbors, who served as the perfect incentive to get my butt out of bed an hour earlier each morning and drag myself to the gym, coffee or no coffee. Located right in my building, a mere elevator ride away, I had no excuse not to be going on a regular basis. I just needed to build it into my daily schedule and commit to it. My not-quite-size-ten body, standing out amongst a sea of fours, was enough shame-motivation to get me there. I didn't need to be a size four, but if my tens fit comfortably again, I knew that would be a huge boost to my self-esteem. And if somehow I ended up a size eight, well, watch out dating world, Tara might just learn how to flirt.

The treadmill next to Jill Presley was open and I parked my water bottle, phone, headphones and a towel in the compartments on the machine's console.

"Did you have fun at the social last week?" she spoke with full control of her breath and had barely broken a sweat as she maintained a steady pace.

"Ugh, no." I began my warm-up. "Had a weird

experience. I hope it's not a foreshadowing of my dating future. I looked for you a little bit later on in the evening, but you were already gone."

"Yeah, I'm on the social committee, so I just stayed a little while to make sure everything was in place." Increasing her speed, Jill's easy strides remained steady. "How long have you been divorced?"

"About a year and a half," I choked out, already out of breath.

"Five years for me." Jill's smile was the tell-all. She did look happy. And healthier than when she'd been Scarlett's teacher. She now had a great, short pixie cut, which only women with gorgeous bone structure can pull off, her weight was down by at least twenty-five pounds and she was wearing the cutest pink tie-dye sports bra with matching Capri leggings. Suddenly my RISD Nads tee-shirt and Nike running shorts seemed like a poor choice, sort of like showing up for a dinner in jeans to find all the other women in cocktail dresses.

"That's such a cute outfit," I couldn't help but comment.

"Thanks. It's C-Kicker. This brand is a Godsend. I can't even tell you how much I love it."

I wondered if it was a Godsend because it wicked away moisture or looked cute and gave her a great ass. Describing clothes as a Godsend seemed a little odd.

The look on my face must've betrayed my thoughts.

"C-Kicker is a line of sports clothing for women who have had breast cancer. They've designed it for post-surgery comfort and for women who have prosthetics. They've really thought through all the details with this line. I know they've worked with actual breast cancer patients to design it," she explained.

Losing my stride, I stumbled for a moment, fighting to stay upright and get my feet planted correctly back on the running deck. Jill's news made my stomach muscles cramp, as I literally felt sick for her.

"I just celebrated three-years cancer free," she delivered the news with a smile.

"Oh my God, Jill, I had no idea, but I'm so glad you are doing well now. Did this all happen after your divorce?"

"No, the initial diagnosis, lumpectomy, and first round of radiation and chemo happened prior to the divorce."

I was floored. Did this douche actually leave his wife when she was in the throes of dealing with breast cancer? And I thought Frank had been a dick. He was a prince compared to this creep.

"Yeah, but we'd been disintegrating for a long time before my diagnosis," she explained. "He was around through the first round, but his demeanor and negativity were just not what I needed when I was fighting for my life."

As her words sunk in, I realized just how fortunate I was. Perspective. Get some, Tara.

"Divorcing Lee and freeing myself from a situation that was making me miserable ended up being an incredible turning point for me. Just a few months after the divorce was finalized, I met the most wonderful man. His name is Ben and we were only together for few months when I had a recurrence and went through my mastectomy." She slowed the speed on her machine to begin her cool down.

"Oh Jill, I am so sorry."

"It was a rough time. But Ben was my rock through it and has been ever since. The man is my biggest cheerleader."

And then, as if reading my thoughts, she smeared the icing on the cake.

"There are still some good ones out there, Tara, and I think we make better choices the second time around. We're smarter now. We know what to look for and what we want."

"And we know when to run," I piped in.

"Exactly. So, even if the social we had here didn't work for you, just get yourself out there. Get online, join clubs, download the dating apps, put yourself in places where you can meet men with similar interests. I'm living proof that there are still great guys to be found." Jill took a swig from her water bottle. "This is just the beginning for you, Tara."

I didn't realize I really needed to hear those words.

# Chapter 7

I'd only agreed to meet him for coffee. My last three dates had some special kind of language processing disorder where the words, "Let me take you to dinner," actually meant, "You owe me sex." I figured a cup of coffee wouldn't even be worth a blow job. Especially since I'd only ordered a small drip. No caramel, no whipped cream, no nothing. Just a small cup of drip with a splash of half and half. No calluses on my knees for a simple cup of coffee, right?

An IT guy for a large law firm in the city, this guy was genuinely handsome. Really, really handsome, in a clean-cut Preppie kind of way. Unfortunately, his hot quotient was the converse and that was directly tied into his personality, or lack thereof. I was fighting for topics where we could get past two exchanges before the dead air moved back in and claimed the moment. And he didn't get my jokes. Not a good thing. Not a good thing at all.

I had spent hours filling out the PerfectDate.com questionnaire with both Laynie and Scarlett looking over my shoulders.

✔ Like poached eggs soft, ~~medium~~, ~~hard~~ (Seriously? Is this guy going to cook for me?)

✔ Prefer sitcoms over drama (Already picturing a couch potato moving in)

✔ Religion is ~~not at all~~, slightly, ~~somewhat~~, ~~extremely~~ important to me

✔ I like a man who ~~acquiesces~~, stands up to me, ~~dominates me~~

✔ I enjoy trying new 5 star restaurants over casual dining (If he thinks chains are gourmet, we've got problems)

✔ My style is to ~~cater to a man~~, share responsibilities, ~~sit back and be pampered~~

I made Scarlett leave the room for the intimate questions which were surprisingly specific.

✔ Will you perform oral sex on a man?
  o If yes,
  • Do you swallow
  • Spit
  • Complete the act prior to your partner's orgasm
  • Depends (Okay, I'll go with this nice noncommittal answer)

✔ Please check your three (3) favorite sexual positions:
  • Missionary
  • Doggie (did they really type that?)
  • From behind on all fours
  • From behind bent over
  o Will you allow your partner to insert a finger in your anus while in this position? (Hell yes!)
  • On top
  • Facing partner
  • Breasts fondled
  • Facing away
  ◊ Anal

- On Back
- On All Fours

*Would all of the above and then some be a bad answer,* I wondered.

"A finger up your ass. My little Tara is a kinkpot. Who knew?" Laynie teased as she poured herself another glass of red wine.

"Keep that up, bestie, and I'm going to send you to Scarlett's room and you won't get to see the rest of my answers. And we haven't even gotten to the sex toys section yet." I, too, poured myself another glass of red wine. We still had four more pages of sex questions to get through.

Nodding as she regarded me through slitted eyes, Laynie laughed. "Now the truth will finally come out about the nipple clamps."

Nearly spitting my wine on the keyboard, I threatened, "Keep it up and I'll pull that third doll out of the drawer and dye her hair red."

Sitting back in her chair and crossing her long yoga pants clad legs, Laynie let me finish the questionnaire in silence.

So, after hours of answering their probing questions, pun so intended, I wondered two things as I sat across from this man, who clearly was not a love connection, just as my past four dates had not been. The first thing that vexed me was: *Do they even use the data they collect* and *How do these guys perfect their online persona (and phone, too) so well and turn into duds when you meet them in the flesh?* Were they all taking some how-not-to-come-across-like-a-loser-before-they-meet-you course?

"I have an early morning tomorrow, Todd," I told my date.

"Let me walk you to your car."

As he took our garbage from the table to the trash, I

shook my head as I admired his tall, well-built frame. What a waste. His build was naturally athletic and I'm sure he turned a lot of women's heads. It had just been such a struggle all night to keep the conversation moving. I was exhausted. Talking to another person should never be that much work.

"Nice car," he commented, running his hand reverently down the hood as if he were stroking the leg of a woman in fine silk stockings. It was kind of creepy.

"Thanks. I like it." Actually, I loved my Audi S5, but I was afraid if I told him that, he'd divulge some strange car kink and I'd never be able to look at my car the same way again.

"Powerful engine," he continued to stroke the car.

"Oh yeah, it's a beast." I hit my clicker to unlock the door. Todd's hand was on the handle to open it and I thought, *even though he is not my type, what nice manners he has.* That thought was fleeting as I quickly found myself pinned up against the car with Todd alarmingly close.

"Have you had sex in it yet?" His smile was a leer.

Alarms were starting to sound in my head as the man's hand slipped around my hip and up the back of my skirt, pulling me into him and his sizable erection. The car really had turned him on!

"I'd like to be the one to help you steal your car's virginity." His eyes and smile told me this guy was dead serious, like together we were going to be partners in committing some forbidden vehicular sex crime.

"If you don't take your hand off my butt and back off, I'm going to hit the panic button on my key fob."

Not moving, the man actually looked offended that I was rejecting his proposition.

"Now!" There was no doubt in my tone that I was not joking.

Removing his hand, Todd backed away enough for me to open the door, slip in and lock it. Without even bothering to buckle my seatbelt, my foot firmly bore down on the accelerator, harnessing the full capacity of 333 horsepower to get the hell out of there and leave that jerk in the dust.

*Where the hell did he get off?* Ugh. He was getting off on my car.

"I'll take care of you, baby." I patted my steering wheel before cutting across three lanes to make a last-minute right turn. What the hell was it with the men I was dating? Was I giving off some pheromone or something? My last date propositioned our barely legal waitress to have a three-way with us after trying to look down her shirt the whole night.

One more block, and the landmark I desperately needed to see was lighting up the night sky. Appearing like a beacon guiding me to safety was the sign for the gas station in my grocery store's parking lot. And yes, it had a 24-hour car wash.

"Don't worry, baby," I said to my car. "I'm going to get that nasty man's grubby germs off you and we'll both feel so much better." Pulling up to the automated pay station, I chose the Super Deluxe with undercarriage cleaning, needing every inch of the exterior of my car scrubbed. Not only did he violate me, the man violated my car. He touched her and she gave him a hard-on. Gross!

As the water, soap and cleansing strips repeatedly pelted the car, obscuring my view out the window, I reveled at being hidden in my own bubble under the bubbles, if only for a few minutes. I had truly forgotten, or maybe just repressed, how hard it was to date. And it was in that moment that I decided to get off the websites, delete the apps and just let it happen organically. If I met someone, great. If not, so what – no big deal. I would be just fine alone. Actually, it would be preferable to suffering through another one of these dates.

Ten minutes later I was home. As I rode the empty elevator up to my floor, I was relieved that Scarlett was at her father's for the night and that I wouldn't have to recap my date for her, leaving out the only interesting part of the evening. Peeling off my clothes and leaving a trail in my wake that led to the bathroom, I couldn't get into the shower fast enough. Standing under a stream of hot water with soap bubbles running down my arms and legs, I treated myself to a cleansing similar to the Audi's, including *my* undercarriage where that creep had planted his unwanted hand.

"Oh my God," I said to no one and began laughing. "This is my life." I continued to chuckle as I mentally recapped my new disastrous dating experiences. It was indeed amusing and I knew I'd be cracking up when I recounted it to Laynie. The only thing I could do was laugh and move on.

As I crawled under my covers, I checked my email one last time. There was a message there from a man from one of the dating sites. Skimming it, he looked good on paper, but they all did. Exec, 42, divorced, tired of the dating scene, hates sushi (Okay, that was a plus). Basically, he had the same generic stuff as everyone else, but what caught my eye was his picture. If this picture was real, then this guy was one of the hottest men I'd ever laid eyes on. He looked like he could be Rob Lowe's brother. Literally, more than Rob Lowe's brother did. What a hottie!

Sorry. Your timing is off. I decided tonight that I am done with internet dating, **I responded.**

**His reply was almost instantaneous.** That's only because you haven't met me.

**LOL… yeah, yeah, yeah…** I messaged back and surprised myself when I realized I was smiling.

**A minute later my private message inbox dinged.** Really, don't give up yet. At least not until after we've met.

**Sorry, this dating thing is just not working for me.** But as I looked at his picture, I felt totally shallow for wanting to look into the blue eyes of this dark-haired god across a pillow upon waking. **Is this your real picture?** I boldly asked.

**Yes. And it's pretty recent. It was shot a few months**

ago at Bethpage Black.

☺ **I recognized the clubhouse.** I was so proud of myself.

**Do you golf?**

**No. It was the ex's favorite public course.**

☺ **It's everyone's favorite public course. How long are you divorced?**

**Fairly recently. Just coming on two years. How about you?**

**I was married for a very short time, a long time ago.**

**Do you have kids?** I asked.

**No. You?**

**Yes, I have a teenage daughter.**

**Do you have custody?**

**Joint.**

**How's it working out? Has she adjusted?**

I was amazed this man was actually asking me about my kid. None of the others were at all interested in knowing about her or how she was doing in the wake of a divorce. **For the most part, yes. She's a very go with the flow kind of kid.**

**That's good. At least that's one stressful thing you don't have to worry too much about. I'm Matthew, btw.**

**Hi Matthew, I'm Carissa.** The minute I typed it, I asked myself *why*? *Why did you do that?* I hadn't lied to any of the other men, but I also hadn't been so attracted to any of the others. Was my attraction to his photo making me want to protect myself? I really couldn't figure out why I had made up the name. Maybe I needed to stay anonymous a little longer after tonight's debacle of a date.

**So, you've hit a string of bad dates, Carissa?**

**You could say that.** Understatement.

**I'd like to help you erase those bad memories.** I'll bet you would, I snickered.

**Yeah, well. I need to think about that.**

**Think about this… I showed up tonight, just at the right time. It's a sign.**

**You're a smooth one, huh!**

**LOL… honestly, I'm pretty hairy.**

Laughing at his joke, I looked at his picture again. He was very masculine looking and I could see the 5 o'clock shadow beginning. Despite that, he was very well groomed. With almost black hair and steel blue eyes, the man was striking. *What the heck was a guy like this doing on a dating site?*

*Damn*, I had just made this decision not to internet date and the cutest guy on the web shows up trying to get me to change my mind. Somehow, I had the distinct feeling he was going to be persistent.

**I need to get some sleep, Matthew. It was nice talking to you. You were definitely the highlight of my evening.**

**Same here, Carissa. I look forward to speaking again. I hope I get the chance.**

As I plugged my phone in to charge and set it down on the night table, I wondered if maybe one more shot at this dating thing could be the one that turned it all around. What if I walked away from the chance to meet the guy I was supposed to be with?

Drifting off to sleep, I was already hoping that when I woke, waiting for me would be a personal message from Matthew, continuing our conversation.

One of the things I'd learned in life was to expect it when you least expect it and after my most unpleasant date, ending the evening on such a pleasant note was highly unexpected.

# Chapter 8

Addiction is so easy to understand was my first thought upon waking. My hand was already reaching for my phone before my eyelids were fully opened. With a flick of my finger my PerfectDate.com account page appeared and the little red heart glowed, indicating messages in my chat threads. *Yes!* Now I just hoped that there was one from Matthew.

Lightly touching the heart, the next screen popped up. There were messages from three people. Someone named Hike4Food, Todd the car rapist, and Rob Lowe's look-a-like, Matthew. *Yes!*

**Brunch**

Just one word. Not even a question mark. *Was the man inviting me out? Hmmm, how to respond?*

**It's one of my four favorite meals ?** I smiled as I typed.

Taking my phone with me down the hall to the kitchen, I placed it on the granite countertop as I hit the coffeemaker's on-switch and stood twirling the K-cup rack, feeling extreme ambivalence at my uninspired choices. I wanted a large Americano with an extra shot of espresso; taste the rich, full flavor seconds before it coursed through my veins, blasting me off like a capsule of focused energy.

As soon as it dinged, my hand was poised to grab the phone.

**What do you like to eat?**

I rolled my eyes at the early morning double-entendre. Dude, I need my caffeine first. **For brunch?**

**Yes, for brunch.**

**The olives in a Bloody Mary. Oh, and the celery and shrimp, too.**

**I have the perfect place for us?**

Bwahahaha, I'll bet you do. **Your bed?**

**If you insist.**

**Forget it, you haven't fed me yet.**

**Well, I WAS trying to get you to brunch first at a place that has a build your own Bloody Mary bar.**

**Hmm, that does sound promising. Do they have shrimp?** My mouth was watering as I imagined the peppery concoction.

**As a matter of fact, they have JUMBO shrimp.**

**Jumbo shrimp sounds like an oxymoron to me. You online guys, hmmph, exaggerating the size of everything!**

**I just spit coffee on my keyboard, Carissa.**

**A man who spits. Hmmm, is it okay if I spit then?** Where was this crazy, forward woman coming from? I was so bold and ballsy, hidden and untouchable behind the electronic wizard's curtain. I was no less a sham than Oz's wizard. I just had better equipment, a rose-gold MacBook and the latest iPhone.

**I love your sense of humor.**

**Thanks.**

**So, come meet me. It's still an acceptable brunch hour.**

**We just met last night. Too fast for me.**

**Brunch next weekend.**

My immediate thought was that I had Scarlett home next weekend, **How about this,** I proposed, **if we are still talking in two weeks, and feel so inclined, we can meet for brunch then.**

**Two weeks???? You know that's forever in internet years. We could own a house together by then.**

**LOL and be broken up** I added.

**I have a feeling you are worth the wait.**

Rob Lowe's look-a-like had me smiling and sighing and by the time we wished one another a good day, I was telling myself that I deserved this, after living through a cheating husband and being "turned in" for a younger model with perkier tits and an ass that was still too young to suffer the devastating effects of gravity, that handsome, amusing Matthew was my due. If he really looked like his pictures and was as normal as he seemed, then I could get over having to find a new dentist.

"Chris isn't in this morning?" I was surprised to see the lights out in my boss' office and his door shut at 10:30 A.M. on a Friday morning.

"No, today's that charity golf tournament thing for the Breast Cancer Resource Council." His admin, Donna, looked up from her laptop.

"I didn't realize that was today. Well, they certainly got a gorgeous day for it." It was a perfect early spring day, not a cloud in the sky and temps in the mid-60's.

The Breast Cancer Resource Council was one of three charities our company, O'Donnell and Associates, supported through both monetary donations and services-in-kind. We often developed pro-bono videos for the BCRC as well as Autism Speaks and the Humane Society and regularly purchased tables at the organization's black tie fundraisers. It was customary for us to invite and entertain our clients at these events which were generally packed with celebrities, as well as scions of business.

My boss, Chris O'Donnell, the company's founder, was a man who walked-the-walk. The only one of three sons not to embrace the priesthood, the charismatic Irishman learned early in life that his easy charm and persuasive powers could be used for good without donning a frock and collar or disappointing the women drawn to his green eyes and sandy-colored hair. A master at hiring, Chris built a world-class video production company recognized for our award-winning work, and he expected all employees' ethos to be synergistic with his own.

Less than a year after he formed the company, a recruiter introduced me to Chris, convincing me that I should talk to the president of this small start-up. "He sizes people up quickly, so don't be surprised if you're out of there in twenty minutes. I've sent him seven graphic artists and none of them have made it past the twenty-minute point."

A two-man shop at the time, I met with the charismatic video producer and knew within minutes why no one had made it past the twenty-minute barrier. Answering one of his questions with blunt candor, Chris pounced on me with a rather intimidating response.

Instead of crumbling, I maintained eye-contact with this handsome guy and just began to laugh at him. "Looks like I've hit a hot button, huh?"

His smile was slow and I could tell by the laughter in his eyes that I had just passed the Chris O'Donnell test. When I left his office nearly two hours later, there was no doubt in my mind that I had found a new home.

"Do you know if he's coming back in at all today?" I asked Donna.

Sitting back, she just shook her head. "I highly doubt it, it's out at the Long Island National Golf Course in Riverhead."

"Oh yeah, forget it, that's over a two-hour drive." My question was going to have to wait until Monday.

"And he had a limo take him," Donna's tone was conspiratorial, as if this were some Earth-shattering secret.

Laughing, "Good for him. And other drivers on the road. Sounds like he's going to be doing business in the clubhouse this afternoon."

Chris was legendary for bringing on new clients in the hours both on the fairway and those that followed at the bar. Our biggest clients came on board over a glass or two or three of Glen Livet.

**Leave work and meet me at the Waldorf Astoria.**

Matthew's daily messages had become the highlight of my days. Logging on and seeing the little green dot next to his name instantly brought a smile to my face. The moment I signed on, I could count on a greeting and a message from him, as if he'd been waiting for the little green dot to light up next to my name. The man had me feeling like a middle-schooler.

It was Friday and our infamous brunch date was now only two days away. After work, Laynie and I had plans for highlights, eyebrow threading and champagne, as I prepped for Sunday's meeting.

**Why? Did Room 69 just open up or something?** I kidded.

**Ha-ha. You just can't wait for brunch to ravage my body.**

This man was so cocky. **Ravage YOUR body? You're the one who just invited ME to the Waldorf.** ☺

Only because I know when you see me you're not going to be able to keep your hands off me. ?

**You are just that irresistible to women, Matthew? Carissa, you are toast.**

I was afraid he was right.

**We'll see. I'm still praying you're not my dentist in disguise.**

**LOLOL. I can promise you that I am not. I can also promise you that you will willingly open your mouth for me. I'm getting hard just thinking about you.**

The man was killing me. All I wanted to do was lock my office door and call him. I needed a cold shower. Suddenly waiting until Sunday seemed ridiculously far away.

I said a silent prayer that he would be as great in real life as he'd been over the past two weeks and that we'd have great chemistry – that went both ways.

"You need to rid yourself of that hairy bush. Maybe just a landing strip." Our highlights were processing, and Laynie was on her second glass of champagne. "I am not letting you walk out of here with that beast between your legs." She was dead serious.

"Please," my tone was meant to shut her down. I took another sip of champagne before shaking my head.

"Tara, you're making sure the hair on your head looks fabulous before you meet him on Sunday. Why would you not make sure the hair for *his* head looks fabulous, too?"

With an exaggerated sigh, "Because his *head* will not be playing *I Spy* with any of my body parts."

"Let me see his picture again." She put her hand out for my phone.

Handing it over, I watched her facial expression morph from interested into pure lust. "Why would you not fuck his brains out?"

"Because I really like him. I'd like to get to know him and see if this could go anywhere."

"Girlfriend, what is wrong with you? The '90s are over, Tar. Time to join this century." Motioning to a tiny woman, "Thao, my friend here needs her hoochie updated. Leave her a little landing strip and put it on my bill. Thank you, doll." She then turned to me. "Not another word," she warned, her pointed finger close enough to the bridge of my nose to feel the heat.

I held out my glass for more champagne and said nothing.

The outfit was brand new. Highlights were fresh and all excess, and potentially offending, body hair had been professionally removed. I'd spent more time in the gym over the last two weeks, since my first online conversation with Matthew, than I had in the past year, as if mega-workouts could miraculously morph my thirty-nine-year old body into its perky twenty-three-year old former self.

"I can't wait to hear what he's like in real life." Jill increased the incline on her treadmill. She was as excited as I was, having lived through the morning updates of my nightly conversations with him.

"I'm really nervous," I confessed. "I just know that if this is a bomb, I'll really miss looking to see if he's logged on and waking to his messages."

"No need for nerves. You are fabulous and smart and gorgeous. And if it doesn't work out," waving her hand, Jill gave me what I already knew was great advice. "Next!"

Handing my keys to the valet at the historic inn that Matthew had chosen for brunch, I stood for a moment on the gravel driveway trying to absorb and memorize the pleasant onslaught to my senses. I took in my surroundings, almost surprised that spring had shown up, as I breathed the brackish air blowing in off the Long Island Sound.

The distinguished establishment was perched high on a cliff overlooking Greenwich, Connecticut on the Sound's far shores. I couldn't help but get swept up into the romance of the white clapboard structure that had been in continuous operation, serving thirsty, hungry and weary travelers in its quaint setting, for nearly 300 years. I wondered what handsome pairs of lovers had sat in the bar, foreheads together, chatting conspiratorially, as they let the spicy citrus hues of their Pimm's Cups rush in waves over their tongues and planned their summers on the island. Perhaps Zelda and F. Scott had passed a Sunday at the inn. Feeling as if I had to duck as I passed through the door, the lintel barely inches above my head, I wondered if Matthew was significantly taller than our nation's forefathers and had to stoop over to enter the building.

My breath hitched at the base of my throat as I caught my first glimpse of him at the bar. The pictures were no lie. Dressed in tan khakis and a light blue polo, the first thing I noticed were the muscles in his thighs straining his pants' leg and then I caught sight of his biceps. They were ridiculously huge. The man was Rob Lowe's buff younger brother. Hot damn!

Slipping onto the barstool next to him. "Matthew?"

As he turned to greet me, I was most surprised by the intensity of his pale blue eyes. The bulging muscles and his square jaw disappeared as I was captivated by the clarity of his irises.

This man was trouble. Very few men looked like this, and those men were not on dating sites. They were models, actors, scions of business. They were not on blind dates garnered via internet and phone apps. With the ease of a U.S. Open contender, I swiped the red flag away with a strong backhand. *Get off my court, doubt!*

"Carissa." His large hand gave my shoulder a squeeze as he leaned forward and kissed my cheek. "You're even more beautiful than your picture," he delivered the line with a practiced ease.

With a smile from the other side of the bar, the bartender asked, "What can I get you?"

"A Bloody Mary."

"How spicy do you like it," he inquired, sliding a glass out of the rack above his head.

"With a good kick." Realizing he was going to be making the drink for me, I was immediately disappointed as I had thought this was the Make-Your-Own place.

Turning to Matthew, "This isn't the Bloody Mary bar place?"

"Ah no, ah," he stammered for a moment. "I couldn't get a reservation there."

The first sip delivered the necessary relaxation potion so that I was able to do more than just stare at this handsome man.

"Do you have a good dentist?" I asked and he cracked up, knowing the story of my dentist's boundary breach.

"Actually I do and she's in the city on 32$^{nd}$ and 3$^{rd}$."

"I like that. I work on Madison Avenue so that's doable

and a woman might be a very nice change." His blue eyes were not looking at me.

"Dude, up here." I pointed to my eyes. The scoop neck on my shift dress was not that low.

His smile had a sneer quality to it, "Carissa, it is hard to focus on anything but how I'd like to be touching you." Reaching out, he ran two fingers along the inside of my bare upper arm. The pressure was focused inward, so while it looked like he was gently stroking my arm, that is not at all what he was doing. This time he looked me directly in the eyes, challenging me and knowing that I wanted to gasp and clench my thighs and yet, with lips slightly parted, I remained silent.

With his free hand, Matthew signaled the bartender for another round of drinks. I was already feeling the first cocktail on my empty stomach and I knew the second was about to obliterate me.

Chomping on my drink's celery stalk, "No jumbo shrimp," I mumbled.

Matthew sneered again, "I'd much rather see that piece of celery disappear down your throat."

"You got me here under false pretenses, you know that." Pointing the remainder of my celery stalk at him, I stared into his beautiful, pale eyes, unable to read them or get a handle on him. "So, what is it you are looking for, Matthew?" The vodka was making me bold.

"Someone I can have fun with. Someone who can just go with the flow." His fingers were back on my upper arm, this time he let his thumb stray to stroke my breast.

Leaning forward, both to hide what he was doing to me and to let him get a good look inside my dress' neckline, just to fuck with him, I spoke low so that he would have to listen, "You remind me of this underwear I used to have."

"Underwear?"

"Mmm-hmm. They had days of the week on them. I

think you probably have women for each day of the week and labeled underwear might really be helpful for you."

Matthew straightened in his seat, letting out a guttural laugh. "So what day are you?"

"Well obviously, Sunday." I took another healthy sip from my Bloody Mary, reaching the bottom of the glass. Once again Matthew signaled for the waiter to bring another round.

"So are you wearing your Sunday undies?"

Laughing, "No. Those were retired long ago." Slowly, I crossed my legs the other way.

"I'll bet you're wearing a black thong." His top lip pulled back into that smile/sneer. He was kind of a Rob Lowe with an Elvis smile going on.

"No, I'm not a thong girl. They are really uncomfortable. I'm all about comfort." I was officially trashed and on the verge of pulling a Sharon Stone move on this player. Trying to focus on the sexual tension and his good looks, I didn't want to think about the disappointment. What had seemed like a promising connection over the last two weeks held no promise at all. The man was a player. A horn dog. Beginning and end of story. I didn't even want to begin to wrap my brain around how many women he'd slept with in his life.

"Comfort, huh? Did you wear your Granny panties for me?"

That made me laugh just as I was sipping my drink and I began to choke. He patted me on the back a few times and I took another sip.

Nodding, "I did. I wore the white cotton ones for you." I kidded, pausing to take another sip of the spicy deliciousness before letting my filter completely disintegrate. With a smile, "I figured they'd be best to absorb any moisture."

His eyes bore into mine as if I'd just reached forward and unzipped his Dockers. "You'd really be better with a polyester to wick the moisture away." His words were incongruous with the intensity of his stare.

"I can't believe you know that," I laughed.

"Yeah, well…" he shrugged, as if that were an explanation, his gaze still holding mine.

I was reaching the bottom of my glass again in an effort to occupy my hands and mouth. Three drinks and no food, my fingertips were numb. Was this guy going to feed me or what?

"Let me run to the Ladies' Room before we get a table." I hoped he'd take the hint and be seated at a table with menus when I returned from the bathroom.

My step down from the barstool was daunting, but my feet hit the floor with more grace than I could've imagined in my highly inebriated state. Smoothing my dress down before I walked away, I caught Matthew's eyes tracking my hands as they moved over my hips.

"Be right back," I smiled.

The hallway toward the restrooms was narrow with uneven wide-planked wood floors. It was hard not to bang into the walls as I walked. My heels didn't like the knotty pine boards beneath them. The second door I came upon was labeled, *Loo*, and with a laugh, I opened the door and felt along the wall for a light switch.

His body was behind mine moving me into the bathroom before I'd even flipped the switch. With one muscular arm wrapped around my breasts, he had moved me into the Colonial-decorated room and locked the door behind him. His other hand swiftly encased my throat, pulling my head back into him.

"You may not have gotten on your knees for the dentist, Carissa, but you're going to get on them for me." The arm that was wrapped around my breasts slid down my body, while his other hand remained firmly around my neck.

Pushing up my dress, he slid his hand under the thin material, his fingers beginning their exploration.

"Commando," he laughed. "I should have guessed." And he continued his journey, maneuvering his hand around to the front of my body, pressing his flat palm against my lower abdomen until I was flush against him.

As his grip on my neck tightened slightly, I felt his warm breath just underneath his hand followed almost immediately by the scraping of his teeth. I shuddered, losing balance on my strappy sandals and melting into him. He took advantage of my unsteadiness, sliding his hand from my abdomen to between my legs.

"So smooth." He ran his fingers over my newly waxed skin. "You did this for me, didn't you, Carissa? You wanted me to explore your sweet, velvety pussy. So, so soft." His hand around my neck continued to slowly tighten as his fingers ventured deeper into me. "You were so considerate, Carissa. I'm really touched. I love ramming into a naked pussy. And to wear a dress with no underwear. Mmm, mmm. Very, very thoughtful. You've made my life so easy today. All I have to do is bend you over that sink and push your dress up to fuck you."

Loosening his grip on my neck, his hand traveled up my face slowly, his fingers entering my hairline like the rakes of a comb until he reached the top of my head, where he filled his fist with my hair. In one swift movement, he wrenched my head to the right, exposing the left side of my neck to his waiting teeth. I yelped, not sure whether it was from the delicious pain tingling along my scalp or the searing sensation at the base of my neck.

"When was the last time you sucked a cock?" his voice was gruff.

I was thinking about his question, trying to remember a time when I wanted Frank in my mouth. Matthew yanked my hair, demanding an answer.

Shaking my head, "Too long ago to remember."

"Your asshole ex had no idea what to do with a beautiful,

confident woman. A woman like you knows exactly what to do with a cock. Not like his twenty-something wife who needs to be trained."

This man was not only hot, he was brilliant. He knew that would clinch the deal. There was no way, especially in my loose drunken state, that I was not going to prove to him that some post-pubescent piece of arm candy had anything on me. I was a woman. A real woman. With the battle scars and newbie little crow's feet, just starting to take up residence on my face, to prove it.

Breaking free of his grasp, I turned to him, my eyes telling him I was up for the challenge as I stared him down before going in for a kiss and reaching for his belt buckle.

"You are a tiger," he laughed.

I didn't bother to answer as I intently focused on sliding my hand in the opening of his boxer briefs and wrapping my fingers around his warm, velvety shaft. I continued to explore, urged on by the power of his expansion and lengthening in my hand. When I could feel his skin taut over his hardness, I pulled him out of the fly of his Dockers.

With my free hand, I grabbed my own hair, twisting it into a ponytail and handing it to him.

The edges of his mouth rose until his top lip formed his sneer-smile. "Nice, nice move. Very sexy," he complimented as I began to sink to my knees.

With an upward yank of my hair, he attempted to take back control.

Looking up at him, I smiled. "I can stop, if you'd prefer."

His pale eyes looked even more transparent in the bathroom light. "Minx," was the single word he spoke before pressing my head down with both hands without letting go of my hair.

It had been so long. So damn long since I'd had a man's cock in my mouth, and a damn fine cock it was. The girth was impressive. Slowly I worked my tongue around him, deliberately making a slow meal of it, just to torment him. My morning's solid intake had been limited to celery sticks, so I wholeheartedly was enjoying this feast as I took him deeper and deeper, inch by inch.

"Fuck," he bellowed, as his crown neared the back of my throat and I tightened my lips around him. "Fuck."

Pulling me up by my hair, he spun me around, bending me over the sink, as promised, then released my ponytail and my hair puddled around me on the cold marble countertop. I could hear the ripping of a condom packet and tried to catch my breath before he plowed into me.

Without a word, he grabbed both my arms and bent them over the small of my back, holding them firmly in place in one of his big hands. I felt his finger from his other hand swiping up and down my slit before plunging in. I groaned at the insertion of just one finger and my reaction made him immediately add a second finger. Spreading my legs a little for him because I wanted more, much more, was the signal he needed to stab a third finger into me, preparing me to accept his significant girth. I wanted it now.

"Give it to me," I growled back at him, lifting my cheek from the cool marble.

Removing his fingers from inside me, he reached up and grabbed my hair, yanking it hard. "When I'm ready."

Although his words rang of control, he immediately edged between my legs. I could feel the pressure of him against me, just starting to sink in and I pushed back into him, so that thrusting into me was his only option, which I answered with a tightening of my muscles around him.

"God, yes," I moaned. I'd forgotten how good it felt. Drunk and fucking in a bathroom. It had been a long, long time. This was so not me and yet so very liberating. It was like a gift for living through all the crap and heartache with Frank and CB, for being the one to put Scarlett back together when her father didn't put her first, for spending the last fourteen years on the backburner putting everyone else's life in front of mine, for worrying about everyone else's happiness but my own.

And I wanted an orgasm. A big, full-throttle, out-of-control orgasm. I wanted to scream so loud that the bartender and half the dining room heard me.

I tried pulling my right hand from Matthew's tight grasp. I needed to touch myself. The more I struggled, the tighter his grip became holding me back from myself. Fuck. I needed my hand. And just as I couldn't focus on anything but freeing my hand to pleasure myself, the thumb of his free hand thrust deep into my ass and my own hand quickly was but a distant memory.

"Yes," I screamed as I started to quake around him. I could feel him stroking his cock with the thumb in my ass and I went far over the edge. So far that he let go of my hands, clamping his palm over my mouth until his body slumped onto mine, his broad chest heaving against my back.

Closing my eyes and feeling his warm breath on me, I realized I could just drift away into sleep, or possibly pass out, right there with my head on the marble counter. There was a comfort feeling having his big body on top of mine.

But it wasn't a moment later that Matthew stirred and began to rise off me. I heard a splat in the toilet as he tossed in the condom and I forced my eyes open, then immediately began to straighten up, smoothing down my dress. Knowing my hair must've been a sight, I reached up to pull it to one side, hoping it created a *look* rather than merely appear as a just-fucked disaster.

As I turned to face Matthew, I realized I was truly ravenous.

"Well that was a good way to work up an appetite." I joked, not sure how to act in this situation.

He almost smiled, but not quite, then the man looked at his watch. "I've got a 12:30 tee time, so I really need to run."

*I can only imagine the look on my face.* Did he really just say that to me? Could he be that huge of a douche?

"So, you invited me to brunch with no intention of ever having brunch." I shook my head. And although I wanted to sarcastically tell him what a class act he was, the fact that I'd just had sex with him in the bathroom didn't exactly spell class act on my part either.

There was nothing to say and without another word, I turned on my heel and walked out of the bathroom.

As I waited for the valet to bring my car around, I prayed Matthew didn't come out before I left. *Tee time. He was so full of shit.* Descending the inn's long driveway, it occurred to me just how much sex had sobered me up. Once on Rt. 25A, I looked for a drive-thru, finding the perfect one to counteract the remainder of the alcohol and provide the sugar and carb comfort necessary after this morning's humiliation. Dunkin' Donuts was my personal savior.

Settled back behind the wheel with a large dark roast coffee in hand, a bagel sandwich with cheese and bacon and a Boston Crème donut, this late morning trifecta served up the perfect comfort food breakfast to help my battered and confused ego on the twenty-minute ride home.

Tossing my keys on the kitchen counter, I dug my phone out of my bag and tapped the PerfectDate app icon. There he was, with a little green dot next to his name. Matthew was logged on. And there were no messages for me. Unlike every other time I'd seen him on the site over the past two weeks, he did not greet me the moment I logged on.

Golfing? Bullshit!

The asshole was not golfing; he was trolling for his next encounter. *Douche!*

Staring at my phone it wasn't clear what was the correct thing to do. Send him a message saying, "WTF?" or "What the heck was that today?" Was he really going to ignore me and not acknowledge that I'd logged on?

In my bedroom, I tossed my phone on the bed and decided I needed a shower. Leaving a trail of clothes on my bedroom floor, I needed to cleanse every inch of myself, let every second of this morning be rinsed down the drain. The excitement of our flirtation of the last two weeks was gone, and I was pretty sure that empty feeling I was left with, was what was going to be the thing that haunted me most. He was a man I'd talked to for two weeks and met once, how could it feel like an actual breakup? I asked myself. It had been a long time since I'd had this overwhelming icky feeling after something ended. But those had been relationships that had lasted longer than two weeks. This just didn't seem possible that I was feeling it and I wondered, was it the intensity based on how the new mediums were so geared toward talking or was I just such a novice at this again? Had hiding behind the Carissa persona actually given me the comfort and the confidence to really share who I was with this person prior to meeting him, and that in actuality, my anonymity had made me more vulnerable?

My mind was spinning and my inner thighs felt strained and tender, not unlike my heart.

With pruning fingers, I finally emerged from the shower feeling as if I'd rid myself of his touch. Swiping the condensation from the mirror, I let out a huge groan. There on the lower left of my neck was a purple bruise from where he'd bit me. Oh great, now I'd have to look at this little parting gift until it healed. Brushing my hair to the left, I decided not to blow it dry knowing a wild mess would probably cover it better.

Sitting on the bed and picking up the phone, I felt that obsessive pull to check the app. Yes, Matthew was still there. No, there was no message for me. And nope, not a word when I logged back on. After staring at the screen for a minute, still trying to decide what to do, if anything, I hit close and opened up another dating app where I deleted my profile information. Over the next five minutes I had done that with all of the dating apps and then deleted the app itself off my phone. The only one left was PerfectDate and I logged on one more time. Matthew was still there and hadn't attempted to contact me.

"You know what, asshole," I said to the phone. "I am not giving you any control. You're a dick and I deserve better. You have skated through life on your looks. You're a fucking hologram." And with that, I deleted my profile from PerfectDate and then deleted the app from my phone.

In fifteen years, I'd slept with two men, Frank and now Matthew. Matthew's purpose was to get me out there in the world again. And that, he did. It was very clear from today that beyond that, Matthew had nothing real to offer me.

If I'm meant to find someone, our paths will cross, I decided. And I smiled, hearing Jill's voice in my head saying, "Next!"

Now I just needed a new frigging dentist.

*Jullie A. Richman*

# Chapter 9

Monday morning's staff meeting had me sporting a pale pink silk chiffon scarf tied around my neck. Not a typical look for me.

"Hiding a hickey or something," Chris teased me.

"I should get so lucky," I laughed. I was feeling out of sorts and was thrilled it was Monday and I was back at work.

"So, I had a very interesting meeting in the clubhouse on Friday afternoon after the Breast Cancer Resource Council golf event and I think we're going to have the opportunity to bid on a really interesting series of Public Service Announcement videos."

"New client or for the BCRC?" asked Jonathan Mills, our Director of Copy and Creative Services. Jonathan was our storyline guy for the videos. I would take his script and come up with the look and then we'd hand it off to production to cast, direct and create the video.

"Yeah, a totally new client. They've been around for a few years and the brand has really taken off. They manufacture workout clothing for women who have had breast cancer," Chris explained.

"C-Kicker?" The question was out of my mouth without thinking.

Chris looked surprised. "Yes, C-Kicker. You're familiar with them?"

"Yes, my friend, Jill, who I work out with is a huge fan. She wears them all the time. The outfits and styles are really cute and their materials are very bright and vibrant. She's always raving about the comfort."

"That's good that you are familiar with them, it'll give you a good sense of direction to go with this. They're looking for a few things; a series of PSA's to run during National Breast Cancer Month in October, focused on women being vigilant about going for mammograms and doing self-exams, and they also want to shoot a series of videos to embed into their website that are real-life stories. We're meeting with them in two weeks, so we've got time. I'd say the best place to start is their website. I think we'll be able to get a lot of the answers right there." He pulled out a piece of paper and handed it to Donna. "Donna, this is the info for the CEO's assistant. Let's have you be central coordinator on this. If any of you have any questions, have Donna send them over."

My mind was spinning, the two ends of the project were so different, public service announcements versus marketing. I couldn't wait to start my research.

"Okay, let's win this," were Chris' last words to us as we emerged from the conference room.

Their fabrics were so bright and happy. The colors just made me smile. All I could think of was rainbow sherbet from when I was a kid. I loved that their photos showed women of all shapes and sizes, from tiny fit women like Jill to women who were older and just beginning their journey toward health.

Peppered throughout the site were motivational stories. Open, compelling and raw, I sat at my desk crying and silently cheering on the strength of these women. How many people did I personally know who were in some stage of fighting or recovery of breast cancer? Too many. Too damn many.

With every line I read, I became more and more committed to being part of a team that joined in with this awesome start-up company. They had been in existence for only five years and between corporate ethos, customer-centric dedication, and a quality product with a fair price point, C-Kicker was kicking butt in the fashion industry and putting a smile on the faces of those who had faced darkness.

Good for them, *I thought.*

I continued to go through the website: About Us, Our Mission, Give Back, Latest Styles, Contact Us. The rest was pretty generic stuff you find on a website.

For a fleeting moment, I thought to myself that the C-Kicker proposal and presentation had truly been a divine gift; the timing could not have been more perfect. I needed a wonderful focal point that helped me to re-center my priorities, move past the debacle of a weekend I just had and make a positive impact. I was all in.

Next step on my mission was to gather more intel so that I had a better feel for the company, and then Jonathan and I could lock ourselves away in a room and start working on the mock-ups of several concepts and story lines to present to the potential client. If we were to bring on the client, once they agreed on a particular campaign, then Jamie Newfield, head of our production team would join us and we'd begin the process of casting, finding locations, scripting, music and all the pieces that would make each piece a short film.

After thoroughly combing through their website, was the Google part of the search. I found that it was often in the "soft" stories that were in the press that I would find what really made a company tick, and at that point, visual concepts would start flooding my brain and Jonathan and I would get down to brass tacks. I loved the research piece of my job, or company stalking, as I liked to kid.

C-Kicker was all over the press, having participated in many breast cancer events as well as sponsoring others. The first link that caught my eye was from last fall's U.S. Open Tennis Tournament. The title read, Cancer Survivors Ace the Open. Arthur Ashe Stadium, Forest Hills, N.Y. – C-Kicker, the hot sports clothing company whose line of workout clothes are specifically designed for women recovering from breast cancer… The article cut off and I clicked to open and read the remainder of the NY Post article.

The page opened and below the headline was a grainy B&W photo. The caption read, GRAND SLAM CANCER KICKERS, C-Kicker CEO, Wes Bergman and breast cancer survivors, Sherri Altman and Maureen Politano raised …

I didn't see the rest of the photo's caption, my eyes kept darting back and forth between the grainy picture and the words C-Kicker CEO, Wes Bergman. Using my PC's snipping tool on the picture, I saved it to PhotoShop and attempted to remove the grain. Able to clear some of the digital noise, I sat there for a long time smiling at the man who was smiling back at me from my computer screen.

I rang Donna's extension, "Do you know the name of the man from C-Kicker that Chris met?" I hadn't even bothered to begin the phone call with a simple hello.

"Yeah, hold on, let me find the card with the info. Okay, here it is. Umm, he met the CEO. His name is Wes Bergman."

"Okay, great, thanks. That's all I needed to know."

Staring at the now blown up, fuzzy picture on my screen, I shook my head. *So, Chris was drinking with you on Friday afternoon, huh? One degree of separation again. I wonder how many times that has happened. I guess it shouldn't be surprising, but now, after all this time, for some reason, it really is. And with your company headquartered in Manhattan, I doubt you are still living in Los Angeles.*

Going back to Google Images, I looked for more pictures of Wes. He still had that gorgeous thick head of hair, but it looked like now there was a little bit of gray in it. Just as I had predicted, this man was better looking now than he had been in his twenties. He still wasn't your standard good looking. He was sexy and charismatic. *I'll bet women trip over themselves for his attention.* He just had *It.* He had always had *It.* But now with the experience and confidence only time can bring as part of his cache, just looking at his picture was making me melt.

The only man I'd ever stayed up with until dawn talking the night away was going to be sitting across a board room table from me in two weeks.

*Wes.* I couldn't wipe the smile off my face. Or stop the overtime beating of my heart. *Wes.* I never got to say goodbye to him and now I was going to get to say hello again.

*Wes. Will you even remember me? Or have you had a million talk until dawn chats with women since our night together?*

*What if he doesn't remember me?* It was a long time ago. But if I closed my eyes, I could see it like yesterday. I could smell the sea air. I could feel my heart soar. I could feel what he made me feel. But what if he doesn't remember?

Picking up my cell, I dialed Laynie's number.

"Have you slit your wrists yet?" was the way she answered her phone.

I had to think for a moment to process what she was talking about. *Oh, Matthew. Fuck. That already seemed like a million years ago. Matthew who?*

"No wrist slitting here. We have to buy me an outfit I don't own yet," I informed her.

"I'm intrigued. Go on."

"You are absolutely not going to believe this. I can't believe this. What if he doesn't remember me?"

"What are you talking about, Tara?" Laynie sounded annoyed and confused.

"Have you heard of C-Kicker?"

"Of course I have. They make the cutest workout clothes. My friend Fawn loves them because she can wear them with or without prosthetics."

"Well in two weeks we are pitching them for a series of projects."

"That's great news."

"That's not the news."

"Well then, what's the news?" Patience had never been Laynie's strong suit.

"Do you remember a gazillion years ago, before I met Frank, I went on a Windjammer Cruise?"

"Of course I remember, I lent you the jade outfit for that trip. I loved that outfit. It was a size two," she reminisced.

"Aww, the jade outfit." I was right there with her. "That was so gorgeous, with the cropped jacket and pants."

"It was my only size two ever," Laynie lamented.

"It was the only night in my entire life that I ever fit into a size two," I confessed, remembering Wes' face when I walked out in that outfit. It was stunning and although he never said anything to me, his face and eyes had said it all.

"So, do you remember I told you about a guy that I met that I had stayed up all night talking to and I really liked him?"

"The Marine?" she asked.

"No, not the Marine. I slept with the Marine, but I never slept with this guy."

"The guy with the actress girlfriend?" Laynie had an amazing memory.

"Yes! Him!" I was so excited she remembered. "I really liked him. Well, you are not going to believe this."

"What?"

"He is the CEO of C-Kicker. And I'm seeing him in two weeks. Oh my God, Laynie, I was just so taken with this man. I don't know that he'll even remember me."

"Of course he'll remember you, Tara. His memory might need a little nudge to place you, but then he'll remember. And you're right, you do need a brand new outfit, because we are going to make sure that he never forgets."

Not even an hour had passed when Laynie called me back.

"Okay, so I've been stalking him on social media. It is so wild. So many of my friends are friends with his friends. This guy is like right there. Like if you reach out, he's there and he doesn't seem to be married."

I immediately logged onto Facebook to take a look. Pulling up his page, the profile picture was a shot of him taken at the U.S. Open event, but it was a different image than what had appeared in the NY Post. This picture was both clear and in color. Wes was smiling. That smile. The smile that made my heart feel like a pinball careening off the walls of my chest.

"Mmm," it just came out of me.

"Did you mewl? Did I really hear that?"

Laughing, "I know, don't get sick. It was gross. But just look at those lips and that hair."

"He's really attractive," Laynie agreed. "You can see even in a picture that the guy is really charismatic."

I sat nodding at her words as I scrolled through his Friends' list.

"Holy shit, Layn, did you see who he is friends with? He's friends with your crazy friend Fawn."

We had been at a mutual friend's wedding and Fawn ended up sitting next to me. For nearly two hours I said "Uh-huh" and nodded at appropriate intervals as Fawn went on and on and on about all kinds of crazy shit. Spying Laynie across the room I mouthed, "Save me." Very goodhearted, Fawn would give you the shirt off her back, but then you'd be forced to listen to a lengthy dissertation on her latest get rich scheme.

"I'm texting Fawn now to find out if she really knows him or if he's just someone on her Facebook page, because as we well know, she collects people."

As I waited for Fawn to answer Laynie's text, I stared at his full lower lip. It still had the same effect on me – all these years later. Closing my eyes, I could feel that dark, star-filled night wrapped all around me. It felt like yesterday. And I was listening to Wes' melodic voice.

"Okay she said. **'Yes, he's a friend from the Hamptons and Fire Island. Really good guy. Haven't seen him in a long time. Do you know him?'"**

**"No, but a friend thought she might."** Laynie responded.

"Well if Wes was spending summers out on Fire Island, he must've moved back from the coast a few years after I met him," I conjectured, suddenly sad that our one degree of separation didn't bring us together back then.

"I know what you're thinking," Laynie's tone was chastising. "But remember, back then GOOGLE and the internet weren't what they are today. And you might've already been with Frank and no longer single by the time he returned from the coast."

Flipping to another picture of him, I acquiesced, "You're right."

"I'm always right." And she usually was.

"It appears the company turned five last year. So, they are a fairly new group. Nowhere in these articles does Wes talk about why, what was the catalyst that made him start C-Kicker. Yes, it's a great idea. And yes, it fills a much-needed hole in a marketplace niche. But it just feels to me like someone would start a company like this when they've personally been touched, when they've watched their wife or their mom go through it and thought *why is no one making clothes designed for their post-surgical needs? Why is no one out there making something useful and comfortable for them?* And then saying, *I'm in this industry. I have the contacts. I'll start the company."*

"I wouldn't be surprised if that is not very close to what happened, T. But the question is whose illness motivated him? It had to have been someone he loved very deeply."

My heart hurt thinking about Wes in pain, but I also knew that I now had the opportunity to help in this quest, in my little way. And I prayed he picked our company to produce the videos.

"You have to come meet me over by my office for lunch," Laynie was insistent later that week.

"Why?"

"No questions. Just come. Thank me later."

"Give me an hour, I'm working on some designs for the C-Kicker presentation." I was so focused on my screen that I laughed out loud when I got a text from Laynie forty minutes later telling me to leave.

**On my way.** I texted back.

**Meet me in Saks in shoes.**

The shoe department in Saks Fifth Avenue certainly sounded like a fun lunch, but I wasn't sure it was going to include food.

Laynie was trying on silver gladiator sandals when I arrived at their fourth-floor shoe department. Sitting down next to her, I was instantly envious of her long legs.

"You need them," I egged her on without any provocation.

"I do," she agreed and told the sales girl she'd take them.

"Where are we going?" I asked. The store was packed for a weekday.

"Just across the floor. There's something I need to show you."

As we walked toward Women's Clothes, my eye couldn't help but be drawn to the vibrant palette of spring and summer clothes lining the racks. The flowers on the sheath dresses made me feel that if I held the fabric to my nose the scent of lilacs and roses would waft up right from the crisp material.

"So what did you want to show…" I didn't even finish my sentence, because as we stood before it, I knew. "It's beautiful."

"I know, isn't it."

"The color…" I was still speechless.

"It's exactly how I remember the jade outfit."

Nodding, "Me too." Reaching forward I let the silk knit dress slide through my fingers. "It must have some small percentage of spandex in it, I can't wear this, it will cling to my body and I'll look like a beast."

"Shut up and try it on." Laynie was halfway to the dressing room with the dress slung over her shoulder.

Grabbing it from her, I let the try-on room attendant lead me to a corner room that was larger than some studio apartments in New York City. Holding up the dress in front of me I could see the jade outfit in my mind's eye. I wore it to the one fancy dinner we had on the windjammer, and I remember catching Wes looking at me approvingly when he thought I wasn't looking. Slipping the dress over my head, it fell over my body and hung. It didn't cling, it hung.

Stepping out of my room, Laynie was sitting in a white and gold boudoir chair texting. Hearing my approach, she looked up and shook her head, no.

"How much weight have you lost?"

"I don't know. I was watching what I ate for the last few weeks before I met that asshole, Matthew, and then again this past week when I found out about Wes. And I've been working out with Jill early in the mornings."

"Well, it shows."

The attendant approached and offered to bring it in a smaller size. When she returned, I held the new one up in front of me. "Not a chance in hell," was my assessment.

"Go try it on." Laynie had no patience for me.

Slipping the new one over my head, I stood there in front of the mirror in shock. The dress actually fit and the way it hugged my curves made me look sexy, not fat. Standing on the balls of my feet to simulate heels, I turned sideways and looked in the mirror. Pulling my hair up, the look was sophisticated, feminine and hot, in an understated way.

"So?" I asked, when I walked out of the room.

"So...I hope he's really not married or you're going to be a homewrecker. That dress looks amazing and if he doesn't remember you, I know it's going to jog a long buried memory."

A few minutes later I emerged with the dress back on its hanger. "Do I get fed now?" I asked.

"Not yet, I was thinking about something."

"Uh-oh, that worries me."

Standing by the register as I paid, "No. Just hear me out. Our senses play a huge role in creating and recalling memory, right?"

"Yes." I swiped my credit card.

"You can hear a song and within the first few notes, you're totally transported back in time to that place where you were listening to it. And it's everything, the visual image, the smell, the temperature. So, we're hitting his brain with a very specific color. Do you remember what perfume you wore back then?" We walked toward the elevator.

"Salt Air & Sweat," I joked.

"Were you wearing the scent Ollie was obsessed with?"

"Oh my God," I laughed, grasping Laynie's forearm. "I hope not."

Ollie was Laynie's prized long-haired dachshund. Like most pets in loving homes, Ollie had no clue he was a dog. He was a little man with a big attitude. A lifelong dog lover, at first I could not understand why this dog ignored me. Ollie would literally dis me every time I walked into Laynie's apartment, until Trésor. For years, I had been wearing Estée Lauder's White Linen perfume and on a trip to the cosmetics counter for a new bottle, a very persuasive sales woman convinced me to also buy Trésor. What was in the perfume that turned Ollie on, I'll never know, but from the first time I walked in wearing it, he would jump up into my lap and stick his long snout into the nape of my neck, sniffing and licking it. He could go for hours. And not in a good way.

"I seriously don't remember wearing any perfume that trip. It was pretty grubby. Hawaiian Tropic was probably my fragrance du jour."

Exiting the elevator on the very crowded main floor, Laynie directed me. "This way. Let's get you a rollerball perfume that screams beach and summer. You are going to assault his senses until his memory becomes his reality."

"My nose is useless. I can't smell anymore," I declared, after the fourth or fifth perfume. My nose was stuffing up. Talk about assaulting the senses.

Laynie continued on her quest, stalking the rack like a cougar on a mission. Reaching out she swiped the next bottle from the display, then the next one.

"Oh too bad, I liked the name and packaging on this one." I held up a bottle of Beach Walk. "There's just something strong and overwhelming in the fragrance that I don't like."

We continued spraying little cards and parts of our arms until Laynie said, "Did you smell this one?"

Handing me the bottle, I sprayed the inside of my wrist and waved it in the air until it was dry before bringing it to my nose. Inhaling the clean scent, I immediately looked at Laynie, my smile giving here the answer.

"It's perfect. It's light and citrusy and it just sings beach on a sunny day." I brought the rollerball up to my nose for another waft. "Perfect."

"Buy it and let's go eat."

Chris held a prep/rehearsal meeting prior to the C-Kicker team's arrival the following Friday morning. Jonathan and I were set-up to play the videos on the projection wall and review general campaign concepts. We'd done several mock-ups that featured different storylines and if given the go ahead, we'd go into full production with Jamie. Joining me, Chris, Jonathan, and Jamie in the meeting were Chris' admin, Donna and account executive, Kim Decker, who would handle day-to-day on the account, if we landed it.

"Did we get a roster of attendees from C-Kicker?" I asked Donna. "We haven't thrown their names and info into the presentation yet."

"No, and I asked for it a few times. I have some info, but not a formal list. I know it's going to be the CEO, Wes, VP of Operations, Julien and a Director of Public Outreach named Renata." She rifled through her notes.

Taking down the info, I typed it into the presentation. Do we have last names on Julien and Renata?"

Shaking her head, "No, sorry and Camilla, Wes'

assistant said something about a marketing person with a scheduling conflict, but that Wes had told her to change it. I'm really sorry, I don't have the info."

Donna was so competent I worried that C-Kicker might prove to be a difficult partner.

Getting up to go back to my office Chris remarked, "That is a great color on you."

Back in my space, I closed the door and took a deep breath. Why was I so nervous? So what if I were going to see a guy I knew for a very short period of time a long time ago. Chances were he would have no memory of me or our night talking until dawn. *Breathe deeply,* I told myself. *If you were seeing an old friend from high school, you'd be psyched and not nervous.*

But it was Wes. Wes who spent his life one degree of separation from me.

I felt as if I were to reach out my hand and he extended his, our fingertips would be mere inches apart and that is how they had been for our entire lives. We were so close yet, remained on opposite ends of a bridge that neither of us could get across. Yet somehow we had come together, just once, and touched for a quick moment in time before being flung back to our rightful, separated places and now our parallel lines were about to converge again.

*Oh God.*

Reaching into my purse, I pulled out the rollerball of Dolce & Gabbana Light Blue that Laynie and I had bought and rolled a touch below each ear and then a longer line in my cleavage. Breathing in, the beachy scent calmed me.

*Okay, let's do this.* I gathered everything I needed and made my way back to the conference room. Donna was setting out an air-pot of coffee and cups, before going to the front to be there to greet the C-Kicker contingent when they arrived.

Kim looked up at me from her laptop screen and

dabbed the corner of her eyes. "I love what you and Jonathan did. I hope I don't start crying when we show these roughs to them."

"You liked it?"

"Tara, you could see the two of you had your heart in this. Pinch me or kick me under the table if I start to cry."

I laughed, "It's a deal." *They're going to love her as an account exec* was my last thought before I heard voices heading our way.

Wes and his staff were here.

Standing, I smoothed down my jade dress and came around the table. *Breathe, Tara.* Chris entered first. He was partially turned around talking to a beautiful Hispanic woman. My guess was that must be Renata. She wore a coral suit that drew everyone's eyes and then didn't let go with its short skirt showcasing her toned, tan legs. Chris laughed at whatever she was saying.

Wes entered next in a deep navy suit with a pale blue shirt open at the collar. Just as I had predicted on the night we met, this was a man who grew into his looks. He owned his charisma now, knowing exactly what to do with it. And he still had all his hair. It was a perfect mess of loose curls with the first hint of grey shyly peeking out at the temples.

Behind him there was another woman, but I couldn't have told you what she looked like. I could only watch Wes as Chris introduced our team to him. He was shaking hands with Jamie and then Jonathan.

"And this is our Director of Graphics, Tara Collins." Chris introduced me.

Our eyes met and I smiled at him, my reaction totally visceral and out of my immediate control. I was looking at Wes. I could feel my cheeks rising as my smile continued on its uncontrollable path.

"Tara," he nodded, extending a hand. *That voice…*

"Wes." I didn't break eye contact as I took his hand,

a slight tremble in mine as our fingers touched, no longer separated by the infinite degrees of the universe. I tried to read what was in his eyes, but he wasn't giving me an answer. And maybe he didn't even have a question.

*Do you know who I am? Anything? Something. "It's me, Wes," I silently pleaded, begging for his remembrance. "It's me, Tara."*

Our hands broke contact and I could feel the space as we were back on our respective sides of the bridge again. But there was no longer one degree separating us or tying us together. It wasn't Chris or crazy Fawn that was the one degree binding us in our separation. We had breached the gap. Again.

As Wes introduced his staff, I was still smiling, just listening to that melodious voice. It didn't feel like a million years since I had heard it last. No, it felt as if the sound had always been surrounding me, pulling me in tight.

Shaking hands with Renata Oliveras, I complimented her on her lovely suit and told her how nice it was to meet her. Next to her was another woman, Kelly Dennis. I was speaking to these people, but I was listening to Wes, hyper-focused on his every word, as my wildly beating heart cut a hasty path toward the surface of my chest and the keyhole neckline of my jade dress. I was a bundle of emotion, trying to appear cool and engaged, but every cell in my body had discovered a new faster frequency on which to vibrate.

Then Wes introduced the tall, good looking man on the end, the last of his employees. I had been so focused on Wes, I hadn't even noticed the man entering the conference room.

"And this guy here," Wes began, "is my right hand and second in command, my VP of Operations, Julien Matthews."

The smile on my face immediately dissipated and I had to consciously tell myself to close my agape mouth and assume a fake grin. It took all the strength I had to prod myself just to breathe. I couldn't freaking breathe, and I wasn't sure that

I even wanted to, because sustained breathing ensured the continuation of this moment.

The man extended a hand, "Tara, is it?" his tone was mocking. As one brow rose, his smile rapidly morphed into his signature sneer.

I forced my hand up to meet his and his sneer deepened as he greeted it with a hard squeeze, causing me to shudder. His pale blue eyes bore into me, transmitting ice cold energy.

And in that very second, I felt my heart stall as I realized that this particular degree of separation would not serve as a connector for me and Wes, but rather threatened to disconnect us, as he was the self-appointed toll taker at the only bridge in sight, the one that crossed over a nearly impenetrable chasm.

*Jullie A. Richman*

# Chapter 10

As the videos ran, I intently watched Wes' face across the conference room table. Professional and composed, most people would miss the nearly imperceptible muscle tic in his jaw that told me of the storm the film clip had just unleashed in his heart. Jonathan and I had been right on the mark with our concept and execution and I was elated beyond belief, not just to do a good job and land an account, but to create something that was meaningful for Wes. *What had happened to him? Who had he lost to this insidious disease?*

When Donna raised the lights, it took a minute for everyone's eyes to acclimate, providing a moment for the room's occupants to compose themselves.

Renata was the first to speak, "That was really powerful." She fanned her face with a piece of paper.

Kelly nodded in agreement. "Just beautiful," was her input as she dabbed the corner of her eyes.

Only Julien sat there with his arms crossed over his chest, his body language suggesting that he was unmoved, or at least not willing to acknowledge the videos' effect on him. Looking straight at me, he broke the emotional hold of the room with his assessment, delivering his opinion with a slight sneer. "I'm sorry but I found it to be derivative and not very original."

Under the table I sunk my fingernails into Jonathan's thigh and just smiled at Julien, "I'm so sorry we were unable to touch your heart." I hoped only he could see the venom in my eyes. *What a douche!*

Wes cleared his throat and my attention went back to him. "I think you hit it on the mark, you captured our mission, our corporate ethos, the message we imperatively need to get out to women. I'm incredibly impressed. This feels like the work of an organization we've been teaming with for years."

My heart soared at his appraisal of our work and Jonathan and I thanked him for his kind words. I could see the smile in the crinkle of his eyes. Damn, the lines on his face were perfect, rugged and sexy. This man had turned into a head-turner, aging beautifully, in a way few men do. Although our eye contact was direct, I couldn't read anything beyond the business conversation. I had no idea at all if he had any inkling that we'd ever met before. Unlike Julien, aka Matthew, who was looking at me like he was going to have revenge sex with me in the bathroom after the meeting.

"I really like this starting point," Wes was speaking again and that melodious voice was like a salve instantly healing scabs Julien was trying to pick open. "Kelly, Renata and I will create a scope of work document, including dates we'll need finished product by. I think we'll be ready to sit down with you again in about two weeks." Everyone pulled out their phones, opening their calendar app. "Two weeks from now on Thursday? Does 10 AM work for everyone?"

Whether it did or not, we would all make it work.

"Is there anything additional you'd like my team to prepare for the next meeting?" Chris asked.

Shaking his head, Wes looked at his staff for concurrence.

"No, I think you did so much prep work for this, we are well on our way. We need to look at numbers and decide how many films we want for both PSAs and the website."

Then Chris threw out a surprise, which was typical of Chris. "I know this is short notice, but I received a call this morning from the Ad Club of New York and they had a table open up at next week's Annual Andy awards at the High Line Hotel. We are up for an award and would love to have you as our guests."

Nodding, Wes smiled. "When did you say this was?"

"Late Tuesday afternoon."

Checking his calendar, "I can clear what I have." He looked at his employees.

The women nodded, but Julien declined, "I can't reschedule my meeting."

"Are four tickets doable?" Wes asked Chris.

"Not a problem at all. We'll have them delivered to your office."

"Excellent and congratulations on the nomination. Though after seeing your work today, I must say that I'm not surprised."

Rising to leave, I came around to their side of the table, shaking hands with Kelly and Renata and sharing with them that I looked forward to working together.

Turning to Wes, I smiled and extended my hand. What do I say? *Nice to meet you.* Or *Nice to see you again.* Or *You might not remember…*

But I didn't need to speak, because he did it for me.

First was the smile that was like an electric shock to my heart, a jolt I felt in every cell of my being, vividly restoring the visual of the first time I saw it as he was spilling a drink all over his bare feet. Reaching out and touching the sleeve of my dress, Wes let the soft fabric slowly glide through his fingers. "This has always been a beautiful color for you, Tara."

*He remembered. Oh my God, he remembered. Not only*

*did he remember me, he remembered the details. He remembered the freaking jade outfit.*

I wanted to speak, but every emotion I possessed was lodged in my throat tying my vocal cords in knots.

He remembered.

Reaching for my outstretched hand and enrobing it in both of his, we looked at one another smiling. I had no consciousness of anything else in the room other than the smile in his eyes and the warm tingle of my hand lost in his.

"One degree," he said softly, his eyes crinkling in the corners.

I laughed, "Our parallel universes converge yet again."

The energy between us had not dissipated over the decade and a half we had not seen one another. Whatever it was the two of us possessed, was still there. I was drawn to this man in a way I was at a loss to describe. Twin flames, maybe? There was something bigger and beyond us at work that was binding us together and I didn't want this moment of rediscovery to end.

"You two know each other?" Chris' surprised voice broke the moment and I was instantaneously transported back to the conference room from the nether-dimension space Wes and I had just occupied.

Wes smiled, his eyes never leaving mine, as he continued to hold my hand in his. "It's been a long time, but Tara and I tend to travel the same path one degree of separation apart, and at times, our paths converge. This is one of those times."

I was the one to break eye contact with Wes as Julien stepped close behind him, assuming a protective stance. My eyes met his and this time I didn't bring anger, I merely tried to convey a message of peace. This was a messy situation to say the least and I just prayed that I could come out of it unscathed, with Wes and I in a good place with one another.

Squeezing my hand, Wes leaned forward and whispered, "See you Tuesday." With his face next to my ear, I could hear him inhale and knew the beachy scent of my perfume had just filled his mind's eye with memories of taut white sails against a star-filled black sky, fruit-laden rum concoctions and our laughter sailing off on the night's breeze.

*Jullie A. Richman*

# Chapter 11

I had been looking forward to the Advertising Club of New York's ANDY Awards, partly because O'Donnell & Associates was up for an award, and it was always great to attend as a nominee, and partly because it was one of the few times a year where the whole New York City advertising community came together and I got to see people I hadn't seen in way too long.

Now there was the added pleasure of seeing Wes and the C-Kicker team, minus Julien, so I was certain a good time would be had by all. And even if we didn't take home an ANDY, since the competition was very stiff in the video category, I was secretly thrilled that Wes was going to hear my name being called as a nominee.

Held in the gothic High Line Hotel, the banquet hall, known as The Refectory within Hoffman Hall was just that, a hall. Long and fairly narrow for a banquet facility, the room, lined with panels of wainscoted wood, soaring clerestory windows and a beamed concave ceiling, included a wood burning fireplace and was truly like no other space in New York City. Historic and romantic, The High Line Hotel was the former estate and mid-17th century apple orchard of Clement Clarke Moore, and it is said that Moore penned *'Twas the Night Before Christmas* on the property.

The room was set with small round tables for six, a raised stage at one end and bars set up on the far end. I first noticed Wes standing in line at one of the bars. He had his left hand on the lower back of a young woman, with waist-length near black wavy hair, an almost embarrassingly short skirt and heels that would have landed me in the emergency room having one or both ankles casted when I tripped over my own feet.

"Tara." I turned to see who was calling my name as Renata and Kelly approached.

"So good to see you," I gave each woman a hug. Renata was again dressed in an eye-turning outfit, this time in fuchsia. I loved that her style matched her outgoing personality.

"Where are you originally from?" I asked her.

"Puerto Rico," she rolled her R's.

I laughed, "You are one hot mama!"

Rolling her eyes, Kelly agreed, "That, she is. Don't let her have too much to drink or she will have this entire room doing a conga line before they serve us dessert."

Wes and the woman turned from the bar, drinks in hand. Her look was exotic and she was quite beautiful. It was her body that surprised me. Small in stature, with a tiny bone structure, she was less developed than Scarlett and my first thought was, oh how sweet, he brought his daughter.

"Wes' daughter is beautiful," I commented to Kelly and Renata. The reaction that I got was certainly not what I expected as Renata rolled her eyes and Kelly pursed her lips. "What?" I asked.

"That's his girlfriend," Kelly's tone was hushed.

"Is that legal?" It was my kneejerk reaction and it was out of my mouth before I could stop it.

Both women laughed. "I like this one," Renata declared.

Sneaking another look at them, my stomach suddenly felt sour. Wes was no different than my ex, hooking up with twenty-something year old arm candy. And for what? To make themselves feel young and virile? What the hell could he talk to this woman about? Would she get his references when he threw in a song lyric circa 1990 or how he felt during an historical event? What the hell was wrong with these men?

*Just buy a freaking convertible,* I wanted to scream across the room at him.

The overhead lights flashed signaling the meal and program were just about to begin. Finding our table with the number 18 sticking out of the centerpiece took some doing.

"Who the heck arranged this," Jonathan bitched, as we sat down. Chris and Jamie were at the next table with Wes and his staff, while Jonathan and I sat with our clients from the Literacy League. It was the commercial we created for them that had earned us today's nomination.

Looking through the program and at all the nominations, I said to Jonathan, "What an honor it is to be nominated with these people. Look at this group!"

"I think either JWT is going to win it for the Macy's Believe Campaign or M. Silver & Associates for 9/11 First Responders' Foundation."

"I think you're right. I'm just really honored and humbled to be nominated with them."

The waiters served our salad course and I tried my hardest not to look over at the next table, but I couldn't stop checking out Wes' girlfriend. I felt like I needed to take her on a playdate with CB or something.

Prior to serving dessert, the program began, with the chapter president thanking everyone for being there and talking about the strength of the organization and what was accomplished within, and created by, the New York group truly shaped global opinion, buying and trends.

They began with the internet advertising awards, clearly

the largest growing category and the youngest, hippest nominees.

"Are they even allowed to drink yet?" Jonathan took a sip of his white wine.

The next category was video-based, first starting with commercial, which took forever to get through and then finally into our area of non-profits and public service announcements. Jonathan and I clenched each other's hands under the table.

"We should all be proud to be nominated. This is so competitive and your message was among the best and really resonated with people," I told our clients.

As they started reading the names I could feel my hand shaking within Jonathan's or maybe it was his shaking that was jostling mine. Although I didn't expect to win, I think it's human nature to hold out hope until the very end. Because you never know.

Smiling at each other and the clients when our names were called, I squeezed Jonathan's hand tight and looked over at Chris at the next table. Momentarily, I caught Wes' eye. The smile on his face was magnificent. Everyone was sharing in this moment of joy.

And then the inevitable, the winners were read, "Mia Silver and Seth Shapiro of M. Silver & Associates for the 9/11 First Responders' Foundation."

Clapping loudly for them, Jonathan leaned over and said in my ear, "If I had to lose to anybody, I'm glad it's them."

I hardly heard him as I focused on the winning team two tables away. With beatific smiles, Mia and Seth high-fived. I had known them for over a decade, not well, but enough that we'd always talk at events. It was what happened after the high-five that caught my attention and raptly held it captive.

Mia turned to an exceedingly handsome man with thick dirty blonde hair sitting on her right and they kissed.

The look they gave one another took my breath away. The love. I felt their love and it made me ache. As she left him to go to the podium to accept her award with Seth, she and the man held hands until the contact broke at the end of their fingertips. And then he watched her, the pride radiating off him like a solar flare. It was then I noticed his wedding band and looked up at the podium to see Mia was wearing one, too.

My heart bloomed with happiness for Mia. I was aware that her affinity for 9/11 charities was not just rooted in being a native New Yorker, but also that she lost her boyfriend in the towers. I hadn't seen her in a while, between work and the divorce, I had missed more Ad Club meetings than I had attended over the past two years.

And now here she was married and probably to the handsomest man in the room, a man who looked to be in his early to mid-40's and I guessed Mia was close in age to me. So why was it that the handsomest man in the entire room didn't need a 25-year old? This man was clearly deeply in love with a woman his age. Why? Why was he not running after child brides like Frank and Wes?

"Tell me this," I asked Jonathan. "Mia's husband doesn't seem to need a 20-something girlfriend and he's better looking than all the ones that do. Why is that?"

"Because that man doesn't have an insecure bone in his body."

"Can you clone him for me?"

"Only if we can clone one for me too." Jonathan pouted. "Did you notice Seth has a handsome Prince Harry redheaded significant other, too?"

"No, I was so busy watching Mia and that man who adores her." Turning to take another peek at them, "I want that."

"Get in line, sista." Jonathan squeezed my hand under the table.

I waited until they began the print awards before excusing myself from the table. Returning from the ladies' room I wandered the ornate building, stepping outside to admire their outdoor bar, Champagne Charlie's. Leaning on the railing, I watched the after work crowd enjoying the balmy spring evening as they winded down the end of the day with a cocktail.

The sleeve of his suit jacket brushed my bare arm, giving me goosebumps, as he leaned on the railing next to me. It was a déjà vu moment of our last night in the Caribbean.

Looking at him, I smiled. "Your daughter is beautiful."

"My daughter?" He looked genuinely confused and I reveled in his discomfort as he was going to have to tell me who she was. "Oh you mean Keiko? No, no. She's not my daughter."

"No?" I feigned confusion. *Say it Wes.*

"My daughter," he laughed uneasily. "Ouch, that hurts." He paused, looking out at the garden and not making eye contact with me. "Keiko is my girlfriend."

Keeping up the charade of confusion, I too looked out at the flower garden and just nodded my head.

"I can see it in your face, Tara. Just say what you want to say," Wes' tone was no nonsense and more than a little defensive, but he had not moved away from me and our arms were still touching.

Without looking at him, I surprised myself by baring my soul. "My ex's new wife is twenty-five," and then I turned to him with a smile, "and a half. Yes, she still counts halves. I call her CB, which stands for Child Bride. So clearly this is my issue based on my own shit." And I shrugged my shoulders.

He nodded. "I can only imagine I dropped a few notches in your estimation today."

Without any true focal point, I stared back out at the garden, because I couldn't look him in the eyes and tell him the truth. The man was a customer. "It's not my place to judge you."

"But you do." He bumped his shoulder into mine.

"It's my shit, Wes."

Leaning into me a little bit, he began to talk, "Six years ago I lost my wife, Lisa, to breast cancer. She'd only been sick, let me rephrase that, we only knew about it for two years. She was asymptomatic for a long time and by the time the cancer started presenting, we had a whole host of issues on our hands."

Reaching across with my left hand, I laid it on his left forearm and gave it a squeeze, "I'm so sorry." I looked at his handsome profile and let my hand remain on his forearm.

He just nodded and continued, "During those two years, I was her biggest cheerleader. She wasn't going to die because I wasn't going to let her. I kept pushing her on, cheering her on. So, when she did die, I went to pieces. How could that happen, I was cheering, pushing, finding new treatments all over the world, working with nutritionists, spiritualists, you name it."

"I'm so sorry," was all I could repeat through my tears. My heart wept for him and his wife.

"After she died, I took off to Mexico and literally sat on a rock in Zihuatenajo for two weeks. Seriously." He looked at me, his eyes sharing an intensity of pain that matched his resolve. "I sat on a rock and didn't move. I couldn't understand how it happened. I'd moved Heaven and Earth to fix it. To fix her. So, how the hell did she die? How?"

Tears were rushing down my face and I could hardly breathe. My hand on Wes' forearm was now more for me, an anchor to hold me up, than it was for him.

"Finally, Stacy came and got me. She made me leave my rock and go home. I was just totally non-functional for a while and then one day when I was doing research, because I hadn't yet let go, the concept of C-Kicker came to me. I knew the apparel industry inside and out and no one was meeting this need. And that is what gave me purpose again and transported me back to the land of the living."

Nodding my head, I was too emotionally devastated to speak.

"And do you want to hear the kicker of all this?" He bumped my shoulder again.

"There's more?" I choked out.

"You know when it rains it pours. Stacy has breast cancer, too. We're dealing with her second recurrence of it now."

"Noooo." My response was low and guttural, another barrage of tears drowning my cheeks.

"She says hello, by the way." Wes smiled at me.

I laughed through my tears, "What? You told her you saw me? I'm shocked that she remembered me."

He nodded and smiled, "Yeah, she remembered you all right. She said she wishes she hadn't been so mean to you. You might be on some long list of people she has somewhere that she needs to apologize to."

"How is her prognosis?"

"We'll see after she finishes this round of chemo."

I nodded, not knowing what to say. We were silent for a few minutes and I wondered if the segue of conversation from Keiko to his confiding his past to me was some sort of explanation for his relationship with her. And if so, what did it mean? That after his wife, he wanted something different? Maybe younger might be equated with health in his mind? I wasn't quite sure. But I was glad he'd confided in me.

"Wes Bergman, why do you always have a girlfriend when we meet?" I shocked myself when what I was thinking came out of my mouth.

The look in his eyes was not one I expected. I was anticipating a joke or wisecrack, but what I saw was a man who was dead serious. He moved his arm from mine on the railing and slung it over my shoulder, pulling me into him.

With lips against my temple, his voice was gruff as he said, "I've never greeted the morning light with anyone but you."

I don't know if he thought it would make me happy to hear that I was the only one he'd ever done that with, but it had the exact opposite effect, and I'm sure it bewildered him as much as it surprised me to feel me stiffen in his arms and look away.

*Jullie A. Richman*

# Chapter 12

"Well maybe he knew she was someone he wouldn't fall for deeply," was Jill's take on the Wes/Keiko situation.

"I agree," Laynie concurred. "I think after what that man went through, he was just looking for something to help him forget and heal. Keiko is not serious material for him. And he wasn't ready for anything serious."

I was on my second glass of wine and instead of feeling happy, the blues were setting in. "Well, it's not like I've got a chance with the man."

Picking the almonds out of the mixed nuts at the center of the table, Jill didn't look up. "Why not, Tara? He's obviously got a thing for you. You two have this special connection."

"We sure do have a special connection and his name is Julien." Just saying it made me shudder and reach for my wine glass.

Jill's blue eyes opened wide with horror. "That's got to be hanging over your head knowing at any time Julien can drop the guillotine," her tone was hushed and dramatic.

A sip of wine was halfway down my throat and I began

to choke, "That's a great visual. The man has already had head from me and now he's going to have my head."

Patting my back, Laynie surmised, "I'm sure if he said something to Wes, you'd know about it."

"Oh, I agree and then look at what a hypocrite I am, judging him on his young girlfriend when I've had sex with his best friend."

"They're best friends?" Jill asked. "Are you sure they're not just business colleagues?"

Shaking my head, and grabbing a handful of the now almond-less nut mixture, "From what Kelly has told me, they've known each other since they are like eight years old. Wes is very loyal to him and Julien is where he is only because of Wes. I think Wes has bailed him out of a few situations in his life."

"Bros before hoes," Laynie muttered.

"Exactly," we all concurred.

"Can we get another bottle of the Syrah and more nuts," I asked our waitress.

"Sorry I stole all the almonds. So why do you think he hasn't said anything to Wes?"

"The only thing I can think is that it's a control thing with him. He's lording it over me. Holding me hostage with it." The whole thing was weighing on me heavily. "Do I tell Wes?" I looked at my two friends sorely needing advice on this one.

Jill was vigorously shaking her head no and I looked at Laynie.

"Not until he's pulling a condom out of its wrapper." My best friend's pointed look clearly said, *keep your mouth shut.*

After weeks of auditions and script tweaks, we were down to final casting on two of the PSA videos with three actresses and two actors doing readings. Wes had joined Kelly and Renata to make the decision and Chris was sitting in with the team, in Wes' presence.

I stopped in to say hello to everyone, since this portion of the process didn't include me. Kim had coffee and danish set-up for everyone and I grabbed a cup.

"Where have you been hiding?" Renata asked.

"Just waiting for you guys to finish casting and then you'll be seeing plenty of me."

I caught Wes' eye and smiled. Why did it feel as if there was no one else in the room whenever he was around? I felt a closeness to this man, yet the distance was evident. Our relationship was purely business, yet it felt like he and I were the only two that shared some colossal secret. Or maybe it was only me, as I really didn't have any idea what he was feeling and the secret I was hiding was massive.

Donna slipped into the room, "Tara, I have Frank on the phone."

It was odd that Frank would call into the main number. "Tell him I'll call him back." I tried to keep my voice low.

"Umm, he was pretty insistent he needed to speak to you." And then she whispered, "It came in through an international number."

"What?" My voice was louder and sharper than I'd expected it to come out.

Shaking my head, I fled from the room. This was not going to be good. Not at all. It was Thursday morning and two days away was the Annual Father/Daughter Spring Dance. If he was overseas anywhere I was going to get on a plane and kill the man with my bare hands.

"I'll put it through to your office." Donna headed back to the front desk.

Visions of castration were becoming clearer as my anger

increased with every step toward my office. Closing the door, I picked up my phone.

"Frank?"

The line was scratchy. "Hey Tar, I've got some bad news."

"Where are you?"

"You see that's the problem. I'm in Paris and won't be able to make it back until Sunday."

"Yeah, that is a problem, Frank, since you've got a date with your daughter on Saturday night."

"I know. I feel terrible."

"No Frank, if you felt terrible, you'd get your ass on a plane tomorrow and come home."

"Look, Tara, my hands were really tied."

"This had better be a good one, like the only surgeon who could reattach your balls is there."

"Ha-ha, good one. You were always funny."

"Spit it out." My anger was flaring.

"It's Crystal's parents' 25th anniversary and she booked this whole anniversary trip for them."

"You have got to be fucking kidding me. How long have you known about this? You both knew this was the weekend of Scarlett's dance. How many times are you going to break your daughter's heart?" Hearing my door, I looked up and Wes was slipping into my office as I got the last sentence out.

"I'll get her something really great. An outfit from a top French designer that her friends would kill for."

"She doesn't want an outfit or any other gifts, Frank. She wants her father with her at that dance. Especially after what you pulled on her with the holiday dance. What message are you giving her? Not to trust men that tell you they love you? You're breaking her heart. As you've already seen, you will have multiple marriages in your life, but only one daughter named Scarlett."

Wes opened the mini-fridge in my office and pulled out

a bottle of Evian. Unscrewing the cap, he handed it to me. My hands were shaking with anger and it splashed all over my desk.

"Can you let her know…" I cut him off.

"No. I cannot let her know. I don't care if it's the middle of the fucking night there, you'd better pick up the phone and call her yourself. You should be ashamed of yourself. That child is too good for you." And I clicked off the phone before he could respond.

Turning away from Wes, I breathed deeply, trying to calm myself. *How the hell could a man do this to his daughter? And now, not once, but twice.*

"Are you okay?"

I shook my head, no. I was trying my hardest to hold back tears. Without turning to face him, I alerted him to that. "If you ever see me cry, run for the hills because it means I'm angry. Very angry. I cry when I'm angry." Dabbing the corners of my eyes with the back of my fingers, I pulled myself together enough to finally turn around.

"What a piece of shit." I exhaled, letting a load of the tension out.

Wes picked up a picture on my desk, "She's beautiful."

"Thank you," I smiled. "And she's a good kid, too. Smart and sensitive and very funny." I motioned for him to take a seat, as I did the same. He continued to look at the picture in his hand. "This is the second time in a row he's done this to her. He did it at the holidays and now for the Father/Daughter Spring Dance."

"When is it?"

"Saturday."

"This Saturday?" Wes looked astonished. "Wow. And what was the excuse?"

"They flew to Paris for his wife's parents 25th anniversary."

"They live in Paris?"

"No. They live in The Bronx."

"Didn't you say she was twenty-five and a half?" He smiled at me, coyly.

Gasping, "I did. Well, there's a little family secret." Shaking my head, "Scarlett is going to be destroyed. Maybe my brother can come in."

"Where is he?" Wes picked up Scarlett's picture again.

"He's in Boulder."

"Colorado?"

I nodded.

"How about this," Wes began. "I know Scarlett is going to be disappointed. But what if we set up a mystery date for her." I could see the crinkles start to appear in the corners of his eyes and then that smile. That damn, heart-stopping smile. *What was it about this man?*

I laughed, "I'm envisioning this board game that my older cousins had. You'd open the door at the center of the board to find out which guy was your mystery date."

"Exactly. What if Scarlett just knows that she has a blind date for the dance and that she's going to have a fun time."

"Okay. So, do we rent a non-asshole dad for the night?"

"Well, I promise not to charge rent." And there was that smile again.

"You?" My mouth was hanging open. "You want to take my daughter to a dance?" I was floored by his offer. It was beyond generous in spirit.

"I would love to. Now, she's a little young, even for me," he joked. "But I'd love to be her surprise date and help make the night a little bit better for her."

"Wes." I was speechless. Reaching for his hand across the desk, I gave it a squeeze. "I don't know what to say."

"Tell me about her dress." He smiled and gave my hand a squeeze back.

"It's beautiful. It's a pale sky blue with a full skirt. Very '50's."

He smiled at the description. "Okay and how is she

wearing her hair."

"We're having an up do done on Saturday. She has that perfect heavy, wavy hair for an up do. And she's doing a mani/pedi on Saturday, too." This man, a virtual stranger to my daughter, had just asked more questions than her father ever had.

"They still do corsages, right?"

I nodded, "They do. It's a big thing for a bunch of girls to put their hands together to form a circle and have someone take a picture from above of the circle of corsages. It's really beautiful with all the colors."

"Dinner?"

"They're serving a buffet there."

"What time?"

"7:30 to get there by 8."

"Where is it being held?"

"At the school. North Shore Country Day."

Wes looked impressed. "North Shore Country Day," he repeated. "Very nice."

One of Long Island's prestigious prep schools, the campus of North Shore Country Day was built on a former Vanderbilt estate. The north shore was dotted with estates that had been summer homes to various members of the railroad tycoon's family.

"Wes, I really don't know what to say, there aren't words to thank you here. I think she will be very hurt by what Frank has pulled, but in the end, I know she will be thrilled that she's still able to go and will absolutely adore you." I know I do, were the words I didn't say.

"My mind is spinning with ideas. We're going to have a great time." He smiled and I felt relief.

"What are you going to tell Keiko? You're going out on a Saturday night."

Looking me directly in the eye and holding my stare. "I'm going to tell her that I'm turning her in for a younger model."

Knocking on her door, "Scarlett, can I come in?"

It took a moment, but finally there was a muffled, "Yeah."

Lying in bed with Five Seconds of Summer's *Castaway* playing on repeat, my heart ached for my little girl and my outrage at Frank's insensitivity stabbed at my gut.

Sitting down on the bed next to her, I gently stroked her beautiful wavy hair. I could feel her hurt and anger in the silence.

*Castaway* was playing for the third time before she spoke. "Why did he do this to me, Mom?"

I shook my head. "I don't know, baby. I'm not inside his head. But it was a stupid, stupid thing to do." How do you tell a fourteen-year old that her asshole father can't stand up to his immature and insecure child bride and is afraid he'll lose pussy access?

"I hate him." The tears rolled down her freckled cheeks.

"Don't hate him, sweetie. Hate what he did." Though I knew she had every right to hate him, she'd looked forward to this for months and he'd promised her he would not let her down again. I didn't want her to have an adversarial relationship with her dad. "So, what if there was a way you could still go to the dance. Would you be interested?"

Lifting her head from her pillow, I could see how swollen her eyes were from crying and in that moment, I hated Frank just a little bit more. "Is Uncle Bryan coming in?"

With a smile, I shook my head. "No. This is a mystery date."

"A mystery date?" I actually couldn't tell whether she

was intrigued or horrified.

"Yes. A mystery date. Just hear me out, okay." Scarlett nodded. "He's father age appropriate. He's handsome, very cool, has got a great personality, and I know you will totally hit it off with him."

"Oh God, Mom, you didn't get him off a dating website or something." Scarlett's blue eyes were wide with horror.

Laughing, "No silly. This is someone I know and he's really psyched to take you on Saturday."

"Are you going to tell me who it is?"

Shaking my head, I smiled at my daughter. "No. It's a mystery date."

"Mom, this better not be embarrassing." How had she perfected teenage attitude already?

Ruffling her hair, "Just the opposite, my love. You are going to have the hottest, coolest date there."

"A hint?"

I continued to shake my head, no. Torturing a teen was a fun sport. "So, is that a yes? Shall I tell him the date is on?"

"I guess," she acquiesced with the obligatory eyeroll.

Pulling my phone out of my pocket, I emailed Wes. **It's a go!**

**"Okay, here's what he says,"** Tell her I can't wait to meet her.

Sitting on the couch with a glass of wine after Scarlett had gone to sleep, I tried to sort out my emotions from the day. Frank could pull shit on me, I was an adult, with the emotional fortitude to handle it, but to fuck over Scarlett that way, well, that was just unconscionable. Was he seriously not standing up to a 25-year old? How hard would it have been to say to her, "You know we can't go away that weekend, I have Scarlett's dance." He seriously couldn't say that? Dickless ass!

As I brought my wineglass to my lips, I had a thought. Something that was probably as juvenile as Frank's behavior, but would make me feel better.

Rummaging around my desk drawer I found what I was looking for. I could feel my smile growing as I pulled the bag out.

"Hello, little dolls," I smiled.

Pulling the male doll from the bag. "Hello, Frank doll. Well this is apropos, because this doll is not anatomically correct. It's missing a dick. And balls. Just like the real Frank. Because you've turned into quite the dickless motherfucker."

Opening the pin box, I looked at all the colorful heads on the pins. "Hmm, which color fits the circumstance. Is there a pink one? Because you are pussy whipped, my friend. So, the pink pin it is."

Putting the doll down on the desk, I took the pink pin and stabbed the poppet between the legs. "If you had a dick, I just stabbed it." I pulled the pin out and stabbed it again in the same spot, just for good measure.

"Take that, you loser." I told the doll before putting it back in the bag and returning it to the desk drawer.

With a final sip of my wine, I felt much, much better.

"Hi sweetie," I answered my cell late the next afternoon. "What's up?"

"Mom, you're never going to believe this." The excitement in Scarlet's voice was at full throttle.

"What? Tell me."

"I just got a package."

"From who?" I started closing down files on my computer.

"From him."

I laughed. I still wasn't getting it. "Him who?"

"My date. It's from my mystery date."

"What did he send?" I packed my laptop into its case.

"It's so unbelievably cool. It's a picture frame that looks like a cell phone. And he stuck a post-it note on it that says, *We need to take one badass selfie for this.* It's like literally the cutest thing ever, Mom."

"It sounds it!" I couldn't believe how Wes was going out of his way to create a wonderful occasion for Scarlett. The man was blowing my mind.

Hanging up with her, I shot Wes a text from my phone.

**You just made someone's day!**

Oh great, she got it! I messengered it over so that she would have it today. Build up the excitement.

My heart melted. How thoughtful was this guy to think about the details to make my daughter happy? I hoped Keiko appreciated what she had, because guys like this were few and far between.

**Wes...**

**Tara...**

**Giving you a virtual hug.**

**You can give me a real one when you see me.**

**Deal,** I told him, wondering how I'd let him go if I were ever in his embrace.

I was on my first cup of coffee Saturday morning, when the doorbell buzzed. Dragging to the door, I looked out the peep hole to see a young man with flowers.

"I have a delivery for Scarlett Collins."

"Scarlett," I called. "Bring me my wallet."

Reaching the door, she gasped. "Are those for me?" She took the arrangement of blue hydrangeas and white roses from the delivery boy.

"And this, too." He handed her a small box wrapped in textured silver foil paper.

Heading back to the kitchen, I admired the flowers on the table. "They match your dress," I noted. "Aren't you going to read this?" I pulled the card.

Still holding the silver box, she looked from the box to the card back to the box, trying to decide which to open first.

I laughed, "Just choose one."

Putting the card down, her curiosity as to what was in the box won out.

"Oh my God, this is like literally so exciting," she exclaimed. And so, it was. In that moment, I thought, had Frank been home and taking her tonight, none of this would have been happening. At 7:30 P.M., he would show up. Beginning and end of story. There would have been none of this preamble to build the excitement and make Scarlett feel special.

*Ah Wes, I bet you are the king of foreplay because you certainly know how to thrill a woman with anticipation.*

Scarlett squealed the minute the lid came off the box. "How did he know? I've been like literally dying for this." Out of the box she pulled a silver Michael Kors bracelet with a pave heart slider.

"That's beautiful." Again, Wes Bergman had rendered me speechless. He had taken this situation where my daughter, who was feeling not very special at the hands of her father, and transformed it into an opportunity to make it one of the most memorable weekends in her young life.

*Keiko, go find someone your own age to play with because Wes is stealing my heart with his beautiful heart.*

Finally, Scarlett was ready for the card.

**Scarlett – Right now I wish I had the superpower to speed up time … just so I could meet you sooner. ~ Wes**

"His name is Wes?" She was beaming when she looked up at me.

I nodded, extending my hand for the card. Smiling at his message, I couldn't help but think that maybe he was a superhero. The White Knight.

"Can't I come over?" Laynie had begged.

"No, I'll take pictures and then I'll meet you for dinner after they leave."

"But I want to see him and I want to see Scarlett all dressed up," she was actually whining.

"You'll see pictures. I think the three of us in the room is going to be overwhelming enough for now."

Coming out of her bedroom, I was entranced by my little girl; she looked perfect and beautiful. But more than anything, what I noted was that my daughter was happy and I could not thank Wes enough for making it so.

"Look at you," was all I could say. "Scarlett, you look gorgeous."

"I look like I'm sixteen, don't I?"

"At least!" I laughed, taking in her fresh-faced beauty.

Playing nervously with her new bracelet, "I hope Wes and I have stuff to talk about. What if we have like literally nothing to talk about, Mom?"

"Don't worry, sweetie," I reassured her. "Wes is this totally cool guy who is really easy to talk to. When I first met him, he and I stayed up a whole night talking, we had so much to talk about. So, I think you'll do okay."

And there he was at the door.

"You ready?" I asked Scarlett before opening it.

Nodding, I could see her curiosity was trumping her nerves.

"Okay, here goes, let the mystery date begin!" I said, as

I opened the door.

Laughing, as he had heard my introduction, there stood Wes Bergman at my front door looking like he was ready for a Tom Ford photoshoot in his white dinner jacket and black bowtie, crazy curls all askew and a florist's box with a blue and white corsage in hand.

Catching my breath was more difficult than I expected as he leaned forward and kissed my cheek.

"You look so handsome." My words were an understatement. Somewhere in my psyche I knew that this image of him was something that would be with me for the rest of my life.

"Thank you." His eyes crinkled and then I watched that smile that always grabbed me and twirled my heart around the room take over his face as he laid eyes on Scarlett. "You are even more beautiful than your picture, Princess."

The moment his eyes were on her and he called her Princess, I watched my daughter do a teen version of swooning. Her right shoulder came up and her chin dipped as she looked up at him through her lashes. *Was I really watching this?*

"I've got another little something for you." He took the corsage, baby white roses set on pale blue lace, out of its box and tied the blue satin sash around her unadorned wrist. "I see you've got my heart." He gestured to the bracelet.

"Just make sure I don't break it," my fourteen-year old quipped.

My jaw went slack as I heard the words come out of my daughter's mouth.

Wes laughed at my precocious child, "Like mother, like daughter. I'm toast," he declared. "Are you ready, Princess?"

"One sec, you two. You are not getting out of here without a picture." My daughter looked very happy under his arm as I shot a few pictures.

"Wait until she sees our selfies," Wes said to Scarlett,

bringing her immediately into a co-conspirator role.

As they headed out the door, Scarlett turned to me and through her smile mouthed the words, "He's cute."

I nodded and mouthed, "Told ya," as my daughter and this handsome white knight left to make their own memories.

It was nearly midnight when I heard from them again.

"Hey Tara, it's Wes."

"Hi, what's up."

"If it's okay with you that I keep Scarlett out just a little later, we were going to stop off at a diner and grab a bite to eat."

"Didn't you guys eat at the dance?"

He laughed. "Not much and we danced it off, so we're starved. Do you want us to come and get you?"

"No, I'm good. Have fun."

"I promise I'll have her home long before daybreak." I could hear the smile in his voice.

Walking through the door at 1:15 A.M., a very happy and tired Scarlett looked at her date and threw her arms around him in a bear hug. "Thank you for making this the best night ever."

Hugging her back, he planted a kiss on the top of her head. "Ah Princess, this was one of the most memorable nights I've ever had. Thank you so much for letting me be your date."

"Goodnight, you guys." She turned around and waved

as she headed to her room.

"Can I get you something? A cup of coffee, perhaps?"

"Definitely," he said, following me into the kitchen. Taking off the white dinner jacket, he hung it on the back of a chair and loosened his bowtie.

"I can't thank you enough," I said, as I handed him a mug of coffee.

"Tara, I had the best time. She is an amazing kid. You should be so proud."

"I am. Did she open up to you at all about the Frank situation?"

He nodded. "Yeah, we talked about it some. I told her that it is his shortcoming and in no way should she think this is her or how she should be treated by men. And that not all men are like that. She's really very mature."

"I don't even know where to begin to thank you, Wes."

The smile was on his face as he opened his arms, "You can thank me with a hug."

He didn't need to ask twice as I closed the space between us, fifteen years of separation rapidly being whisked away. As his arms closed around me, I let myself enjoy the barrage of sensations, his heat, his scent, his strength, realizing that I'd been waiting for this very moment from a few hours into the night we met. And now here we were, a lifetime away, and I was finally enjoying the comforts of Wes' embrace, yet knowing that it didn't mean what I'd hope it would. And now, it never could.

"You don't have to be so strong all the time," he whispered in my ear.

"Oh, but I do. Because as you saw it's not just me to worry about and I can't count on anyone. I have to be strong for her."

Wes tightened his hold around me. "You amaze me, Tara. If there's anything you need, I'm just a call away."

Letting my head find its comfortable spot on his chest,

I closed my eyes, momentarily spiriting away to that place that I could pretend, just for one second, that Wes didn't have a girlfriend who wasn't me.

I was having strange dreams of Wes when the phone woke me out of my restless sleep.

"Hello," my voice was barely a croak after three hours sleep.

"Tara," the voice sounded far away and broken.

"Yes, who is this?" I couldn't yet pry my eyes open.

"It's me, Tara. It's Crystal," she sounded as if she'd been crying.

"Is everything alright? Where are you? Are you in Paris?" I was now sitting up in bed, raking my hair from my face.

"Yes, we're still here."

"Crystal, where's Frank? What's going on?" I was starting to feel panic set in.

"Frank's in the hospital, Tara," she began to sob.

"Oh my God, what happened? Is he okay?"

Through her sobs, she squeaked out, "He passed two kidney stones."

My half-closed eyes opened wide. Kidney stones. Massive penile pain. Twice. Holy shit!

My worry of anything major subsided and I had to hold back my laughter. "Is he alright?"

"Yes, he's resting comfortably, but he was in so much pain last night."

"I'll bet he was." I nodded.

"He said it was like being stabbed."

Moving the phone from my mouth so that she wouldn't hear my snickers, I took a moment to collect myself before speaking again.

"Oh, that sounds terrible," I managed, picking at a thread on my comforter.

"It was. It was horrible. I was so worried and it ruined my parent's whole anniversary celebration," she was now whining.

Seriously? Did she really expect me to commiserate with her on her ruined party plans after what she and Frank pulled on Scarlett? Could she be that clueless?

"It is really hard to have to handle all the health issues you older people have."

*You older people?* Did she just call me that?

"Okay Crystal, I'm hanging up now. Tell Frank I hope he feels better and have a fabulous rest of your trip." Click.

Two kidney stones. Two pin stabs. Holy crap, this was truly getting scary. First Crystal and the toe stub. Now Frank and the kidney stones. Maybe that old toothless lady in Dominica wasn't kidding, maybe these dolls had voodoo powers. These coincidences were crazy. Could it be just putting the thought out there in the universe was creating the energy to make these things happen?

Holy shit! I was slightly freaked out, but at the same time loving it. Take that, Frank. Hurt your daughter and I'll stab your dick again, you coward.

Curling back under my covers, I couldn't help but smile. Scarlett had a wonderful night at the Father/Daughter Formal with Wes and Frank's dick basically went up in flames in Paris. It was a good night. A very good night indeed.

I couldn't wait to tell Laynie and Jill.

# Chapter 13

"Tara, Tara, Tara." There was a mocking tone in his voice as he entered my office and slithered into a guest chair across the desk. "I don't know if I'll ever get used to calling you that."

"I know the feeling, Matthew. I mean Julien." I smiled, as I turned from my computer screen to face him.

"You're really not quite as amusing as you think."

While maintaining my smile, I began chanting in my head, *"He's a client. He's a client. He's a client."*

"So, what's up?" I knew he wanted something. Julien Matthews was not parked in my office for a social visit.

"You tell me, Tara." The emphasis was on my name.

"Your visit. Your agenda."

Picking up the frame with Scarlett's picture, he looked at it, then at me. "Cute kid."

"Thank you."

Without putting down the frame, "Pretty sleazy move there to use your kid to hook Wes."

"What are you talking about?" I could tell there was a look of disgust on my face and I immediately tried to get back to neutral. I was reacting and that was just what he wanted.

"Wes has done well with the ladies over the years. You've obviously seen Keiko so you know he attracts beautiful women. You don't stand a chance. So, to use your kid as bait is really a desperate move, Tara."

Reaching across the desk, I plucked the picture frame out of his hand.

"Julien," I shook my head, "do not take a really lovely gesture on your friend's part and turn it into something ugly, because there was no underlying evil or nefarious scheme attached to Wes helping out."

And with a sneer on his lips, the man rolled his eyes at me. Choosing not to continue down that road, I pivoted.

"You know those weeks we talked, I really enjoyed our conversations. We appeared to have a lot in common and quite a bit to talk about."

"Appearances can be deceiving." He smiled at his success in turning my words on me.

"Yes, they can." I paused to let that sink in. "But, you know, I really think we do have a lot in common."

"So what? You want to be *friends?*" Venom dripped off the last word.

"I don't know if that will ever happen. I do know never say never. But we are colleagues and what I'd love to see is a good professional relationship and maybe peaceful co-existence on a personal level. Julien, we have no reason to hate each other."

"You got off the dating site pretty damn quickly."

So, that's what this was all about. Even though he'd "dumped" me, he wanted me to come back for more and had obviously looked for me and I was gone before he "released" me. I didn't come begging. What a flipping control freak this guy was.

"Oh Julien, it wasn't for me." I decided, let's see how

the man reacts to honesty. "I really enjoyed talking to you for those few weeks and you lose friends as quickly as you make them on those sites. I can't do that."

"Maybe you shouldn't hook up with everyone." His sneer was saying checkmate.

As I maintained direct contact with his icy blue eyes, I certainly was not going to tell him he'd been the only one. The last thing this dude needed to know was that he and my ex were the only two men I'd had sex with in over fifteen years.

As he got up to leave, I cursed myself for wasting the male poppet doll on Frank.

*Jullie A. Richman*

# Chapter 14

I shouldn't have been this emotional. Scarlett had been attending this sleepaway camp since she was ten. But for some reason, being alone for the first time in the new condo was making me feel as empty as the space I was inhabiting. I missed my daughter. Her laugh, her eyeroll, her obsession with the boys in Five Seconds of Summer.

Walking the halls, I couldn't get comfortable in my own space those first few nights. I hoped the feeling would subside as I got used to being alone. Scarlett's absence made it brutally clear that my life revolved around my daughter and my job and somewhere in there, Tara had been lost. *Was I doing this because it was safe,* I wondered?

"Why don't you take a vacation?" Laynie asked over lunch that week.

"I'm swamped at work. We're still working on the C-Kicker campaigns for launch in October during National Breast Cancer Awareness Month, and we just picked up Food Bank for NYC as a client, so a long weekend is probably all I'd be able to get away for and I'm going to save that for Parent's Weekend at camp."

"You need something more, you know that," she pressed.

I know Laynie was expecting to get an argument from me, defending that everything was fine the way it was, but I surprised her when I agreed with her. "You're right, I do. I just don't know what. I don't know how to be single and socially active. I kind have dug myself into the holes of being highly successful at being single and alone, single and a great mom and single and a workaholic. But I don't know how to be single and socially successful."

"You need a pool boy." Laynie was dead serious.

"That would work much better if I had a backyard and a pool." I lamented.

"Excuses, excuses." She shook her head while focusing on cutting a slice of grilled eggplant.

"Bitch."

We both laughed, but I was no closer to figuring out how to keep the loneliness at bay that was invading the sanctity of my nights.

"Hey, what are you doing here?" It was a surprise to see Wes walk into my office. Renata and Kelly were the two we had the most contact with and it had been at least a month since Wes had been onsite.

"There were some rushes that needed my approval."

I was surprised we hadn't just uploaded them to him.

"And I have to meet Julien in about an hour. Our biggest fabric supplier is in from the Far East and we have a last meeting with them out by Kennedy Airport before they head home, so I figured I'd stop by here first.

"Sit down." I motioned to the chair.

He picked up the picture of Scarlett and smiled. "So, she seems to be loving sleepaway camp."

"You two are in touch?" I was shocked.

Wes laughed. "The mom's always the last to know. Yeah, I get texts from her every few days."

"You do? That child tells me nothing." I shook my head.

"That was some bruise she got falling off that horse, but she says she feels fine," his delivery was casual.

Gripping the edge of my desk, I sat up straight. "Scarlett fell off a horse and the camp didn't call me?" My voice rose an octave.

"I guess I wasn't supposed to say anything. She's fine, Tara."

"Wes, show me that picture." My hand was outstretched for his phone.

Scrolling through their text thread, he came to the picture and handed me the phone.

"Oh my God, she should have been x-rayed," I gasped, looking at my daughter's purple thigh.

Scrolling down the thread, I was amazed at their rapport and the wonderful advice he was giving her on friends, life and boys.

"And who is this?" I turned the phone around to show him a picture of a boy.

Wes laughed, "That is Cameron."

"Cameron?"

"Yeah, Cameron lives in New Hampshire and is captain of the camp soccer team."

"And I assume my daughter likes Cameron?" I asked.

With a shit-eating grin, Wes filled me in. "I guess you could say Scarlett and Cameron are an item." He just sat there smiling at me. "If you weren't holding my phone I'd take a picture of you right now to send to your daughter. Subject: Freaked Out Mother."

"I can't believe I don't know any of this." I think Wes

finally read the sadness in my eyes. "She used to tell me everything."

"And she will again, Tara. I think she's just excited to get a male perspective on guys. I'm a safe place that's not mom or dad."

I nodded. "Well, thank you for being there for her. I really do appreciate it."

"And honestly, I didn't realize she wasn't sharing some of this stuff with you. But now that I know that, if it's anything important, like falling off a horse or falling in love, I'll make sure you're aware of it."

"Thank you," I began to say, as his phone buzzed in my hand. The screen flashed Keiko. "Oh, for you." I awkwardly handed his phone back to him.

"Hey, what's up?"

I suddenly felt like the outsider in my own office. *Do I give him privacy? Step out into the hall?*

Wes' demeanor changed at lightning speed, a crease forming between his brow as his spine stiffened and the tic in his jaw pulsed.

The tsunami of tension from across the desk slammed me unexpectedly and I knew I needed to vacate immediately or I was somehow going to go under. Standing, I grabbed my cell and came around my desk toward the door. Wes' right hand shot out, grabbed my forearm and held me there. It was in that moment that I realized he was not pulling me to safety but using me as an anchor and I threaded my fingers through his, squeezing his hand tightly.

"That's fine," his tone denoted anything but fine. "Just make sure everything is out by the time I get home today. And I mean everything, Keiko. Garbage comes tomorrow."

*Holy shit.*

"Well, clearly that is too much of an imposition on you and Lord knows, I would hate to impose." I hoped never to hear him use that tone on me.

He sat listening for a moment and then finally said, "Are you done? Because I am." And clicked off his phone.

This was like watching a train wreck and I just wished I was a few car lengths back instead of getting a front row view of the carnage.

Leaning back in his seat, Wes shook his head and smiled. "She was supposed to drive Stacy to chemo today and hang out and wait for her while I was at this meeting with our fabric supplier. She felt that it was too much of an imposition and more than she'd signed on for in our relationship."

Giving his hand another squeeze, I weighed in. "Well, she just showed you all you needed to know about her." Probably not smart to trash his girlfriend, but I didn't care.

"She sure did." Looking over at me, he smiled. "It's strange, but I feel nothing. I just want her to go."

"She doesn't deserve more than that."

Wes squeezed my hand. "You speak truth, woman."

And we both laughed.

"Crap, I need to call Julien and let him know I won't be meeting him."

"Hey, hold on a second," I interrupted him. "How about if you keep your meeting and I take Stacy to chemo." I didn't know I was going to offer until the words were out of my mouth. "I definitely owe you one."

"Tara, you owe me nothing. Taking Scarlett to the dance was my pleasure."

I had to laugh. "Well, I don't know that taking Stacy to chemo will be a pleasure, but I'm more than happy to help you out here."

His eyes crinkled as that smile took over his face. "She's going to shit when she sees it's you."

Swinging his hand, I laughed. "I can't imagine it will make her wish she'd been nicer to me. Don't tell her, I can't wait to see her face when I show up."

"Tara, I owe you."

"There's no debt between friends. Just don't hesitate to ask when you need me, okay."

This was a small price to pay for the friendship and stability he had selflessly been providing to my daughter.

I let Chris know I was leaving the office and made a few stops for supplies before heading home to pick up my car and go get Stacy. Pulling up in front of a 1940's red brick house, I wondered if this was where Stacy and Wes grew up.

Climbing the three steps to the front door, I could not suppress my smile. I rang the bell and waited. Oh, this was going to be good.

The shock in Stacy's eyes when she flung open the door made my day. Expect the unexpected.

"Not Keiko," I exclaimed with false cheer.

"Fuck. You keep turning up like a bad penny. Didn't I get rid of you like fifteen years ago? So, where the hell is that bitch, Keiko?" I had officially been greeted by Stacy Bergman.

"Bitch be gone."

"Gone? Like she's meeting one of her twelve-year old looking friends for lunch or gone, like you should be?"

I laughed. "Shit, Stacy. It's good to see some things never change. Hey, you are damn lucky your brother is in the garment industry, so he can get you free scraps of fabric for your head." I motioned to her scarf covered head. I guess I had been expecting her long thick dark brown hair and the paisley head covering was the harsh reality simmering beneath our banter, one that caused a jagged ache. Both for Stacy and Wes.

"Fuck you, Tara. So, where the hell is Keiko?"

"Gone. And Wes had a meeting out by the airport, so

you're stuck with me today."

"Ugh," said Stacy, grabbing her purse. "And I thought cancer was bad." She blew by me on the front steps, heading for my car. "Come on already, we're going to be late," she barked at me.

*How the hell did she get such a terrific brother*, I wondered?

Much to Stacy's chagrin, there were empty lounge chairs in the infusion room and a very sweet nurse who invited me to come in. I sat silently as they readied her port and the nurse asked questions.

"So, how did you feel after the last infusion?"

"Tired. More tired than I've felt with previous infusions," Stacy shared her side effects.

"I'm not surprised. As you know from your last round, it tends to be cumulative. How severe has the nausea been?"

"Days two and three are my worst."

"Do you need anything for it?"

"No, I think I'm still pretty good with my Compazine."

"Are you eating?"

"I try."

"Drinking plenty of water?"

"Yes." Stacy rolled her eyes at the nurse.

"Just looking out for your well-being. Any mouth sores?"

"No."

Listening to the litany of questions, I was sad for Stacy, that this was her reality.

"How often do you come?" I asked.

"Every three weeks. But I only have a few more to go."

Nodding, I took in the room. Leather recliner chairs

lined three walls. There was a large TV high on the fourth wall playing *House Hunters International,* and I wished I was with the British couple looking at cave houses in Santorini.

"Those things kind of freak me out." I gestured toward the TV.

"Why?" Stacy looked at the handsome couple weighing the pros and cons of three properties.

"I don't know. Being in a room without windows is a bit spooky and the thought of an earthquake or something and being trapped in a cave totally wigs me out."

"You're weird, Tara. Look at that Infinity pool overlooking the Mediterranean. I would love to be there."

Digging into an oversized beach bag, I gave Stacy a mysterious smile.

"What? What are you going to torture me with now, Tara? Besides your mere presence."

Laughing, "Damn woman, you are such a treat." And I pulled out what I was looking for and handed one to Stacy.

She looked at the paperback's cover and flipped it over to read the blurb on the back.

"Is that Claudia Bustamonte's new book?" A fiftyish woman was getting her infusion three chairs down.

"Yes," I nodded. "It is."

"I just read her *Time Slips Away* Trilogy. I could not put it down."

"I loved that series." I agreed with the woman.

Looking at the copy in my hands, Stacy commented, "So, you bought us the same book?"

"Yes, I thought we could both read it and then we'd have something to talk about."

Before she could answer, the other woman chimed in, "What a great idea."

"Would you like my copy," I offered her. "I'll just download it on my phone and read it there."

"I couldn't," she began to protest.

Getting up from the lounge chair, "Please, it will be fun to all do this together. I'm Tara, by the way." With a smile, I happily handed her my copy.

"Well, thank you so much, Tara. I'm Andie."

"This will be fun to talk about." Andie's smile was beautiful. "Will you be here with us in three weeks?"

"I could be," I answered with a shrug of my shoulders, looking over at Stacy.

She was already on chapter one when I sat back down. "Ugh. You're actually a nice person. No wonder why my brother likes you so much," she mumbled.

My day had just been made.

It was about 8 P.M. that evening when I heard from Wes.

"Hey, I just wanted to thank you for today. I hope she didn't give you too hard a time."

I laughed, "She's as ornery as I remember her."

"Oh no, that bad?"

Pouring a glass of red wine, I moved toward my couch as if it were an oasis in the Sahara, kicked my shoes off and spread out. "Nah. Not too bad at all. So, how are you? Are you okay?"

"Yes, I got home and as she promised, all signs that she'd ever been here, are gone."

"I'm sorry, Wes."

"Getting dumped is no fun, but honestly, Tara, this has been over for a while. I knew she didn't have any place to go, so I didn't push it." He sounded tired.

"I guess she found a place." The minute it came out of my mouth, I hoped it didn't sound snarky.

He laughed and I was instantly relieved that he didn't

take it that way. "Thank God." He paused for a moment. "I would like to thank you for today. Do you have plans Friday night?"

I could feel my cheeks making my eyes crinkle. Was Wes Bergman actually asking me out on a date? Never did I ever think this would happen. "I don't know. Do I?"

"You do." And I could hear him smile.

"What am I doing Friday night?" To say I felt giddy would be an understatement. I had wanted to spend time alone with this man from the night I met him, but that was a dream I was convinced would never happen in this lifetime. And now, what was this? Was it really happening?

"You're having dinner with me on my boat. I'm going to fire up the grill and cook for you." The man sounded proud.

"You have a boat?" This was a surprise, but having met him on a boat, I was excited to be on a boat with him again. I probably should have been more surprised that he was going to cook for me. Frank had never even scrambled eggs for me.

"I do," he laughed. "After a certain windjammer trip, I made myself a promise that I would buy myself a boat as soon as I could afford it."

"Well, I would love to have dinner with you on your boat. What can I bring?"

"Just you. I'm at the Brewer Capri Marina up on Manhasset Bay. I'll text you over directions and a map to the boat. Eight o'clock work for you?"

"Sounds perfect." And I knew exactly what I was bringing.

Laynie and Jill had watched and laughed as I tried on half my closet. I ended up in a pair of white jeans shorts, a turquoise tank top and a white boat neck sweater with thin turquoise horizontal stripes.

"You look very Ralph Lauren," Laynie commented as I tied the straps from my turquoise espadrilles around my lower shin.

"Love the shoes." Jill gave me the nod of approval. "Anything that ties around your leg like that is sexy in a totally casual way."

"Do not forget the perfume," Laynie marched into my bathroom, coming out with the Dolce & Gabbana Light Blue in hand. "He's recreating the boat thing, so you're going to help him fill in any memory gaps."

It was fun having friends over to help me get ready for my date and cheer me on.

"How is his evil friend?" Jill raised her brows.

"From what I've heard, he's over in the Far East for like a month. Wes didn't want to go out of town with Stacy undergoing chemo."

"Ugh, he's still on the planet. Too close for comfort." Laynie stretched out on my comforter.

"He's like this black cloud hanging over me. I'm waiting for the other shoe to drop, for him to tell Wes what happened and Wes to want to have nothing to do with me." I could feel my nausea rise to a fevered pitch just verbalizing it. Rationally, I knew it was before Wes came back into my world, but the emotional part of me told me that Wes would not be happy hearing about it. I wanted to tell him, so that he would hear it from me. But I also just wanted to ignore it and maybe it would just go away.

"You guys, I have to tell him. Or it's always going to be there weighing on me. Choking me. Plus, I'd rather he hears it from me and know I wasn't hiding it." I didn't realize I'd been wringing my hands, until I noticed Jill staring at them. "And Lord knows how Julien would spin it. He could make it even worse, just to be a bastard."

I was not in an enviable spot and I needed to come clean with Wes and accept whatever consequences ensued.

Julien. Julien. Julien. Oh, how I wish I'd never met you.

# Chapter 15

With a map in hand, I navigated past gorgeous sailboats and yachts in search of Wes' berth. Trying to walk with confidence, big purse slung over one shoulder filled with everything I might need – or not, weighty freezer bag firmly planted on the other arm, I was beyond nervous, as if the world were riding on this, a date with a man I'd waited half my life to date. *Why did the stakes feel so high?*

And there it was. I was wondering what the name would be. Named for his lost wife? His company? Some obscure reference? And then I was upon her. *Second Wind.* And I immediately loved the hope and freedom it implied. There was an optimism and that really spoke to Wes and his entrepreneurial spirit – taking his heartache and turning it into something that brought brightness into others' lives. The possibilities were endless when you were given a second chance. A do-over, per se.

"Hey Wes," I called out, stepping onto the deck.

He bounded up from below, full smile. "You found me."

*Oh yes I did. Again.* "This boat is beautiful." I took in

the teak deck and navy blue appointments.

Laden with bags on my shoulder, I pulled off the freezer bag, thrusting it toward Wes instead of approaching him with any kind of hug.

With eyes widened, as did his surprised smile, he relieved me of the pouch. "Damn that's heavy. A new boat anchor?" he kidded, taking it over to a built in wooden table. Unzipping the bag, he pulled out the huge, oversized pitcher of slushy frozen rum and somethings and laughed at the plastic cups I'd brought for us to drink them.

"Most excellent," he exclaimed, that smile stealing my heart yet again. "I'll try not to spill them on you this time."

Biting my tongue, I just wanted to tell him to spill away as long as he licked them off my toes. But I just laughed.

Pulling out two thick royal blue reclining seat cushions, Wes placed them side-by-side on the deck, with the rum pitcher and cups between them. "Be right back." He bounded down the stairs with lithe grace, returning a moment later with a platter of cheese, crackers, fresh fruit and dip.

Easing onto the comfortable pad chair, I fiddled with the back to get the right recline.

"Here, let me get that for you," he offered, positioning it perfectly for relaxation while still a safe angle for eating and drinking.

With our first rum whatevers safely in plastic cups, we clinked too hard, both spilling and laughed.

"You know we had to do that," I couldn't contain my smile. "For old times' sake."

Raising his glass, his eyes crinkled, "For new times' sake."

*New times.* I liked that. A lot.

Both taking big swigs of the mixture I know I put way too much rum in, I had the feeling that we both needed a little shot of confidence. While I'd kept thinking about it as one bridge dividing us, there were multiple and we needed to cross them one by one.

"So when did you come back to New York?"

"It was probably less than a year after the windjammer trip."

"Really. I would have thought you would have stayed out there. I think you're one of those rare personalities that can adapt to both coasts and really thrive."

He smiled and I could tell there were memories flooding in. "Actually, you kinda ruined that for me."

"Me?" I choked on my drink. "How did I do that?" Sitting up in my chair, I faced him, untying the silk straps on my espadrilles and setting the shoes aside.

"Honestly?" His brows were raised and I knew he was asking if I were ready to really talk.

"Yes. Of course." I picked up the pitcher and refilled both our glasses. We clinked again and laughed at the need for liquid confidence.

"Okay, so I went back to L.A."

"We never said goodbye." It was out of my mouth, not meaning to interrupt him, but I could feel the desperation in my gut that I had that morning. I had missed the chance.

"I know," he whispered.

"I looked for you. You were down the gangplank, entering the terminal. I called out, but it was so loud. And then you disappeared and by the time I made it into the terminal, you were gone."

"You did?"

I nodded and he reached forward, squeezing my hand, the revelation of a moment he'd missed over a decade before sinking in, aided into his blood stream by our rum redux. There was a warmth in his eyes when he looked at me.

"That makes me feel really good." Taking a deep breath, he continued. "So, I went back and at first things felt okay. I was happy to be home, probably just happy to be away from Stacy, who you know was miserable that trip. But my contentment didn't last very long and I was feeling like a fish out of water, in a pond I no longer was sure I wanted to be in. I felt like I was trying to fit in and it was work, as opposed to just being and everyone getting you and still liking you."

"Well, there's a lot to be said for shared history with people," I interjected.

"Yeah, but it's more than that. Shared sensibilities. Shared goals. Shared ethos."

Smiling, "Okay, so I get that. But how did I ruin things?"

Wes' melodious laugh was hearty as he gave me a *Really, Tara* look. "That freaking night, Tara. How do you have a night like that and then sit amongst people who seriously don't get you?" Pausing, he took a sip. "Especially one you are sleeping with and really doesn't understand the fundamentals of what makes you tick. So, that night became this comparison point for me and although that probably was not fair to my girlfriend, it really shone a light on things that were missing." Wes took another sip of the drink. "I remember thinking all that glitters might not be gold and this kind of false California reality began to look decayed in the bright sunshine."

I remained silent because I could see his mind going a mile a minute as memories were plowing in fast and I wanted to hear every word he had to say, experience every thought, all the feelings I'd wondered about for so very long as I questioned for years, in the back of my mind, *was that real?*

"There were a group of us out to dinner one night. Some vegetarian place, of course," he laughed. "It was fall and I just wanted it to feel like fall. I wanted to put on a sweater, sleep with the windows open and no one even understood that. So, that night when we got home, I said to Alicia, my girlfriend, I'm booking us two tickets for a long weekend back east, we'll try and hit peak foliage, check out some apple orchards, get cider."

I know my smile was huge just listening to him as he described the wonderfully simple things nature brought to us that were a timeless gift. Those perfect few weeks of Indian Summer when the northeast was a magical tapestry of color, smells and crunches of bright leaves underfoot.

"What happened?"

"There was not a damn fucking thing she liked about fall in the northeast."

"What? How is that possible?" I truly was shocked. Just listening to Wes, all my senses were filled with the splendor of autumn. Apple cider. I could taste iced cold apple cider in my mind.

"Right? How is that possible. She literally counted down the hours till we got back to Los Angeles."

"Wow." I was speechless, so I continued to drink as if the rum whatever was going to give me some insightful answer to impart.

"I couldn't figure it out, so being a glutton for punishment, I said, okay let's try a Christmas trip to New York. Rockefeller Center, store windows, the Rockettes at Radio City Music Hall. Quintessential Christmas in New York."

"And?"

"It was like I was torturing the poor girl."

"I don't understand." I just shook my head and reached for a chunk of cheddar cheese. "I mean, it might not be what she grew up with, but people come from all over the world. The energy is magical here from the fall through the holidays. The weather is generally beautiful and everything is so festive. I can't think of a more feel good time or place to spend that time of year."

"It was hard to go back to L.A. after that and feel good about things. I tried for a long time to convince myself that the lifestyle made me happy, but I really felt alone."

"I'm sorry."

"And Tara, you popped into my head often because I knew, because you showed me, that there are people who are naturally on the same wavelength you are on. You don't have to try. It's natural and organic and it is there. And I remember being angry at my own circumstance. That when I met you, I wasn't free to explore a relationship with you. And I hated that our timing was off. I hated that we just walked out of one another's lives. Although our time together had been short, I felt like I'd lost a best friend. Now, had it been today, I would have Facebooked you or something when I moved back. But it wasn't. And a year had gone by. But I knew as soon as I was back, that it was right. This was where I belonged and if I could have a relationship with someone who got me the way you got me, that I could be happy."

"And you did." I was thinking about his wife.

"Yes. I did." Wes smiled at me. "You two would have liked each other a lot."

Reaching out, I took Wes' hand. "Of that, I have no doubt. And I'm really glad you think so."

Squeezing my hand back. "Are you as nervous as I am, Tara?"

Nodding, I felt instant relief hearing him verbalize that. "We set a memory bar very high. And we have a work relationship, which does complicate things." *And then there is Julien. The ghost hanging over me. Which I regret because he shouldn't be marring us. But he was before you came back...* I wondered what he knew. If anything. Julien was a 220-pound gorilla sitting on my chest, choking the joy out of me. I didn't want to give him that power, but I just couldn't push all his negative juju far enough away, even though he was currently on the other side of the world.

"Wes, we've had a connection from the second we met. And I think we both get how special that is. That night we met was like meeting my best friend for the first time and that doesn't ever happen. I make friends slowly and have a small circle that are close to me. You have this big personality – I don't think you've ever met a stranger, and that is an amazing talent. So, I never really knew if that night was just a normal night for you, just the way you relate to people or if our connection was different."

I was shocked to see the stricken look in his eyes and the deep crevasse form between his brows. "Tara, seriously?"

I nodded, "Seriously." I needed to hear him tell me.

Moving the food tray and pitcher from between us, he shifted his seat over, adjacent to mine, slinging his arm over my shoulder and pulling my head close, and in that moment, it felt right to settle in there. Bridge one had just been crossed. It took over fifteen years.

His voice was gruff when he spoke. "I met my best friend for the first time. I can't think of a better way to describe it. You were there, and as every minute flowed effortlessly into the next hour, you were inextricably more a part of my life, immediately – both past and present, as if there had never been a moment without you. Our crazy one degree of separation was uncanny and it was clear we were supposed to meet. It had been like we'd been playing this parallel game of hopscotch our entire lives. We were always so close, yet one step away. So no Tara, the level of instant connect that I had with you, is not the level I get to with most people – at least not for a very long time," he paused, then added, "if ever. Never. Just once." He took a sip from his drink. "I really didn't know what to do with it. I knew what I wanted to do with it. And I couldn't and I was so at odds because of that. I'm not a cheater. That's not who I am. But I also knew, on some deep, cellular level that letting you walk out of my life was a tremendous loss that shouldn't happen. I never should have left that ship without a way to stay in touch. And I regretted that. I regretted it deeply. And that stayed with me."

Lifting my head from his shoulder, I shifted in my chair to face him. I needed to see his eyes. "We weren't ready.

Our paths weren't ready yet. We both had other destinies to fulfill."

"Ready now?" He raised his brows, questioningly.

"Almost." Taking a deep breath, I gathered courage I prayed I possessed. *Please don't let this be the end,* I prayed.

"Almost?"

"There's something we need to talk about."

Wes shook his head. "No, Tara. We don't."

"We do. We can't have this between us," I implored, sick to speak the words about to come out of my mouth.

Adamantly, Wes continued to shake his head. "Trust me. What you think you need to tell me, you do not need to tell me. It is a conversation we should not have."

Could he possibly be talking about the same thing? Had Julien already said something to him.

"We have to. You have to hear this from me."

"No, Tara. Trust me on this. I do not. It is best *not* to have the conversation you think we need to have. Trust me. I know me and I'm telling you. You do not need to verbalize this."

"I don't want it between us."

"It's not going to be between us."

"Are you sure?" I searched his eyes. He had to be talking about me and Julien.

"I'm positive and it is nothing I ever want to discuss. Please trust me on this one."

Looking down in my lap, I studied the shade of pink on my fingernails. "Okay, I'm going to honor that. I just want to say one thing." I looked up at him. "I would never do anything to intentionally hurt you. And I hope you know that I think the world of you and I consider our paths crossing again to be a huge, huge gift. One that I really cherish. I hope you know that."

"I do know that, Tara and that is exactly why the conversation you think needs to take place really does not need to take place and would actually be detrimental. This is about moving forward. From here. Now. Not the past."

He knew. *He knew.* And he still wanted to move forward with me. I closed my eyes and let the relief wash over me. What Wes and I felt for one another. The potential of what we could be was so much greater than Julien's toxic energy and games. I let the power of that wash over me as if cleansing my soul, which hit rock bottom that Sunday morning when I mistakenly and naively believed that Julien Matthews actually had a heart, foolishly allowing him to use and disregard me in his sick and misguided quest to prove his manhood. I had momentarily given him power, which yes, I did regret, but I had cut it off before that day even ended. Something he made very clear to me that he resented. The man did not like having his power usurped.

Picking up the pitcher of rum and somethings, I filled both our glasses with the slushy concoction.

"To exploring us. And really getting to know one another. Finally." We clinked glasses, both taking a sip and laughing.

"I've never felt more right about anything." Wes' smile had the effect on me it had had fifteen years before.

"I'm so nervous."

He laughed. "I know."

"Like I don't know how to do this. I don't want to mess this up."

"No pressure. As much time as you need for things to feel right."

I nodded, glad he wasn't pushing me into the physical aspects, even though I'd yearned for that from the night I met him. Here I had jumped into things with men around him, but with Wes, I needed to do this right.

"I appreciate that. But there is one thing."

"What is that?" he asked, his smile warm.

"Your lips. I've always been a bit obsessed with them.

They look so soft." Leaning forward on my knees, I raised my right hand to his cheek as I brought my lips to his. I could feel his smile as I softly tasted his rum sweetened lips beneath mine and he began to kiss me back, a soft exploration that grew in intensity, leaving me breathless, as I always knew it would.

Taking my face in both his hands, he covered my lips in kisses. Strong kisses with his full lips, kisses that clearly told me his intentions to make me his lover. Claiming kisses. Now that I'd tasted his lips, he left no question in my mind. Wes Bergman knew exactly what he had just done.

It was finally our time.

Finishing marinated chicken kebobs and foil packets of zucchini Wes had prepared on the little propane grill, I sat back with a smile. "Oh my God, that was delicious. Thank you." We had stayed docked at the marina and were just enjoying the lights on the harbor and music from other boats.

"So, in that big oversized bag you brought, I'm hoping you've got a bathing suit and clothes. Overnight stuff?"

"I do have a change of clothes and a bathing suit."

"Okay. Well here's what I'd like to propose. I can certainly lend you tee-shirts, plenty of toothbrushes and toiletries on board. I've got two cabins below, so no pressure. If you don't have plans, we could get out early, at first light, sail east, either a leisurely sailing day or see how far toward the east end of the island we can make it. Just figure it out as we go. Catch a great sunset. If we don't go as far, we can be back tomorrow night, if we end up out toward Greenport, we'd be back Sunday night. What do you think?"

"I think you're going to need to lend me a tee-shirt or

two."

His light-hearted laugh made me smile. "My pleasure. I'll have to pick you out some good ones."

The thought of sleeping in Wes' tee-shirts made me smile. Getting up, he quickly bounded down the stairs and was back in a moment, spreading out maps on the teak table. As I slid in next to him on the bench (versus across from him), I couldn't contain my smile. "This is going to be so much fun."

Showing me our routes along the shoreline, we talked about all the other possibilities along the Sound, both on the Long Island and Connecticut shorelines and my heart soared that this wouldn't just be one isolated weekend, but something we could enjoy together, even just an escape dinner cruise out into the harbor to watch sunset. And in that moment, I felt hope that I didn't realize I'd lost when I'd found out that Frank had been cheating on me, when I had to remain strong for our daughter. I'd spent every day trying to rebuild. But there were two things that had evaded me. Hope and Happiness. And I'd been afraid to feel them because I feared I didn't have the strength to have them stripped from my heart yet again.

But as I looked at Wes, a man who'd experienced devastating losses, I realized he wanted to take me on a journey with him. A journey where hope and happiness were possible. Because out on the open waters, there was a second wind and I had the choice to let it swirl around my face and blow my hair all askew or not. But I was being given a choice. And that in itself was a gift.

"Okay, daybreak is going to be here soon. Let me get you set-up."

Going downstairs, he led me to the larger aft cabin, pulling out a fresh toothbrush for me. Disappearing, he arrived a few minutes later with two tee-shirts and a wide-grin. In his left hand was a Ramones shirt, in his right The

Clash.

"Hard choice." I laughed.

"Why is that?" He was being coy.

Looking up at him through my lashes, I reached out and grabbed The Clash shirt. *Should I Stay or Should I Go*, playing on full blast in my head.

He laughed, "Well, if you get lonely, you know where to find me." The man was now torturing me.

"Don't make me be the aggressor."

He nodded. "Okay, I'll remember that."

It was sometime before dawn when I felt him wrapped around me, melted into him and fell back to sleep.

Sunrise and the start of our adventure would be quickly upon us.

# Chapter 16

"T."

I felt his hand brush my hair from my forehead and the mattress depress as he sat down next to me. My nose twitched at the smell of strong coffee and I knew I was smiling before I'd even opened my eyes.

*T.* I liked that. He called me *T.*

"Hey." I stretched, pulling myself up on the pillows and taking the steaming mug he was handing me. "Mmmm."

"It's a little before sunrise. I thought it would be fun to sail into it."

"Sounds perfect." I leaned forward to kiss his tantalizing lips – just because they were there. And I could.

Wes laughed. "No. *That's* perfect." And with a ruffle of my hair. "See you topside." And he left me with my coffee to pull it together.

It was just so easy to be with this man.

As I climbed up on deck, we were just pulling away from our slip and heading out into Manhasset Harbor. The sky was still black and dotted with stars. This was truly a fitting restart to where we'd once stalled so long ago and I was loving the synergy of the continuation. Where we once before ended at dawn, today it signified a new beginning.

With the marina's now shimmering lights behind us and the edges of the eastern sky brightening, I went and stood next to Wes in the cockpit as we watched dawn break together. It was officially a new day.

"Can I be doing anything to help? Cook breakfast? Hoist sails?" Even I had to laugh at the last suggestion.

"I could eat."

"So how do you like your eggs, Mr. Bergman?" I really knew so little about him.

"There isn't an egg I don't like, T. Surprise me."

Smiling. "You got it. Sail on, sail on, Sailor." I quoted The Beach Boys and disappeared down into the salon.

Opening every little cubby in the kitchen and marveling at its efficiency, I should not have been surprised at how well Wes had it stocked with great foods and fine herbs. Immediately in my glory, as cooking was a Zen thing for me and always a way of sharing love, I immediately began chopping herbs and separating egg yolks and egg whites. The minute I saw the smoked salmon, fresh dill and muffin tins (the man had muffin tins on his boat), I got this idea for baked eggs with salmon drizzled with a dill hollandaise sauce. Add some English muffins and fruit and we'd be good to go until later in the day.

"Something smells amazing down there," Wes yelled down at me.

"Few more minutes." I was ladling the sauce over the perfectly browned muffin-shaped eggs, feeling very proud of myself.

I bounded the steps, bringing everything to the teak table in a few loads and called to Wes.

"Tara. Holy smokes, this looks amazing."

"Now let's just hope it tastes that way. Would really hate to poison you the first time I cooked for you." We sat down across from one another; Wes with the smile of a Cheshire cat.

Taking his first bite, he closed his eyes, the grin on his face sublime. "Oh my God. I'm kidnapping you and never letting you off this boat. Gorgeous and she can cook."

"They did come out good." I was relieved, as I dug in, my appetite more voracious from the fresh air than I'd expected.

"This is delicious."

"Well, you had great ingredients for me to play with and I love to cook. I see fresh herbs and I'm in creative heaven."

"I'm now embarrassed by my chicken kebobs." His smile was sheepish as he took another egg muffin from the tray, poked a hole in the top and poured a drowning dose of dill hollandaise into it, until the sauce covered the plate to its edges. "Would it be rude to lick my plate?"

"Your boat. Your rules."

"Licking is fully acceptable then."

"Good rule," I muttered. "I'll keep that in mind."

"I think I'll save some of this sauce." Wes' smile was playful. "For dessert."

"I'd forgotten what a cute town this is and how hilly." With a slip secured at Danford's Hotel & Marina nestled in Port Jefferson harbor, we wandered in and out of the town's little shops.

"Taste this." Wes had speared a piece of salami on a toothpick and was about to feed it to me. The look on his face made me want to eat more than the single slice of salami. I could see his amusement and feel the sexual tension building between us in the farm-to-gourmet store.

With a smile, I opened my mouth for him. "Oh yum, that is good. I love the fennel in it."

"That is produced at a local farm just east of Riverhead," the woman behind the counter informed us. "Have you tried the Chianti Salami?"

We shook our heads no and she produced a long, thin salami from the case, cutting slices for each of us. The minute the taste buds on the side of my tongue savored the salt, I turned to Wes, who was looking at me like someone was giving him a hand job. The man was on the brink of a new kind of oral gratification.

"Okay, can we get a half pound of this and a half pound of the fennel, thinly sliced? What cheeses do you like?" He turned to me.

"I love the triple crèmes and any kind of blue cheese or gorgonzola."

"We are so damn compatible," he laughed, leaning in for a kiss and I could feel my greed rising as I yearned for the softness of his lips. Lord help those poor women who had to kiss thin-lipped men.

Out on the street, he pointed to a local coffee shop. "Want to grab us some coffees and I'll run down the hill and put the food on the boat."

"Sure, what are you drinking?" Thrilled I didn't have to climb back up the hill, I was glad to let him go alone.

"Cappuccino," he called over his shoulder with a smile, already loping down the sidewalk toward the harbor.

Grabbing our coffees and a table, I pulled my phone from my purse and immediately laughed at the barrage of texts sitting there from Laynie.

**So?**
**I need details?**
**Are you alive?**
**If not, I hope he fucked you to death.**
**Where the hell are you?**

**You know you are killing me.**

Taking a sip of my latte, I answered. **All is well. We sailed out to Pt. Jeff. Walking around the town. Wes just went to put some stuff on the boat.**

**OMG you are alive. Details, please.**

**Having fun. Not much to report yet. Taking it slow. He is so easy to be with. He is just one of those rare good guys.**

**He'd better be or I'll have to stab him with pins.**

I choked on my coffee at Laynie's last text.

**I see him coming up the hill. Talk to you later.**

**When are you coming back?**

**Sailing back tomorrow.**

**Have fun. And show him how a grown woman fucks!**

I laughed at her last swipe at Keiko and CB. *Damn right I will!*

As Wes approached, I couldn't help but smile. The man was timeless cool. The hair, the sunglasses, the ease with which his body moved. I wondered how many people passed him thinking, what band is that guy with? Isn't he somebody famous?

I could see that he was talking on the phone, observing as his face broke into a huge smile when he noticed I was watching him. Sliding into the chair next to me at the little wrought-iron café table, he put down a small paper bag and picked up his Cappuccino, mouthing, "Yum. Thank you," after the first sip.

"Yeah, she's right here. You have a bone to pick with her? And you really think I'm going to hand her this phone." He was smirking.

"Oh no, what did I do now?"

"No clue." He shook his head, handing me the phone.

"Hello," I was pretty sure I knew who was on the other end of the line.

"You bitch," she exclaimed.

Yup. I was right. "Hey Stace."

"Stace? Wes is the only one that calls me Stace."

Laughing, "Well, now there are two of us. So, what did I do now?"

"Oh my God, that book. It ended in a cliffhanger. I'm dying here. I can't even breathe. I hate you, Tara."

"Well don't hate me for too long," I was smiling at Wes, as I spoke to his sister. "You're getting something in the mail today. So, now it's all up to your mailman."

"Well that fucker better not be late. I'm going out now to check the mail."

"Okay, well enjoy."

"Don't hang up. I'm taking you with me to the mailbox." I heard some scraping. "It's here," she exclaimed. "Shit Tara, do you have a tape fetish or something?"

Choking on my latte, I looked directly at her brother, "A tape fetish? Are you asking me if I like things tightly bound?" Now I was smirking and Wes was choking on his Cappuccino.

"Oh my God, Tara, what do I do?"

"Hit the power button. That will bring you to your library of books."

"The rest of the series is here." I couldn't help but smile at the excitement in Stacy's voice. "I have all the books."

"Yup."

"Tara."

I was biting my lip, not wanting to have an emotional moment with Stacy. "Now stop bitching at me and you can get off that damn cliff and find out what happens next. Here's Wes." I handed him the phone.

"Yeah, I'll call you tomorrow night when I get home," he told his sister before hanging up. "What did you do?" He was looking at me with that glorious smile.

"Okay, well Stacy, this woman Andie who's on the same chemo schedule and I all started reading this book series together. I thought it would be something fun we could all talk about during treatments. But I didn't know if Stacy would be into it, so for the first book in the series, I bought paperbacks. When I saw she liked it, I ordered her an eReader and downloaded the rest of the series and some other books I thought she might like." Wes was silent, smiling at me. "So the first book ends on a huge cliffhanger, which is why Stacy was cursing me out. But little did she know, in her mailbox was her new eReader with the rest of the series."

Wes shook his head, "You are a gem. A true gem. That you are even thinking about ways to make things better for her is so selfless and beautiful."

"It's really nothing. I've always been a voracious reader from the time I was a kid. And a good book transports you to a different world and sometimes, we all just need a break from the world we're in. So, I thought this might be good for Stacy and then Andie joined us, so that makes it even more fun."

Sliding the paper bag over to me, Wes cocked his head to the side. His voice was a little choked when he spoke. "I saw this in a shop down the hill and it made me think of you."

Smiling, I just looked at him.

"Open it," he urged.

Reaching inside the bag I could feel a small box, telling me this was some kind of jewelry and I think the shock registered on my face, because Wes just laughed at my reaction. As I pulled the small rectangular box from the bag, I couldn't stop smiling. "What did you do?"

"You'll see." And there was that smile. That smile that begged to have my lips all over it.

Opening the small box, I gasped. This man. This amazing man. Sitting on a cottony pillow was a silver chained necklace with three long rectangular bars of sea glass. Jade sea glass. The exact color of the dress I was wearing when we met again.

"It matches my jade dress. It's beautiful, Wes." I searched his eyes and could see the joy he received in giving, in making someone else happy. "Thank you so much. Will you put it on me?" I asked, knowing it would look beautiful against my white tee-shirt. Handing him the ends of the necklace, I lifted my hair, the afternoon breeze making me shiver slightly. Before fastening the chain, Wes dipped his face to my neck, his soft curls brushing my shoulder, exacerbating my previous shiver. Feeling the touch of his full, soft lips before fastening the chain brought a full-on quake in my chair. His chuckle sounded self-satisfied and I knew I was both blushing and ready to pull this man into a back alley.

Turning to him, "How does it look?"

"Perfect."

Digging in my purse, I pulled out a mirror. "It does look perfect," I agreed, running my fingers over the rough sand blasted glass. Leaning forward, I kissed Wes softly. And again. "You are so thoughtful."

"The color caught my eye as I was passing the shop and all I could think of was the jade dress and that cute outfit you wore years ago. It seemed like it would be a perfect match for that dress. Which, by the way, you look very hot in." And there was that smile. Melt.

Laughing, "I didn't know if you even recognized me."

Wes laughed. "The moment I walked in." Shaking his head with a smile, "Lady, don't you know you are unforgettable." Lightly, he ran his fingertips down my forearm and across the back of my hand. "I thought you recognized me. But I wasn't totally sure. I kind of kept going back and forth throughout the entire meeting. *Does she realize that we know each other?*"

"You didn't hear me screaming in my head the entire time, *Wes, it's me!*"

"Tara, I'm not surprised that fate has brought us

together again. We both knew, from the moment we met, that we were destined to be a part of one another's lives." And with a wry laugh, he added, "It just took a while."

Taking a sip of my latte, I let his words settle in. "This is a gift. It really is. You see, you were the best boyfriend I never had."

"I guess we both needed to get to this place to be ready."

"And to appreciate," I added.

"I think you're right," Wes agreed. "I'm not walking off a boat without you this time, Tara."

"That was one of the best meals I've had in a long time." I rubbed my full belly as Wes and I walked, hand-in-hand, through the historic village toward the waterfront.

"That's because you had great company."

"So true," I laughed.

Reaching the *Second Wind*, Wes pulled out the reclining pad chairs and I eased down onto mine.

"Be right back," He called over his shoulder with a smile, disappearing below deck.

Relaxed and contented, I breathed in the salty air and got comfortable in my chair, stretching out my legs. It had been a perfect day. A long, exhausting perfect day. The fresh air and activity had totally wiped me out and closing my eyes for a minute, I knew I might not reopen them for another eight hours.

"You're not falling asleep on me, are you?" I opened my eyes to a smiling Wes standing over me, holding two brandy snifters. "Cognac?" He bent down to hand me a glass.

"Mmm," was all I could say as I accepted the glass and he lowered himself to the pad chair next to me. "To a perfect day." I clinked my glass to his, before sipping the amber liquid. "Are you trying to get me drunk?" I asked.

"It may not have been the best idea." Wes smiled. "Because I think it is just going to put you to sleep."

"We are definitely not pulling an all-nighter tonight. I don't have the energy I had in my twenties," I admitted.

"I hear ya." Wes laughed and then craned his neck to the left to see where a very loud Duran Duran song was being blasted from.

"I think it's two boats over. Maybe we'll get an 80's concert." I laughed and sipped my brandy, enjoying the glowing warmth in my chest, that I was sure Wes could see like some sort of fluorescent black light poster.

The Duran Duran song was followed up by Katrina & the Waves *Walking on Sunshine* and Wes jumped to his feet, reaching a hand out to pull me up. "We can't not dance to this."

Kicking off my shoes, that was all the invitation I needed as we danced on the teak deck acting more like twenty-somethings than we thought we would be doing. Katrina & the Waves were followed up by Dexy's Midnight Runners' *Come on, Eileen.*

"Wow, someone is totally doing some MTV flashbacks," my breath was choppy from dancing. "This is better exercise than the gym."

"And more fun." Wes twirled me around.

At the song's end, the highly recognizable first strains of *Walk Like An Egyptian* filled the night air. "Follow me," I called over my shoulder to Wes, as I began what were more robotic movements than I assumed were vintage Egyptian. After doing a full trek around our deck, I climbed onto the dock, my Egyptian walk still in time with the music and headed over to the boat playing this awesome, nostalgic mix. Wes was right behind me, funky moves and all. As we approached the boat, two couples started cheering us on.

"This is the best music," I called out. "We couldn't help ourselves." One of the men reached out a hand to help me onto their boat and Wes followed. Without missing a step, we fell right into our Egyptian stroll.

"I'm Wes and this is Tara," I heard from behind me. Inadvertently, I smiled. We were being introduced as a couple.

"Jimmy. Debbie. Kelly and Richie." The man who helped me onto the boat pointed to himself and his friends.

Soft Cell's *Tainted Love* was up next and had the six of us singing on the top of our lungs as we danced under the stars. I couldn't remember a time where I'd had so much fun with absolute strangers. Two notes into Modern English's iconic hit, *I Melt With You*, Wes pulled me into his arms and following the singer's lead, my body and lips melted against his, as we simultaneously kissed and sang into one another's mouths.

Laughing and kissing, we continued to dance with our new stranger/friends, all singing at the top of our lungs to Bon Jovi's *Living on a Prayer* and Bruce Springsteen's *Dancing in the Dark*.

"This truly is the best workout. No wonder why we were thin when we were young." I was out of breath. "Jimmy," I called out, "this is the best dance mix ever." I got a thumbs up from our host, who didn't miss a step.

"I have so much fun with you." Wes planted a kiss on my lips that didn't end until the last note of the song. "Let's get outta here." And there was that smile that stole my heart on the night we met.

Returning his smile, I nodded and we waved, bidding goodbye to our hosts.

As we stepped down onto *Second Wind*'s deck, Spandau Ballet's *True* began. With a smile that melted my heart, Wes extended a hand, "One more before we go below deck?"

Taking his hand, I smiled back as I glided into his arms, resting my head on his shoulder. "This has been a perfect day."

Wes kissed my forehead softly and whispered, "It's not over yet." His arms tightened around me in response to the shiver that wracked my body as it responded to his words. "Ooo, shivering in anticipation. I like that."

As the song ended, I fell against him, exhausted from the long day, yet wired with anticipation at finally becoming lovers with the man who had hijacked my heart well over a decade before. I was fighting the age demon that kept swimming across my sea of consciousness taunting me with visions of what my body looked like in my twenties, before gravity, childbirth and sedentary corporate life had taken their toll. Trying to drown the little troll and exorcise it from my thoughts, twenty-something Keiko and her twelve-year old's body were the next to invade.

*Go away! Get the fuck out of my head!*

Wes must've felt me tensing in his arms, as his embrace tightened to comfort me. Trying to dig deep within myself, I attempted to unearth my waning confidence. *You're smart. You're attractive. You're a good person. You're fun. You're successful. You're a great mom. And you're freaking hot – so get the heck over it now!*

"Are you getting tired?" Wes asked.

I nodded, without saying anything, and he took my hand and led me below deck and to the back cabin.

"As fast or as slow as you want to take this, T," he reiterated, looking at me with sincere eyes.

Sitting on the edge of the bed, I unlatched the sea glass necklace and gently laid it on the nightstand. "Come lie down next to me." With faces now mere inches apart, we smiled at one another from our pillows. "I love being with you, Wes."

The smile on both his lips and in his eyes was the perfect answer. Reaching out, he brushed my hair from my face, gently placing it behind my ear. "T, there is no better dream I could have asked for than our paths crossing again and you becoming part of my life. I feel like it was divine intervention."

Gently, I ran my finger down the lines of his face, tracing the heartache and triumph that were finely etched around his mouth and eyes. There was nothing I wanted more than to be this man's love, tonight and forever. But after two years of continuous disappointments, my fear was that my heart would be decimated.

"What do you want?" I asked the question haunting me.

"I want you in my life." He didn't skip a beat.

"As what?"

Wes shrugged. "As whatever we become."

I laughed, "Well, that's pretty nebulous."

Laughing back at me, "I love that you're smart. I'm not trying to be vague. I just want to figure this out as we go along, but if what you're asking me is, *Is this a casual fling?* Then the answer is no. You're not a fling. You're not a rebound person. And I understand, it's not just you. It's Scarlett, too. And I respect that."

With my hand still on his cheek, I drew him closer for a kiss. "I think I'm putting a lot of pressure on myself with this because I feel like this is an incredible second chance. A dream come true."

Wes smiled at my words. "I understand."

"And I'm just afraid I'm going to fuck it up. Or it's somehow going to get fucked up and Wes, to be totally honest, I don't know how to engage in something with you without going in with my total heart. And that scares me. There, I said it. Out loud."

"T, you aren't alone. I feel the exact same way. You scare the crap out of me because it is impossible not to fall in love with you. And it's kind of a double whammy, because I absolutely adore Scarlett too and I don't ever want to let her down. So, I get how you feel."

Reaching out, I let one of his loose curls slide between my thumb and forefinger as I searched his eyes. My heart told me his words were true and that I needed to see where this took us, just as he had said.

Tapping the tip of my nose with his forefinger, his grin became mischievous. "Wait here," he ordered and jumped up from the bed.

I could hear sounds in the salon of cabinets opening and closing, then quiet, followed by a ding.

"What are you doing," I laughed.

"Patience, patience," he called out.

With the same mischievous smile, Wes re-entered the bedroom holding a small white ceramic cup. Propping myself up on the pillows with my elbows, I looked at him questioningly.

"What's that?" The grin on his face told me he wasn't bringing me a cup of tea.

"You'll see." Sitting down next to me on the edge of the bed, "Shove over and lie back."

"Why? What are you going to do to me?"

Laughing, "You'll learn soon enough. Now move over."

Complying, I inched toward the center of the bed.

"Keep moving and lie back," he pressed.

His take charge attitude was getting me hot. *What was he up to?* I followed his direction and continued to move, lying my head back on the pillow.

Wes lifted my shirt, baring my stomach.

"What are you up to?" I protested, laughing.

"Shhh. Have faith, T."

I felt something warm on my stomach, as if he were painting me. His finger continued to draw across my entire abdomen with the warm liquid.

"Okay, you can look now."

Raising up my upper body, I noted how proud of himself he looked. Across my bare midsection WES was written in Hollandaise sauce.

"Have I just been branded?" It was impossible not to smile.

Wes nodded. "You have. I have branded you. I'm marking my territory."

"Okay, well this is better than getting pee'd on."

Bursting into laughter, "I should say. And that's not all. The clean-up is pretty good, too."

Dipping his head, Wes began to lick the W off my stomach. I squirmed and laughed as the tip of his tongue tickled my belly.

"You're going to make this very messy, T." He looked up for a moment to give me a stern look. It was the same look he'd given me on the night we met when I'd laughed at him for spilling his drink on his feet.

"I am so ticklish," my words erupted in bursts between laughs. "My brother used to hold me down and tickle me until I couldn't breathe."

Wes smiled, "Oh poor T." And he continued slowly licking the letter E, sending me into hysterics as I tried to roll away. "Mmm mmm mmm, you need to stay put until I'm done." He held down my arms to keep me from rocking.

"Weeeeesssss," it was somewhere between a gasp, a laugh and a whine.

"I have one more luscious letter." Slowly his tongue curled over the S.

Trying to hold in my laughter, I threatened, "You will pay, Mr. Bergman. You will pay."

Finishing the top swirl of the letter, he looked up at me from my stomach. "Who would've ever guessed you were so ticklish." The look in his eyes told me that I was in for future torture.

"Oh my God, my brother used to torment me when I was little. He would hold me down and tickle me and I would scream out for my mother and he'd say, 'Why are you screaming? Mommy can't hear you. She can't help you.' It was horrible what he used to do to me."

"Oh, that is pretty harsh." Wes smiled, not looking at all remorseful.

Playfully I whacked him on the side of the head. He just laughed and dipped his finger in the ceramic cup and slowly brought it to my lips. With a smile, I opened my mouth and sucked the Hollandaise off his fingertip.

"Damn, that is good."

"It really is." He followed with another taste for himself. "With breakfasts like that."

I cut him off before he finished his sentence, "No. No. No. Don't you start thinking about me cooking you breakfast every morning. That's way too much work."

Laughing, "Well, you're in luck because I love to cook and I make a mean breakfast."

"Will you make me breakfast in the morning?"

"If you're too worn out from tonight. Sure." And there was that smile.

"Well, wear me out." The truth was, I was already worn out, totally exhausted from the long day and fresh air.

Wes obviously could see it on my face. "I think that mission has already been accomplished." Pulling off his shirt and shorts, he crawled under the covers in just his boxers.

Taking a hint, I stripped down to my tank top and bikini underwear and turned off the light as Wes spooned behind me.

"C'mere," was all he said and I smushed back into him. "This feels so good."

"It does." I turned my head back to kiss him, knowing he was as exhausted as I was, but excited to see what sleep and the morning would bring. I listened to his breathing, enjoying the comfort and warmth of his body wrapped around mine. It was a perfect moment, in the perfect place with the perfect man. I wanted to savor the experience, remembering every detail of his touch and his scent, but fatigue was the victor as I quickly faded into sleep.

His hand slowly stroking up and down the outside of my thigh is what roused me from my dream state. It was so soft and tender that I was getting more and more turned on with every movement. With my eyes still closed, I enjoyed the sensation. It wasn't until his lips started brushing my shoulder, that I was unable to stifle a moan, revealing that I was awake.

"Good morning," his whisper was hoarse.

"Mmm, good morning." I stretched my body against his and turned my head to see his face hovering over mine, before our lips met.

"Sleep good?"

"Surprisingly, I did. I was so exhausted. Sorry for passing out on you last night," I apologized.

"I think we both passed out the moment our heads hit the pillows." Wes' hand had migrated from my thigh to my stomach, where he softly drew circles with his fingertips.

Rolling over to face him, I pushed my hair out of the way, silently praying my humidity enhanced curls didn't make me look like a deranged housewife, scaring the erection right out of the man. Slinging a leg over his thigh, I instantly got my answer. The crazy morning coif was not a cock killer. *Thank God!*

"You're a morning person, I see." Hiding my smile was not a possibility.

"Yeah, I am," Wes laughed, moving closer to me, his eyes filled with the unmistakable desire to become lovers, something I'd dreamed about on the deck of a windjammer long ago.

"You can wake me up like this anytime." I needed to let him know it was okay. He'd said he'd take it as slow as I wanted it and what I wanted right now was a slow rhythm of him plowing into me. Hard.

"Are you hard to wake up?" He was pressed up against me.

"I think you'll figure out the secrets to rousing me."

"You've already figured out the secrets to arousing me." His voice still had that sexy edge of morning roughness to it, making me want to skip all foreplay and have him inside me.

"I'll bet you have a few more secrets I can discover," I said against his lips, as I shifted the leg I had slung over him, pressing my heat and wetness against his already throbbing cock.

Wes groaned and I could feel his smile against my lips. "You know you're going to make it impossible to make slow, sweet love to you."

"Good, because I don't want it slow and sweet."

Wes flipped me onto my back, "I can easily accommodate your wishes. Are you on anything or do I need to…"

"We're good," I assured him.

"Yes, we are." He kissed my neck, then swiftly pulled my tank top over my head tossing it to the floor. "We're going to be really good together. Of that, I have no doubt."

And I knew he was right. Being with this man had been so perfect from the night we met. We meshed with ease and the result was pure joy.

The warmth in his eyes and smile made my breath catch, and in that moment, I was flooded with overwhelming emotion at how much I wanted him. How much I'd always wanted him. It was more than lust, beyond the heat of the moment. Wes Bergman was the man I had always wanted, from the night we met. That was clear to me now.

"I vote we skip the foreplay." I wriggled out of my

underwear.

"You're on." His smile told me he was taking on the challenge.

"You're in," I gasped, my breath catching in my throat, surprised at the swiftness with which he filled my request.

"Ah fuck, you feel good."

His face was hovering above mine. Lacing my fingers through his hair, our lips met and I wrapped my legs around him. With his arms embracing my shoulders, he rocked back to his knees, lifting me with him and sinking deeper into me. Breaking our kiss so that I could watch his face, I slowly lifted up the length of him until I could feel the head of his cock against me. Leaning forward, I bit his full lower lip before slamming down onto him.

"Oh God, yes," he groaned, grabbing my hips and repeating the motion again and again. "Damn, Tara, I have wanted to fuck you since the night I met you." Grabbing my hair, he pulled me to him for a kiss. When our lips broke, he asked, "Why are you smiling? What's going through that head of yours?"

"Well, besides the fact that this feels so fucking good and that you like to talk during sex, too – which I guess I should not be surprised at, I'm smiling because I'm thinking, *Finally! Finally, he doesn't have a girlfriend."*

Laughing, Wes softly kissed my neck, as he continued to pound me up and down on his cock. "Ah, but I do have a girlfriend. I've got a great girlfriend."

"Oh yeah?" I pushed him onto his back so that I was now straddling him. Squeezing him as tightly as I could, I asked the question, "Am I the other woman?"

Reaching up to my shoulders, he pushed me back in one swift move, until my back was on the mattress. Pulling me to the edge of the bed so that my ass was hanging over, he stood on the floor, raising my feet to his shoulders before plowing back into me.

"Other woman?" He cocked his head to the side, driving into me fully with force. "You are *the* woman. The only woman. You got that?" There was not a hint of a smile left on his face. Reaching forward, he slowly rubbed my clit as he continued his steady pace of filling me.

Lost in the sensation I closed my eyes, unable to answer him, at least not with intelligible words. What started out as soft whimpers, grew quickly in volume and intensity as I neared my peak.

"T, open your eyes," Wes demanded.

Complying, I looked up at him, panting and moaning and fighting for my breath. With a smirk, the pressure he was applying to my clit intensified.

"Fuck," I yelled out, my breath ragged. "Oh my God, Wes."

At the sound of his name, he pulled me flush against him, groaning as his orgasm released in waves and he collapsed onto the bed next to me. Pulling me to him, Wes buried his face in my neck as he regained his breathing rhythm.

Like with everything else, the man who seemed to be totally in sync with me was also thoroughly sexually compatible. This hadn't seemed like a first time, trying to figure out how to please your new lover, and sometimes failing miserably, but rather like making love to someone whose cravings and body you were already attuned to, bringing them to the heights of pleasure with the ease of a duet singing impeccable harmonies.

"Wes," I whispered, holding onto him tightly, "Thank God we got a do-over."

# Chapter 17

"Taste this."

Wes held up a wooden spoon of his Special Sunday sauce to my lips. Blowing on it to cool down the molten delicacy, I opened my mouth, accepting his offering.

"Oh my God, Wes. Where did you learn to cook Marinara sauce like this?" The complex depth of flavors had me wanting more. I didn't need meatballs, pasta or garlic bread. I could eat this sauce like a bowl of soup or just pull my hair back and lower my face into the steaming pot – it was that good.

"From our next-door neighbors growing up, the Colucci's. Their grandmother was from Sorrento and she lived with them. Every Sunday, Grandma Colucci made "gravy." So, not only did I eat there on a lot of Sunday evenings, but I would hang out in the kitchen and watch her cook."

Sticking a spoon in to steal another taste, I had it in my mouth before Wes could shoo me away. "This should be illegal. Too addicting."

Leaning over to place a kiss on my lips, "You should be

illegal."

Laughing, "Why is that?"

"Because you're intoxicating and addictive and I crave you."

We'd been together for six straight nights and I couldn't get enough of him either. I needed a constant fix. We'd made love throughout my apartment: bed, couch, rugs, shower, chairs. Texts throughout the work day had me hungering for his touch, yearning to touch him. I was riding a high so powerful that I was lost in my own fairytale. And that scared me. After two years of heartache, it was difficult to relax and to let go of the specter of the other shoe dropping. But then he'd touch me or I'd hear his voice and I was lost to the dream that I could possibly have a happily ever after with this loving, charismatic man.

"Chill out and enjoy it," Laynie had yelled at me earlier in the week. "You're too uptight, Tara, and you're going to make this a self-fulfilling prophesy."

I knew she was right.

"Hey, this might sound a little odd, and please feel free to say no. In two weeks, Scarlett's camp does this combination end-of-the-season Parent's Weekend along with camper pick-up, would you like to come with me for the weekend?"

Wes turned from stirring his pot. "Damn, I would love to and I'd love to see Scarlett, too. But I've got Julien returning that weekend and I've got to get him from the airport. Can't wait to see Scarlett again after that, though."

Julien returning. Crap. It had been so pleasant without the man, that I'd let myself forget he even existed in the last few days. Life without Julien in the picture was so much simpler.

"Bummer," was all I said, trying not to give away anything. Two more weeks. I had two more weeks with Wes before that albatross showed up. Having no idea how he'd react to our coupling, I feared the worst. The man was a vindictive son of a bitch. And he hated me.

My gut told me he wasn't going to play nice.

"Do you have summer allergies?" Stacy's dry cough seemed to be getting the best of her the next time I picked her up for chemo.

"I do and I think the mold count is high today from all the rain last week. I have this stupid itch in my throat."

"Ugh. I hate when that happens. I always feel like I want to take a metal coat hanger and get in there to scratch my throat," I laughed.

"Well, that might be excessive." Stacy coughed and looked out the window. "So what's with you and my brother?"

Shrugging my shoulders, "I guess you could categorize it as we're seeing each other."

"Good," Stacy nodded, coughing.

"Good?" I was shocked. Did Stacy Bergman just approve of me dating her brother? Did I hear that right?

She turned in her seat to look at me. "Yeah, good. You make him happy. You've always made him happy and I want Wes to be happy."

"I want him to be happy too, Stace. He is truly a fine man and that is such a rarity in today's world. He's really very special." And I meant that with all my heart. Just talking about him, I could feel the swelling in my chest. I knew I was in love with him. Deeply in love with him, although neither of us had yet uttered the words.

I also knew that my feelings for Wes were on a level so much deeper than what I'd felt for Frank. I had loved Frank, but not like this. With Wes, it was like he was intricately woven through my heart and soul in a way that could never be separated without irreparable damage being done. I knew, to my very core, that this was the person I was put on Earth to be a part of their life.

"I'm glad you guys found each other again." Stacy's words were blowing me away.

"You know what, Stace, I'm glad we did, too. But what I'm also thrilled about is that you and I are getting a chance to really know one another." As brusque and as off-putting as she was on the outside, I was quickly being exposed to the caring and loyal side of Stacy Bergman.

She just nodded her head in acknowledgement, coughing a few times.

"Should we have the infusion nurse call in the doctor to check out your cough." I had gone into mama bear mode.

"Nah. It really feels like allergies. You know how when you're getting sick you feel overall icky, but when it's just allergies it's just that one isolated thing that's bugging you. Well this is that one thing and it's itchy versus hurting. Plus, they said on the news this morning that the mold count was off the charts high and mold always sets me off."

"Okay," I acquiesced. "I wonder if Andie has finished the trilogy yet?" We stood waiting for the elevator to take us up to the third floor.

"Oh I hope so, because I want to talk about it and I don't want to have to censor what I say." Stacy paused and laughed, "Not that I ever censor what I'm saying."

"That's a freaking understatement," I laughed. "As you were the woman who once told me to stay away from your brother."

"A lot of good that did me. You two found one another again and he's crazy about you."

"He's crazy about me?" I so wanted to hear her say those magic words.

"Crazy about you. Well, that's an understatement. I think head over heels would be a more accurate description."

I know I had a loony smile on my face as we emerged from the elevator. "Head over heels." I repeated.

"Certainly that's no shock how crazy he is about you." Stacy was very serious.

"Well, it's nice to hear and also good to know that I'm not wandering down a path by myself," I admitted, letting a fear surface.

"C'mon Tara, you know that you and Wes have always had that special something – from the moment you met. There's no one else in the world when the two of you are together. No one else."

I wondered how much Wes had confided in Stacy about our relationship. Obviously some, and it was comforting to know that I had someone on my side not telling him to stay away from me.

*Jullie A. Richman*

# Chapter 18

"I can't believe you zip lined, Mom!" Scarlett squealed at the end of the course, as I was unhooked from the harness.

"It wasn't my first time." I slung my arm over her shoulder as we walked away. "But I haven't done it in a very long time. It was before I even met your father."

Frank and CB had waited for us in the dining hall. CB's outfit for the day was not conducive to participating in any of the Camper/Parent activities.

"So, am I going to get to meet Cameron?"

A long, drawn out, "Mom," accompanied her blush. "Did Wes tell you?"

"Well, I was scrolling through his phone after he told me about your fall from the horse." The bruise on her leg had faded significantly, now appearing almost green and yellow in hue.

"Scrolling through Wes' phone?" Scarlett raised her eyebrows and gave me a pointed look.

"Yeah, well that's kind of my news. We've been seeing each other."

Stopping dead in her tracks on the dirt path. "And you complain I don't tell you like anything? This is literally like so huge. And you didn't tell me this, really?"

"Well, it's pretty new."

"I can't believe he didn't like tell me. I am like literally so mad at him right now." She had become very dramatic over the summer.

I laughed. "Well, bitch at him. I want to see Cameron. You don't have to introduce me if you think I'm going to embarrass you."

With an eye roll, we headed over to the soccer field. "He's number 12." She nodded her head toward the right side of the field.

Elbowing her with a smile, "You've got good taste, little one. He's a cutie." With thick blonde hair and a preppie look, I could see why my daughter had fallen for him. "How about if I take off and get your father to load your trunk and your bags into my car, so that you get a chance to say goodbye to Cameron and then meet up with us in the dining hall."

"Okay," Scarlett agreed with a smile, visibly relieved that she would get to say goodbye to him alone.

"See you in a little bit." Taking off toward the dining hall, it was time to get Frank off his butt and working or we'd never get Scarlett packed up and on the road home at a decent hour.

As I climbed the hill to the dining hall, I pulled out my phone. I had one bar of phone reception and my data was reading 4G. 4G? I hadn't seen that on my phone in centuries. There were no text messages from Wes and my heart took an immediate tumble. I needed a Wes fix. And then I chuckled, thinking once I get to a place with decent cell signal, my phone is going to blow up and all the messages will show up at once and my craving for him will be satisfied.

**Just saw Cameron. He's cute. My daughter has a bone to pick with you. And I miss you. Big time!!!**

I didn't know if my text would actually reach his phone or just float around in the ether for a while until we were back in civilization. I hadn't realized that I would feel so incomplete without him by my side and that made me both happy and sad. I couldn't help but wonder what he and Julien were doing. Pushing that thought immediately from my head, I didn't want Julien anywhere near my thoughts. It had been so pleasant not having him around.

"So. what's new, Tara?" Frank asked as I sat down next to him and CB.

"Not a damn thing." I certainly wasn't going to share my personal life with him. At least not yet or he'd be counting down the days until he could stop paying alimony. "I'm going to pull up my car as close as I can get it to Scarlett's bunk. I need you to load her stuff into my trunk."

"You can't do that?"

"No. I can't. Don't worry, Countess, you won't break a nail." I pointedly looked down at Frank's manicured fingers and wondered how I'd ever been married to him. Immediately I was slammed with a painful pang. I missed Wes so much. Had he been here, we would've just loaded up Scarlett's stuff, it all would've been positive and there would have been none of this negative energy expended trying to get the ex to get off his pampered butt.

It annoyed me to no end that I had to tell him to load the car. This was the fifth summer we'd done this. The man knew the drill.

Around the time we hit the interstate, cell signal had returned and Scarlett began texting her camp friends. Lifting my phone to check for texts, I was surprised not to see any. Julien certainly must've been keeping Wes very busy.

"So we need to start school shopping." I attempted to get my daughter's attention.

"Okay. Can we ask Aunt Laynie to come with? She literally has like the coolest taste."

"Text her and ask," I said, silently laughing at my daughter's vernacular and wondering if I'd ever hear a sentence for the next five years that didn't include the words like and literally.

"She says of course and wants to know if you want to meet for dinner tonight."

"Tell her yes. After this drive, I'm sure as heck not cooking."

We were still an hour and a half out of New York City, when my cell signal chirped. Finally! Lifting my phone, I was surprised to see it was from Stacy.

**Just admitted to Memorial Sloan-Kettering**

"Oh my God."

Alarmed, Scarlett turned to me, putting down her phone. "What's the matter?"

"Wes' sister Stacy just got admitted to Memorial Sloan-Kettering."

"The cancer hospital?"

"Yes, she's being treated for breast cancer. Will you do me a favor and text her back on my phone. I don't want to text and drive at the same time."

"Sure."

"Okay, say **OMG, are you okay? What happened?**"

**Cough got worse. And I'm running a fever. Going down for a CT Scan in a few.**

"Tell her **I'm on my way back to the city with Scarlett. Will drop her off, then be by to see you.**"

"Are you okay with just dinner with Laynie?"

"Sure."

"Okay text Aunt Laynie and tell her the situation."

As we continued down I-91 heading toward New York, my stomach was in knots for Stacy. And for Wes. No wonder why I hadn't heard from him.

*Please let this be nothing more than an infection from being run down by chemo. Please,* I prayed. Trying to keep my thoughts positive, I knew I needed to keep my strength and energy up to lend support to both Stacy and Wes.

*Jullie A. Richman*

# Chapter 19

I was nauseous as the elevator ascended to Stacy's floor, begging a higher power to please let her be okay, please let this be something antibiotics could fix. By the time the doors opened, there was an acidic burning at the back of my throat.

Wes was standing next to Stacy's bed when I reached the doorway. My heart sighed in relief at the sight of him. Turning toward me, he began to approach. Something looked different. *What was it?* I had just crossed the doorway's threshold into Stacy's darkened room when he reached me, ushering me back out into the harshly lit hallway. Under the fluorescent light, I could finally see what had altered his appearance.

My hand immediately shot up to caress his swollen and bruised left cheek, but he caught my arm just before it reached his face and led me down the hall, finding a small waiting room that was empty and steered me inside.

"Wes, what happened? Are you okay? What's going on with Stacy?" My senses were on high alert. He had not yet uttered a single word to me and the sinking feeling in my stomach was becoming more pronounced. Whatever was going on was not good. "Talk to me," I begged. "Please talk to me."

With a deep exhale, he began. "Things are not good with Stacy. The cancer has metastasized to her right lung and she has an infection in there on top of that."

"Oh God." Hot tears, that were impossible to control, spilled from my eyes. "That's what that damn cough was about, wasn't it? Shit!" I closed my eyes.

Wes just nodded.

"Oh Wes, I'm so sorry," I continued. "What are the doctors saying?"

"Nothing yet. They need to clear up the infection. But, it's not good. The chemo didn't stop it from spreading." He gazed at his hands as he spoke.

Reaching out, I laid both my hands over his. His reaction was immediate and visceral as he pulled his hands away from mine, leaving my outstretched hands holding only air and my rapidly crumbling heart.

"Wes?"

Looking up at me I could see the crevasse between his eyes and the tic in his swollen jaw. I'd seen this once before and the feeling of déjà vu was suffocating. *Garbage comes tomorrow,* he had said to Keiko.

"I can't do this, Tara. I'm trying to cope with the fact that I'm going to lose my sister, that she is falling prey to her battle with breast cancer. That I am going through this again and losing the last member of my family."

"I know, Wes, I understand. And I don't know what I can do to help you. But I'll be there for you."

His eyes met mine and there was no warmth or compassion in them. Where was my Wes?

He just looked at me for a moment. "Just like you were there for Julien?"

My blood ran cold. Opening my mouth to speak, the

suffocating lack of oxygen bound my vocal chords in knots, leaving me momentarily both speechless and lightheaded as the room swayed. *He hadn't known until now?*

"That is what I was trying to discuss with you the weekend on the boat when you didn't want to talk about it. From your response, I assumed you already knew and didn't want the past to get in the way of the future."

"The past?" he scoffed.

"Yes. The past. I didn't know you and Julien knew each other. I didn't even know you lived on the east coast. It had been over fifteen years."

Waving his hand at me, I could tell he wasn't even listening to what I was saying. He wasn't getting past me and Julien having sex for the other pieces to have any bearing on his feelings. Couple that with Stacy's horrendous diagnosis and Wes' past, and I knew there was no winning for me in this conversation. But I still had to try.

"Wes, listen to me, please. Julien was before us. From the moment you and I walked back into one another's lives, it's only been you. It's always been you, Wes. You have to know how I feel about you. How deeply I care." I could hear the desperation creeping into my voice as I watched his body language telling me clearly that he was retreating more and more with every sentiment I professed. But I couldn't stop. I couldn't let him go. "Wes…"

He held up a hand. "Stop, Tara. I have enough to deal with emotionally with my sister. I can't handle this."

"Please don't push me away. Not now. Let me be there for you."

With closed eyes, he shook his head, his lips forming a grim line. Slowly, he looked up. "Julien?" And I could see the pain in his eyes.

"I didn't know you'd be coming into my life again."

He remained silent.

"Don't give up on us, Wes." I couldn't believe he was

going to walk away from the happiness we brought to one another.

"I can't deal with this."

"I want a do-over," I whispered.

"Well, you can't always get what you want."

There was no use in furthering the discussion if he no longer wanted us. His pain was a mish-mash involving all the people closest to him. The man was gutted. That was clear to see. Standing up, I looked down at him. "I'm going to see Stacy."

And I left him alone in the waiting room and walked down the hall in my own personal, surreal fog. Annihilated. Totally annihilated.

Wiping my eyes before I entered the room, I squared my shoulders and collected myself. Leaning over, I gave Stacy a kiss on the cheek and pulled up a chair.

"That fucking cough," I shook my head.

"Did you speak to Wes?"

I nodded, my throat closing. Suddenly I was fighting back tears and I didn't want to burden Stacy, who had bigger issues than me getting dumped.

"So, you're not having the greatest day either."

I shook my head and moved the subject off me. "So, what are they doing for you here? What have they told you?"

"Not much. Just that there is a mass in my right lung. It might be operable, but first we need to clear up this infection."

Reaching over, I squeezed her hand. "How are you feeling?"

"Ironically, physically not so bad. Emotionally, I'm still processing it. I'm not happy that the chemo has obviously been ineffective, but the oncologist was by earlier and he said we still have options with chemo that targets my type of breast cancer and potentially surgery when this infection clears up."

"Okay, so this sounds hopeful." I was relieved to hear they were presenting viable options to Stacy.

"Hope. That's all we've got."

I nodded, but couldn't speak.

"Don't give up hope on Wes, Tara." I could see the sadness in Stacy's eyes. "He really cares about you."

"I don't think Wes wants to have anything to do with me."

"Give him some time. He'll come around. He's crazy about you. He's just overwhelmed right now. And it's like he's living his worst nightmares all over again."

Nodding, "I can only imagine what seeing you go through this is doing to him."

"I know," Stacy agreed. "But that's only part of it."

"I'm not sure I understand." I really wasn't quite sure what she was getting at.

"That fucking Julien." The look of distaste on Stacy's face was evident.

"I feel so terrible," I admitted, trying to hold back my shattered emotions.

"You have nothing to feel terrible about. Julien's just a douche and this hit way too close to home for Wes."

"I don't understand, Stace."

Pressing the button on the side of her bed to elevate the upper half of her body so that she was now in a sitting position, Stacy rearranged her blankets before she started speaking. "Although they are the best of friends, there's always been something of a rivalry between them, back to when we were all in school. If Wes liked a girl and Julien knew about it, he'd pursue her and face it, he's a really good looking guy, so usually he'd get her and Wes would end up in the friend zone. It happened all the time when we were growing up. And Wes has always been so good to him. Like bringing him into C-Kicker when he got laid off from his last job. So, when Lisa was so sick, my brother was just so dedicated to her. There wasn't enough he could do for her, finding doctors, trying to make sure she was comfortable and had everything she needed, trying to keep her spirits up and a few months before she died, she became really withdrawn and he was so devastated, feeling like he was already losing her and he wasn't ready to let go. Around that time, she started confiding in Julien and it was really weird, they got very close. There was nothing physical going on. Lisa was physically weak and certainly not doing anything like that, but there was definitely this emotional *thing* going on between them and I know it hurt Wes deeply that she was turning to Julien for support and not him. So, what I think he's reacting to is a combination of what is going on with me and this bombshell Julien dropped on him."

"Oh God, Stace, I feel so awful for him."

"And they must've really had it out based on what my brother's face looks like."

"Julien did that to him?" I was shocked and now hated Julien even more in that moment.

Stacy nodded. "Yeah, they got into a huge fight. And I think it was events both past and present that brought it to the boiling point."

I was sick listening to how Julien took advantage of their friendship and I could only imagine how he had trashed me to Wes. Unfortunately, I didn't feel very hopeful that Wes would reconsider and I was angry at him for not having more faith in me. In us. But Lord knows what Julien had said to him. Had he embellished to make me look even worse? Not that it needed it, just spewing *facts* from his stilted perspective would be damning enough.

"Does Wes always forgive Julien for his bad behavior?"

I asked, already knowing the answer.

"He hired him and gave him a big job after that crap with Lisa. My brother has a big heart." Stacy shook her head.

Regrettably, that heart no longer had a place in it for me. What was the old saying? *Bros before hoes.* Wes would continue to take Julien back and that was a relationship I was never going to come between. The odd man out here was me and I just needed to walk away.

Pulling into the parking garage I knew exactly what I needed to do. It had come to me on the way home and although I knew it was a longshot, I had to try it. What had Stacy said? *Hope. That's all we've got.* Well maybe there was some magic in that.

Entering the condo, all the lights were off. I had beaten Scarlett and Laynie back home and I was glad to be alone to do what I needed to do. Immediately, I went into the kitchen and got what I needed, then headed to my bedroom, situating myself in the center of my bed.

"Here goes." I held the dark-haired doll firmly in my left hand and raised the blue-headed pin with my right hand, stabbing it with force into the right side of the doll's chest. Raising my hand, I did it again, the pin landing near the last stab. And then again. And again. And again, with more force accompanying each successive blow.

"Die motherfucker," I spat from between clenched teeth. "I'm going to kill every single one of you. Obliterate you. You don't stand a chance against me. Against my power. I'm going to destroy you." And I stabbed and stabbed and stabbed and stabbed. As tears rolled down my cheeks and into my mouth, I swore, "Don't you understand. I'm not going to lose them. Either of them. I love them both. I want them in my life. Need them in my life. So die, you motherfucker. Just die." Viciously, I continued to stab the doll's chest. "Die," I screamed through my tears. "I need you to die."

And with every stab, I screamed. "Die." Stab. "Die." Stab. "Die." As I sobbed, I could barely see the doll in my hand with the now ripped open chest. When there was no fabric left to stab on the right side of the doll's chest, I continued stabbing into the stuffing before moving to obliterate the left side of the chest. "I'm going to kill you. I'm not letting you rob everything from me. You get nothing, you motherfucker. I will destroy you." Tears dripped onto the poppet as I relentlessly decimated it.

"Mom! Are you okay? What are you doing?" I could hear the terror in Scarlett's voice, but it sounded as if she were on the far end of a tunnel, her voice echoing off the graffitied, concrete walls.

Surprised by the interruption, I hadn't heard Scarlett and Laynie enter the apartment and now I needed to finish this fast. I wasn't done yet and through my tears I continued to stab, now reciting the death incantation in my head. Or so I thought.

"Mom, what is wrong with you? Stop!" I barely heard my daughter.

I couldn't stop yet. I wasn't done. I needed to complete the job or it wouldn't work.

"Aunt Laynie," Scarlett screamed.

A moment later, Laynie was on the bed next to me. Scarlett remained in the doorway, her fingers clenching the wooden doorframe.

"Tara. Tara. Stop," Laynie implored. "Tara, stop!"

But I couldn't. I needed to finish. I couldn't stop yet. And I stabbed and stabbed again.

"Tara, who is this doll?" I didn't answer and Laynie repeated the question. Finally, grabbing my right arm mid-air, she asked the question for the third time.

With my wrist tightly in her grip, I choked out, "Stacy. It's Stacy." I needed her to let me go. Let me finish.

"Tara, why are you killing Stacy? Did she do something to you?"

Shaking my head, I sniffed, trying to breathe through my stuffed nose. "I'm not trying to kill Stacy. I'm trying to save her."

"What are you doing?"

"I'm killing the cancer cells, Laynie. I have to kill the cancer cells in her lungs. I need to get them all," I cried and wrenched my wrist free of her grasp so that I could continue on my mission to heal Stacy.

Laynie's arm went around me, "Okay Sweetie," she said softly. "Kill all those nasty cells. Kill them all," her voice choked up with emotion.

Scarlett joined us on the bed, flanking my other side as I continued to stab. When the poppets chest was just batting, I stopped.

"Julien told him." I looked at Laynie, fresh tears making their way down my cheeks.

"I thought he knew."

"Me too. But obviously not."

"Holy crap. And he heard it from him first. Well, what did he say to you?"

Trying not to totally break down, though after what my daughter had already witnessed tonight, there was very little left that I could do that would shock her. "He ended things."

"Oh Tara." Laynie's arms went around me tighter.

Scarlett remained silent, but laid her head in my lap. Softly, I ran my fingers repeatedly through her long hair, the repetitive motion calming me.

"So, it's been a pretty shitty night. Stacy's chemo didn't work and Wes told me to take a hike."

"I wish you had an extra doll for Julien," Laynie muttered.

I actually laughed. "I've thought that on more than one occasion."

"So, why the blue pin?" she asked.

"You know how a beautiful blue sky makes you feel good, that anything's possible? The sky's the limit. It's like infinite hope. And right now, we need hope. We need infinite hope."

# Chapter 20

As I went to enter Stacy's room, I saw a tall, white-coated doctor by her bedside and remained in the hallway, so that I could give them privacy.

"Tara," Stacy called to me. "Come on in."

"Hi." I approached judiciously.

The doctor turned to me and extended his hand. "Bray Hamilton."

Taking his hand, instead of uttering an appropriate hello, the words, "You are beautiful," sprang forth from my lips.

Stacy laughed, "I know, isn't he? Dr. Hamilton, this inappropriate woman is my friend, Tara."

"Nice to meet you." He smiled and to his already overwhelming features, dimples were now added. Tall with an athletic build, Bray Hamilton was of mixed race. With high cheekbones, green eyes and skin the color of Cappuccino, he was one of the finest looking men I had ever laid eyes on.

Turning back to Stacy, "Okay, let me take a listen to your lungs. Breathe in deeply for me." He began with his stethoscope on her chest. Moving it, "Again." And now to her back, "Take another deep breath for me. And another." Moving the stethoscope again, "Please say the letter E for me." Stacy complied. "And again. Okay, you can lie back now. I'm now hearing some crackling in there, so I'm going to order another set of x-rays."

"What does crackling indicate?" Stacy asked.

"Well, it could mean fluid," he explained.

"Like pneumonia?" It was the first time I heard alarm in Stacy's voice.

"That is a possibility." He was frank, but calm.

"But I'm already on antibiotics." Stacy searched his face.

"What we've got you on for the type of lung infection you have is not something we typically use to fight pneumonia. Let's get them in here to take some pictures so that we know what we're dealing with and come up with a course to address it. Let me go put in those orders now."

"Fuck," Stacy screamed as soon as he left the room.

"Let's think positive until we know what's what." Hope. We still needed hope.

"I think it's going to come back positive. My upper back is killing me."

Shit.

"Have you heard from Wes?" she asked.

"No." I shook my head.

Stacy sighed. "What a dumbass. This is when he needs you most."

"I think that windjammer has sailed, Stace. I can't imagine Julien letting up on trashing me to Wes."

"Well, Julien's a piece of shit and he doesn't deserve to ruin my brother's life and rob him of his happiness and he should not be allowed to do that to you either."

Shrugging my shoulders, "I really don't know what I can do. The damage is already done and Lord knows what he's already said to Wes."

"Wes loves you, Tara. He doesn't want to be without

you. He just got hit with a double whammy and doesn't know whether he's coming or going. He's bracing for pain and loss and in some deluded way, he thinks what he's doing will minimize that."

"I don't know how to get through to him. And I don't want Julien to do or say anything else that could hurt Wes."

"You love him, don't you?"

I nodded. "How could I not? He's going to be a very rough one to get over."

"Well, you need to have some hope, Tara."

Here was Stacy, in the throes of fighting for her life, trying to convince me to keep the faith. Amazing. "I don't want to set myself up for something that's not going to happen. And with Julien by Wes' side every day, I don't stand a chance."

Taking a deep breath and nodding her head, Stacy said, "I'm going to tell you something that very few people know about. I know it, Julien knows it and my two best friends from high school know it. Wes does not know it. Use it if you want. Or don't use it. I'm telling you this so that you have an ace up your sleeve to protect yourself, okay."

"Okay." I was dying to know what she had to tell me.

"When I was sixteen years old and Wes and Julien were nineteen, I slept with him a few times. I actually lost my virginity to him. He was so good looking that I didn't even care what a total dick he was. I was young and stupid and I got pregnant. I was in 10th grade at the time and I didn't know what to do. I told Julien about it and of course his first response was how did I know it was his."

"What a douche. Why is Wes even friends with him? Wes is such a quality human being."

"Wes' downfall – he sees the best in people."

Stacy read the look on my face as I silently asked the question, *Why isn't he seeing the best in me?*

"Give him time, Tara. He's on overload, but he'll come

around. Anyway, I asked Julien for money to help me pay for an abortion and to please come with me. He threw half the money at me like I was some cheap whore, not his best friend's sister who he had watched grow up. He also promised to come with me and drive me, and on the day of the appointment, he no-showed and wouldn't answer my phone calls. My friend Ali came with me and we had to take the bus there and back."

"Just when I thought I couldn't despise him more. And you never told Wes?"

Stacy shook her head. "I was sixteen and scared."

"It's hard to imagine you fearing anything."

"I was afraid my brother would never look at me the same. And I was ashamed." Stacy paused. "So, if he fucks with you, Tara, tell him you know all about April 22, 1994 and that you've got proof."

"Proof?"

Stacy grabbed a pen and paper from the tray next to her bed and began to scribble a note.

*Wes,*

*Tara is telling the truth. On 4/22/94, I had an abortion. The baby was Julien's. He called me a whore and then stood me up and made me take a bus to get the abortion. Ali came with me. I'm sorry I never told you. I love you.*

*~ Your Brat*

"Trust me, you will never, ever need this. This note will not see the light of day. But if Julien attacks you, you have that. And Wes will know I wrote that."

I noticed that my hands were shaking as I held the

note. I was beyond angry at this man and angry at Wes for not seeing through him. "Wes is a savvy guy, Stace. I don't understand how Julien has continued to dupe him."

"The man is a great actor and Wes has always had a soft-spot in his heart for him because Julien lost his parents very young. They were in a car accident when he was eight and Wes kind of adopted him into our family after that. For some reason, Wes has always felt a responsibility to him as if he were the third sibling. And you know when it's family, sometimes you're more forgiving."

An x-ray tech entered wheeling in a mobile x-ray machine. "Stacy Bergman?" he asked.

"That's me."

"I've come to get a couple of pictures of your lungs." And then turning to address me, "This will only take a few minutes."

Grabbing my purse, I stepped out into the hall. Checking my phone, there was a wave of disappointment that there was nothing from Wes. Which after three days shouldn't have come as a shock. But I was still hoping beyond hope.

The door to Stacy's room opened and the tech wheeled his machine out. "You can go back in now."

"Wow. That was quick," I said to Stacy, sitting down by her bed again.

"So, you were pretty funny with my doctor." Stacy smiled at me.

"He looks like a movie star."

"The nurses were telling me his mother is some big socialite here in the city." As soon as Stacy finished her sentence, he walked into the room, followed by a nurse carrying an IV bag. "Speak of the devil."

"Hopefully good things," he smiled.

"We think you should be a movie star."

Dr. Hamilton laughed, "I'm a New York boy. I'd be a

fish out of water on the west coast."

The nurse hung the bag from the IV pole and began to attach it to Stacy's IV.

"So, you do have fluid in both lungs and I'm adding a second antibiotic that we use for pneumonia, called Avelox."

"So, do I have pneumonia?" Stacy asked for clarification.

"Yes. In both lungs."

"Shit," she hissed.

"We're getting you started immediately on Avelox, which is a strong and targeted antibiotic. Do you need me to give you anything for pain?"

"Yes."

Dr. Hamilton said something to the nurse and she left the room.

"We're going to inject a painkiller into your IV that will help you rest comfortably. It's going to make you drowsy. I'm doing rounds, but I'll come back and check on you in a little while, okay."

The nurse re-entered with the syringe. "This is going to make you sleepy and help you rest comfortably." She emptied the syringe into the injection port in Stacy's IV line.

"I'll stay until you fall asleep."

Stacy reached out a hand and I stood up and took it. "Tara, take care of my brother."

"I'm not sure that he'll let me." She was already asleep before I finished the sentence.

Placing her arm under the covers, I leaned over, kissing Stacy on the forehead, my heart heavy as I silently prayed that this rough and tough lady would kick pneumonia to the curb so that she could get on with her treatment.

Once out in the hallway, I pulled out my phone. 6:15 p.m. I assumed Wes would be leaving work soon and heading directly here. Whether he wanted to hear from me or not, he was going to. With Stacy passed out from the pain killer, I could fill him in on the details of what had transpired.

**Leaving hospital now. Stacy has pneumonia in both lungs. They've started her on Avelox and gave her a shot of pain meds that has knocked her out. She just fell asleep.**

I didn't expect a response to my text. Not after our conversation a few days earlier. As I reached the parking garage, I could hear my cell buzzing in my purse. Once inside my car, I dug it out.

**Thx. On my way.**

I was glad I'd be long gone by the time he arrived. The fragments of my heart were stabbing me, wounds so deep that I felt like the obliterated poppet. As much as I wanted to throw my arms around him and give him strength, I knew that anything but staying away would result in shattering what was left of my already fragile heart and ego. And I couldn't let that happen.

I needed to preserve. If not for me, then for my daughter.

Stacy was sleeping during my next visit. The first change I noticed was the oxygen cannula in her nose and I hoped that was just there to help her rest easier. Taking a seat next to the bed, I quietly pulled out my phone and opened my reading app. I knew she needed her rest and I didn't have the heart to wake her.

After about forty-five minutes, I rifled through my purse for a piece of paper and wrote her a note telling her I'd been there, but didn't want to disturb her sleep.

Leaning over to gently kiss her forehead I could feel the searing heat from her body on my lips.

Two nurses were sitting at the Nurse's Station.

"I just came from Ms. Bergman's room. Her fever is spiking."

A small, dark-haired nurse rose from her chair. "I'll go check on her."

As with my last visit, I knew the right thing to do was pass information to Wes.

**Just leaving Stacy. She's resting comfortably but her fever is spiking. I alerted the nurses. Shouldn't the Avelox have kicked in by now?**

His response was identical to the prior time.

**Thx. On my way.**

# Chapter 21

C hris rapped lightly on my office door before entering. Looking up from my computer screen I smiled, then saved my work file.

"Hi," I greeted him.

Taking a seat, he said, "You probably already know this."

I searched his face, shaking my head.

"Donna got a call from Wes Bergman's assistant. He lost his sister this morning."

"Noooooo." My hand flew to my mouth. "Oh my God. I went to see her two days ago." The rest of what I was going to say stuck in my throat, as a hazy Chris swam before my watery eyes. Biting my lower lip not to cry, I composed myself enough to ask about arrangements.

"Service is at a funeral home in Queens on Thursday morning. Donna has all the info. I'm going to go let the rest of the team know." Chris got up from the chair. "If you need to get out of here." He didn't have to finish the sentence.

I stared at the wall in my office for about twenty minutes,

paralyzed. Unable to move from my chair. Stacy was gone. Her poor chemo-weakened immune system couldn't stand up to pneumonia's powerful onslaught. Shit. Shit. Shit.

Putting my head in my hands, I let the tears flow. My heart ached for the memories we would never make together. The conversations we would never have. This brash woman turned out to have a bigger heart than anyone I knew. Underneath the prickles was a loyal and caring woman, who made me laugh with her pointed barbs. After the Julien story (seems we all had our Julien stories), no wonder why she didn't let people in. She'd been a sixteen-year old with a secret. Embarrassed. Made to feel cheap and worthless for wanting to be loved.

I *understand, Stacy. I understand. And I don't judge you.*

*Oh Stace. I am so, so sorry. I really am going to miss you so very much. Never in a million years did I ever expect our paths to cross again and I certainly never would have ever guessed that you and I would become friends. But I'm glad we did. You know you really got under my skin – and I mean that in a good way.*

*I don't know that I'm going to be able to honor your last request to me, to take care of your brother. Lord knows I would love to, so that you can rest in peace. But that is truly up to Wes. I can't want him to want me in his life. It was a cruel twist of fate to find the two of you again after all these years, just to lose you both. I really saw us as all becoming family and I'm heartbroken that the three of us will not be growing old together. I feel like I'd been given this great gift, only to have it robbed from me.*

*Bitch, I'm going to miss you!*

*I'm fighting with myself now about calling or texting your brother. I want to reach out to him. Comfort him. But he made it clear that he can't deal with me and wanted space. And I know I should respect that and just give him my condolences on Thursday. But it's so hard not to reach out, because I want to be there for him. That is what you do for people you love. And I do, I love him. And I loved you too, you ornery bitch.*

*Damn, I'm going to miss you.*

There was only one right thing to do. And I knew that. Whether he wanted it or not.

**Wes – Chris just told me. I am so, so sorry. I just can't believe it. I'm really going to miss her a lot and I'm glad we had the opportunity to become friends. If there is anything you need, please don't hesitate. I'm here. ~ T**

Curled up like a cat on my couch with her legs tucked under her, Laynie took another sip of her wine. "Do you want me to come with you tomorrow?"

"Thank you, but no. I'll be okay. There's a whole work contingent going. So, I will just blend in with them."

"Have you slept? You look like shit."

Rubbing my burning eyes, I shook my head. "Not very much. I'm just devastated over everything. My heart actually hurts. I wasn't ready for the two of them to be ripped away from me."

"Have you heard from him at all?"

"No. I'm sure he has his hands full with arrangements and dealing with the situation with me would be overload." I reached for my wine glass on the coffee table.

Laynie gave me the look that says, *I call bullshit.* "I'm sure he is overwhelmed and hurting. He lost the last member of his immediate family, but he owed you a phone call to let you know what happened. You were taking the woman to chemo and visiting her in the hospital."

"I know. You're right. This just reaffirms that he wants me out of his life. So, I will stay out of his life. I need to get through tomorrow and the Breast Cancer event in October and that will be it. I'm sure after this round of videos, he won't be using O'Donnell & Associates in the future. So, he will be out of my life again and I will move on. It's not like I haven't done it before."

"Are you sure you don't want me there tomorrow for moral support?" Laynie looked concerned.

Shaking my head. "No. I'll be okay. I'll have Jonathan and Chris there with me."

"Yeah, but I know how you are." Laynie was referring to my almost phobic fear of funerals. "This way you could take a little something to relax before you leave and I could drive."

"I'll be okay," I assured her. What I didn't admit was that if I took something, I was fearful of having my guard down and being around Julien. If he dared to verbally accost me, I wanted to be sharp and able to defend myself.

I made sure I didn't leave too early. The last thing I wanted was to be there with a lot of time before the service began. My plan was to stay for the service, give my condolences to Wes and exit as quickly as was socially acceptable. I didn't think it was appropriate for me to attend the graveside service after the funeral home or the repast that was taking place after that. Paying my respects here allowed me to properly say goodbye to Stacy without becoming a burden for Wes. I needed to grieve. But I needed to do that privately.

The O'Donnell & Associates team was in a pew about halfway back. Sliding in, I sat next to Jonathan.

"Hey Sweetie." He kissed my cheek. "Have you seen Wes?"

"No. Not yet." I noticed the front pew was empty.

"I think he went off with the funeral director."

My eyes focused on the simple wooden coffin at

the front, covered in a blanket of purple irises. They were beautiful and I wondered if they were Stacy's favorite flower. It was hard to imagine Stacy lying in that box, she had been such a force to be reckoned with. Pulling out a tissue, I started dabbing my eyes. *Change your thoughts, Tara,* I told myself. *Think of something totally nasty that Stacy said.*

"The first time I met her, she made me cry." I whispered to Jonathan.

"Oh no, what did she do to you?" He looked shocked and amused.

"She told me to stay away from her brother. She said he had a girlfriend who was an actress that looked like Sharon Stone and that he'd never leave her for me."

Dramatically, Jonathan's hand flew to his mouth. "She did not."

Nodding my head, I laughed. "She did. She wanted me nowhere near Wes." I looked at her coffin with a smile. "And the bitch got her way. Never in a million years would I ever have guessed that she and I would end up being friends."

From a side door, Wes, Julien and several other people emerged and made their way to the front pew. I could see the tightness and stress in Wes' face, the sadness in his heart evident in lines that appeared more deeply etched than the last time I'd seen him. My heart broke yet again. I so wanted to give him comfort. And seven rows back represented a million heart miles, as I'd been relegated to the status of business associate.

And then there was Julien, about to take a seat next to Wes. Before he sat down, he turned around, quickly surveying the pews.

"Does he have the remnants of a black eye?" Jonathan whispered in my ear.

"Sure does," I snickered. What had he said about me that incited Wes to punch him in the eye. It must've been a doozy. Yet, there he sat at Wes' side. And in that moment, I felt my anger spike. *Fuck you both. Bros before hoes.*

We began with the 23rd Psalm. Not good. I could never make it through without mumbling and crying and today was no different. The man speaking was a Methodist minister. Stacy was not a member of his congregation, but he had grown up down the street from Stacy and Wes and known them his entire life.

"Stacy Bergman was a difficult person to get to know. Earning her trust was not easy. She always told it like it was and if she didn't like you, she let you know. In no uncertain terms." He paused as the attendees laughed at the truism. "Once you earned her trust, Stacy was a loyal and giving friend. And you became a friend for life. She would have your back through thick and thin and if anyone talked trash about you, Stacy Bergman would put them in their place with one clean swipe. She was a woman you wanted on your side. Always. Deeply passionate about causes she believed in, she was tireless in her efforts. Although not a mother herself, Stacy was a generous supporter, both in the giving of her time and funding, to the Special Friends Organization, a non-profit providing respite programs for children with special needs. A talented artist herself, Stacy could be found every Saturday at Special Friends running art classes and planning art shows for the students."

As I sat and listened, I learned so much, realizing we had more in common that I'd ever thought.

"But more than anything, Stacy loved her older brother, Wes." As Wes bowed his head, I could see his shoulders heaving. "I remember from the time we were small children, Stacy followed Wes everywhere. At the local Little League games, Stacy was his biggest cheerleader, bragging, and rightly so, about her brother's athleticism. She was devoted to her brother as he was devoted to her."

I was at the point where I almost couldn't breathe, my tears were choking me so.

"Fighting a valiant fight against Breast Cancer, Stacy was a warrior, never for a second giving up hope, and in doing so, inspiring everyone around her to be hopeful about the endless possibilities in their lives."

Stacy and I had just had the conversation about hope. She had told me not to give up hope on Wes, and I could feel my heart shredding and hopeless, as I stared at the back of her brother's head. The sob that escaped from me was surprisingly loud. Everyone turned to look, including Wes, and I was glad when Jonathan pulled me to him, so that I could hide my face in his suit jacket and muffle my crying.

Hope. That light had been snuffed out. I'd hoped Stacy would beat this. I'd hoped Wes and I could talk through everything and make amends. I'd hoped Julien wouldn't do anything to destroy us. I'd hoped I'd finally found my happily ever after. Hope didn't feel very much like an ally to me.

And the only thing I now hoped was that the ceremony would soon be over and that I could leave.

After the minister, a few friends got up to speak, but I didn't hear a word they said. When I saw Wes rise, I reached for Jonathan's hand and squeezed it tight. I needed strength from somewhere.

"Thank you all for coming today to honor my sister and celebrate her life. I'm going to make this very brief. Little sisters are put on this Earth to drive their older brothers crazy and my sister was certainly exceptionally talented at that. Growing up she was like my shadow and by the time she was ten, it felt like she was my manager." Everyone laughed. "My sister always had my back and I knew I always had her love. I can't even begin to imagine how much I'm going to miss her and I'm just really fortunate that I had a sibling as great as Stacy." Looking at her coffin, "I'm going to miss you, Brat. Thank you for loving me and believing in me so much." Wes' voice cracked. Wiping his eyes, he stepped down to where her coffin resided and bent down to kiss it before returning to his seat.

Crying so hard that I couldn't breathe, I was afraid to look down at my chest for fear that my blouse would be shredded and stuffing would be hanging out. The searing pain made me feel as if I were the destroyed poppet. Stacy had not yet been diagnosed with pneumonia when I decimated the doll. *If only I had known,* I thought and then stopped myself at the lunacy of the thought pattern.

Chris bent forward and whispered, "Are you going to the cemetery or repast?"

Shaking my head, no, "I'm just going to relay my condolences to Wes and then go home and work from there today, if that's okay."

He nodded his head.

The ceremony ended with the playing of Stacy's favorite song, Train's *Drops of Jupiter.* Wiping my eyes again, I turned to Jonathan, "Pat Monahan wrote this song after his mother's death. Part of it came to him in a dream. Best song he ever wrote," I whispered.

Announcements were made about the burial and repast as everyone stood, allowing Wes and people I assumed were his cousins and an elderly aunt to exit to the outer room. It was time for me to convey my condolences to Wes and my anxiety was peaking at just the thought of approaching him. When I reached where they were gathered, he was surrounded by people. So, I stood off to the side and waited.

Almost pulled off my feet, Julien had grabbed hold of my upper arm and started dragging me off.

"Get your hands off me." I wrenched my arm free. Pointing my finger at him, "Do not touch me again," I seethed.

"I think you need to leave," his voice was a low, harsh whisper.

"I'll leave when I'm ready." People were milling past us, unaware of what was going on.

"Don't you think Wes has been through enough today without having to deal with you?"

I laughed. "Seriously, Julien? When have you ever cared what Wes was going through or put Wes first?"

"What the hell is that supposed to mean?" The man was looming over me imposingly.

"You want to know what it means?" I smiled. "It means I know a lot more than you think I know. And you'd better be careful around me or I will blow your life apart."

"Those are some big words."

"Yes, they are. And it would do you good to heed my advice." With that, I turned on my heel and headed back to where Wes was standing. Still surrounded by guests, I no longer cared about being polite and negotiated my way into the center of the circle until I was face-to-face with him.

"I just wanted to let you know how sorry I am and how fortunate I feel to have had the opportunity to really get to know Stacy and become friends. I really enjoyed the time she and I spent together."

Nodding, Wes smiled. "She felt the same way. And I haven't thanked you for all you did taking her to treatments and visiting her in the hospital and keeping me updated on everything. I really did appreciate it, Tara."

I nodded. There were no more words. None that were appropriate to speak in this setting. Leaning forward, I hugged Wes, taking him by surprise. His hands went on the sides of my waist, but not a hug. "I'm sorry for your loss," I whispered and turned away, hoping to find the closest exit quickly.

I'd taken maybe three steps and Julien was upon me. My index finger immediately shot up to an inch from his nose. "Don't you touch me," I seethed and kept walking. Turning back to glare at him, I saw the stunned look on Wes' face as he took in the encounter.

Finding the exit, I made it out to my car, my hands

shaking as I tried to hit the right button on the remote to open the doors. Once inside, I immediately turned the air conditioning onto high and put my head down on my steering wheel. I'm not going to cry here, I decided. I will drive to a parking lot and pull in if I need to lose it.

Lifting my head from the steering wheel, I watched as they loaded Stacy's iris covered casket into the hearse. Wes emerged from the funeral home, unbuttoning his suit jacket and pulling out his sunglasses before he slipped into the limousine. My heart seared with the pain of losing him again, except this time I wasn't calling his name, trying to get his attention. Maybe we were always meant to stay on our respective sides of the bridge, running parallel, but leading separate lives.

As the hearse began to pull away, the heaviness in my heart took on additional weight. I had lost a friend who died way too young. A woman who brought art to kids with special needs. I was going to miss her sharp tongue and our sparring.

*Oh Stacy, I'm not going to be able to accomplish what you asked of me. And I'm sorry for that. But Wes and I need to go our separate ways and rebuild our lives. I am the last person he wants taking care of him.*

*But what I can do is try to lessen the void in your art students' lives. I can't replace you or what you've given to them, but maybe I can make sure art stays in their lives through graphic arts and other forms of artistic expression. That I can do. I can try and carry on your work and make sure what you started with these kids continues. I would be honored to do that.*

Putting my car in drive to leave, I began to feel better. While I didn't have a lot of hope for myself, I could make sure that it wasn't lost for the special kiddos that meant so much to Stacy.

# Chapter 22

B y the second week, I realized Saturday mornings were becoming my personal savior. They pulled me from a dark space that enveloped me too much of the time. I had never dealt with depression and wondered if this is what it was or if I just needed to work through grief at the loss of two people I cared about deeply. Sunday through Friday, with effort, I was just going through the motions and I was doing it because that is what I owed my daughter.

Now Saturday, that was a different story. There were seven children in the art class. They had different degrees of communication skills and all of them were very unique. Scarlett joined me to lend a hand, as did her BFF Emmy. Working hand over hand with some of the students, they expressed themselves in bright colors and patterns on canvases that told stories many could not verbalize. It was a joy to witness their personalities and creativity come alive through their creations.

Assisting nine-year old Simone to grasp her paint brush, I asked her to show me what color paint she wanted to use next. Her hand moved to a neon pink and together we dipped the brush into the bubblegum colored paint.

"That is a very happy color, Simone." The little girl looked up at me with a bright smile and together we ran her brush across the canvas using a broad stroke. "Very good," I complimented her.

Gazing over at my daughter, I couldn't help but smile as she stood between two of the children, helping them to create their latest masterpieces. I knew this kind of experience would shape her in so many positive ways, potentially setting the direction for her future and I had Stacy to thank for this.

As we were cleaning up the room, the director popped her head in and pulled me out.

"How did it go today?" she asked. Camille Toussaint was a small, energetic woman and my gut told me she was probably a champion kickboxer.

"I think it went well. Everyone left with a canvas suitable for hanging and a big smile on their faces."

"Well, I've got some good news for you. We have a patron who will donate laptops for the graphics program you talked about."

"Tux Paint. And the program itself is free. We can just download it onto the laptops. This is so exciting. It will not only teach them about art, but help hone computer skills. This is amazing."

"What else will you need?" the program director asked.

"A photo quality printer and ink cartridges so that the kids can print and take home their work."

"Well, I think we can pay for that with our budget."

"Camille, thank you so much." I wanted to hug the woman, but I got the vibe she wasn't a hugger and I'd end up flat on my back on the cold, hard floor after she flung me down with a perfect self-defense move.

"Don't thank me. It's our generous donors."

"Is there someone I should be thanking for this?" I was beyond elated at the usable skills I was going to be able to teach these kids under the guise of fun. What they would learn would help them in school and someday out in the work world. There was nothing better than teaching skills that could be generalized across environments.

"No. Our donors prefer to stay anonymous."

"I understand. But please thank them for me for the generous donation and I promise it will be put to great use."

Back in the classroom I announced to Scarlett and Emmy, "We're going digital! Brand new laptops are being donated for the kids."

"That is awesome, Mom."

"And a lot cleaner," Emmy added, her smock looking similar to many of the canvases that walked out of here today.

I laughed. "Yes, it is. You can actually wear cute clothes here knowing they won't be ruined. No more neon slashes across your shirts."

My head was swimming with the possibilities and I knew I had to break it down into simple steps that built on one another so that the kids would have success and want to continue.

"Well, you two," I said to the girls. "Let me pay you for your morning's efforts in food. Where would you like to go? And make it someplace where we are served. No drive-thrus."

"Are you sure you don't want me to stay?"

Looking up from my book, "Of course not, sweetie. It's your time with your dad. Go enjoy yourself."

Sitting down next to me on the bed, Scarlett smoothed out the cream silk comforter. "But Mom, you just like seem so sad all the time. The only time I literally see you smiling and energetic is when you're teaching the art class."

"That's not true." I reached out and tucked her hair behind her ear.

"Yes, Mom. It is. You were not this sad when you and Dad got divorced."

I laughed, "That's because I was so damn angry." Which was odd, because anger was usually my trigger for tears.

"Yeah well, guess what, Mom," my sage teen began, "now you're like literally so damn sad."

Hearing her say those words broke my heart. Opening my arms, she came in for a hug. "I'm sorry, sweetie. I will push myself to get to a better place. You deserve that."

"So do you, Mom." Her big blue eyes told me she was dead serious.

"You are very smart. And you are right. I do deserve to be happy. And since I'm the one in charge of my happiness, I need an attitude adjustment."

"You like literally do, really. Maybe you and Aunt Laynie should like go out for Margaritas or something." Scarlett smiled at me.

"You know you inherited your brilliance from me."

"Of course I did," she laughed.

"Okay, I promise to call Aunt Laynie and get my butt out of the house tonight."

"That makes me happy, Mom." Scarlett gave me another tight hug before going back to her room to finish packing.

"She's right, Tara. You are significantly more miserable now than you ever were during your divorce." Laynie was giving me that tilted head, raised eyebrow look. The one that screams *you know I'm right, so don't even think about denying it.*

"It was a hope thing, I think. I let myself believe that

Wes was the one I was always meant to be with and could be my happily-ever-after." Taking a sip of my wine, "Just verbalizing that sounds pathetic, doesn't it? Ugh. I just felt like I had this soul attachment to him. But clearly, I was just another expendable woman."

"I don't know about that. I think the timing just sucked and he emotionally melted down. He knew he was going to have to deal with his sister's death, even without the pneumonia, just the fact that the chemo wasn't working and it spread. So, I think he had the hope pulled from him. And basically, at the same time he gets blindsided with the news that this woman he is crazy about, his happily-ever-after, had sex with his best friend in a bathroom. And not that you did anything wrong, because you didn't, but he lost a lot in the blink of an eye. The two women he cares about most were being ripped from him. And although it's not right, I'm sure his anger at Stacy's situation got displaced on you."

Signaling the bartender for another glass of wine, "Can you make this next one the Silver Oak cabernet, please. Thanks." Turning back to Laynie, "I just have to get through the Breast Cancer event and then I think I'll feel like I'm out of limbo and can start moving forward again."

"Well, you'll have us there with you, so that should help make the evening less awkward for you."

Back when we'd first been chosen for the project, I'd purchased extra tickets for Laynie, Jill and Scarlett to attend the white-tie event. I thought it would be an inspiring night out for all of us and now I was glad to have my posse with me. I was a little concerned about Scarlett seeing Wes, I didn't want her to feel brushed off by him over the situation with me. When I'd asked her recently if they'd been in touch, she shared not often, that she'd checked on him after Stacy's death and he thanked her for it. And then one time after that, she'd reached out to see if he was okay and he'd answered back that it was a rough time for him and he was trying to get through it one day at a time.

Later that evening in bed, I stared at the ceiling, unable to find a comfortable position and stop my mind from racing. What I was finally letting my conscience admit was just how stressed out I was about the fundraiser. It was business and my work was being presented there. I had a commitment to professionalism and I had to be there. The dread I felt in being at the same function with both Wes and Julien was overwhelming me. I knew I could count on Wes to act professionally. The worst-case scenario was that he would ignore me and although that would rip at my already tattered heart, I just needed to keep my chin up and act like a lady. I knew the true grieving would begin after that night.

Julien Matthews, on the other hand, was a wild card. Lord knows what shit that man might pull and that scared me. Knowing he wasn't above pushing my buttons to make me look bad in front of Wes, just for him to then be able to say to Wes, "Aren't you glad you got rid of that crazy bitch." There was no telling what he'd do to get back at me for not coming back for more, begging him and humiliating myself.

I looked forward to the day Julien Matthews was a footnote in a very short chapter in my life. But for right now, being with him and Wes in the same room for that fundraiser filled me with dread.

And tonight, I was feeling hatred toward Julien for being such a malicious dick. Toward Wes for not even giving me the courtesy of a conversation and for bailing on us and for choosing and believing Julien, and finally toward Laynie, for making up excuses for Wes, which was the exact opposite of where she'd been. I understood her sympathy toward him, but what about sympathy for me? I had let myself dream. Really dream. And the reality of it was crushing me.

*When was it ever going to be hoes before bros?*

# Chapter 23

To say I was freaking out about attending the Breast Cancer Fundraiser would be an understatement. I was obsessing about it, making myself sick, having totally OCD thought patterns that were totally fucking with my head. Every day, all day, I played a *What-If* game with myself.

What if Wes ignored me?

What if Wes was there with another woman?

What if he was physical with her in front of me?

What if Wes was shitty to Scarlett and broke her heart?

What if Julien made a scene and embarrassed me publicly?

What if the attendees hated the videos?

What if I went totally apeshit on Julien and embarrassed myself personally and professionally?

I was driving myself crazy, totally assured the worst was going to happen. My dream had turned out to be a lie. And the biggest *What If* of all was what if I had just deleted all my online accounts as I had planned to after my date with the car groper, then there would have been no Julien in my life?

But the *What If* that hurt the most nudged its way in right after that one. What if Wes had just talked to me and didn't push me away? What if he'd let me tell him that night on the boat? What if I hadn't let myself fall crazy in love with him? What if we'd just remained on our opposite sides of the bridge.

Walking into my living room, I looked out at my terrace and the view beyond with the pinpoints of twinkling lights in people's homes as the evening sky darkened and the first stars made their way onto the faded blue, blank canvas. Sliding open the glass door, the cool Indian Summer evening felt refreshing, I stepped outside and I breathed it in with a sad sigh. Wes and I had made love out here. There weren't very many spots in my condo that we hadn't christened.

*The sun was a mesmerizing red ball sinking into a layer of humidity and smog. Wes stepped out onto the terrace, wrapping his arms around me from behind and pulling me against him snugly. The heat of his lips on my neck made me shiver.*

*"Shivering in 95 degrees?" he laughed.*

*"You make me tingle."*

*Grinding his hard cock against my ass, he laughed again, "I could say the same thing about you."*

*Turning my head back to kiss him, the thought of having sex out here in the open, although eighteen floors up, was getting me as wet as his kisses. Without any provocation, I pulled my tank top off over my head revealing a pale mint green lace demi-bra.*

*"Oh so unfair, you know I'm now toast."*

*With a playful smile, I took his hands and placed them on the lacy cups. "I think your toast may have been in the toaster too long…it's hard." And I pressed back into him.*

*"Just like your nipples," he whispered in my ear, as they obediently responded to his touch through the lace. "So, are we going to christen this terrace?"*

*Leaning my head back on his shoulder, "I think it's our*

duty," I said very seriously, actually keeping a straight face and unhooking the front clasp on my bra.

Wes moaned in my ear, his hands now fully on my breasts, "I don't think you have any idea just how hot you are and that is such a turn-on."

Hearing those words from him, the one man I wanted to see me as sexy, a man with such commanding appeal, gave me a confidence I didn't think I still possessed after being dumped for a millennial.

Turning in his arms, I pointed to one of the chaise lounges. "On your back, Bergman."

He never took his eyes off mine as that slow, sexy smile of his made my breath quicken. Unbuttoning his cargo shorts with slow deliberate moves, he knew exactly what he was doing to me, as his eyes took on a playful cast while he removed them.

Standing there in just my white jeans shorts, I too slowly unbuttoned the top button and made a meal of leisurely lowering the zipper. Once it was down, Wes stepped forward, slipping his hands inside and molding his palms around my ass cheeks, kneading them hard.

"You're killing me," I choked out.

"Good." He smiled, kissing my jaw.

I could feel a band of sweat forming along the hairline on the back of my neck. The humid summer air was enveloping us and I was both sweating and shivering at the same time. Closing my eyes, I put my hands on Wes' shoulders, his skin was already moist under my palms. The balmy night was making it harder to breathe and amping up the intensity of the moment. This was not going to be lovemaking; this was going to be gritty, nasty sweaty fucking and we were both jumping at each other's touch.

After another squeeze of my ass cheeks, Wes tugged my shorts down and I stepped out of them. I was down to a pale mint lace and silk thong.

"Get naked, dude. I need you on your back." I pointed to the chaise. "Now."

"*You want them off me,*" *he was referring to his gray boxer briefs,* "*then take them off me.*" *There was a challenge in his tone.*

*Slowly, I approached, holding eye contact. Running my hand up the outside of the soft fabric, I traced his hard cock with my fingers.*

*His sharp intake of breath almost did me in and my touch became firmer. Moving my hands around to the back, I slipped them under the waistband, cupping and kneading his ass like he had done to mine a few minutes before and pulling him against me.*

*From his look, I could tell he liked me as the aggressor, a role I didn't take on until extremely comfortable. But out in the open that night, in my brand-new lingerie, with this confident, sexy man, I felt his equal partner. We were right together. This was the way it was supposed to be. Finally.*

*Peeling his underwear down to his thighs, I caressed the length of him, feeling him grow rock hard to my touch and leaned forward to place a kiss on his delicious lips. Pressing into him, I forced him to walk backwards until the back of his knees were against the lounge chair.*

"*You don't have to ask for a third time.*" *Lowering himself onto the thick lemon colored pad, he peeled off the boxer briefs and opened his arms to me.*

*Laying down on top of him, I could feel the sheen of sweat on both our bodies. There was no friction between our skin as my legs glided over his.*

*Taking my face in both his hands, he kissed my lips hard, his tongue seizing control of any coherent thought pattern onto which I was still holding. I could only feel his sweaty stomach under me, as I rubbed on him, my thong still in place. Lowering a hand from my face, Wes began to tug at my thong and I reached down to pull it off, laughing as I was trying to kick it down my legs and not being as graceful as I'd hoped. Finally, the offending garment was gone and we were slick skin to slick skin.*

*Our lips once again meeting, I rubbed my wetness along*

*the length of him, until I was positioned in just the right spot and Wes thrust up into me.*

*"Yesssssssss." I gasped, staying very still for a moment, savoring the sensation of him filling me. I smiled down enjoying seeing his curls mat with sweat on this sultry night, as I began to ride his cock. The look on his face every time I pounded down was incentive to drive harder, knowing the pleasure I was bringing him.*

*As I watched the handsome man he'd matured into, my heart was brimming with emotion. From the first night we'd met, Wes had been intricately woven into my life in a way that even I didn't understand. We were fated to meet. Of that I was sure. And we were fated to meet again. I knew I was blessed. I had never been so right with another man and I didn't think there was anyone else out there who complemented and completed me in the way he did. The way he always had.*

*I'd been lost in my thoughts and when I returned to the popping sounds of our sweaty bodies, my legs sliding off his, Wes was smiling up at me.*

*Smiling back, "What?" I asked.*

*"You're finally mine."*

*The truth was, I was his about three hours into a conversation more than a decade before, the night I met the man it was clear I was destined to meet.*

*"Finally," I whispered.*

"Mom." Scarlett broke my reverie and I jumped. "Sorry, I didn't mean to scare you."

Holding my heart and breathing hard, "Oh gosh, I didn't hear you come out here."

Sitting down on the chaise next to me, she clutched her

cell phone tightly and let out a big sigh.

"What's up, sweetie? Is everything okay?" I sat up in my chair as there was clearly something she wanted to tell me.

"I just got a text from Wes." I could see her trepidation as she waited for my response.

"Oh really? What did it say?"

Scarlett handed me her phone.

**Saw your name on the guest list for the fundraiser. Made my day.**

**Can't wait to see you again.**

**Save the last dance for me.**

I smiled at the message. I could now take the *What if Wes treats Scarlett badly* off the table. His message to her was very sweet.

"That's nice." Smiling, I handed the phone back.

"You're okay with it?" Scarlett's loyalty and protectiveness were coming through.

"Of course I am, baby. What's going on between me and Wes is our deal to work out or not work out. But the two of you really like each other and I'm glad he's not letting our stuff get in the way of that."

"But Mom, he hurt you. Like really bad. I've like literally never seen you so upset, not even over Dad and I'm like really mad at Wes about that."

"I understand. Sometimes people hurt each other unintentionally and things snowball and other factors get in the way and just make a bad situation worse. Well, I think that's what happened with us."

"Are you going to be okay seeing him?"

I thought for a moment before answering. The reality was probably not. My heart was going to burst the minute I laid eyes on the man. But this was a business function for me, a work event and the onus was on me to conduct myself as a professional and that is exactly what I was going to do.

"Yeah. I'm going to be just fine. And I'm going to look

so damn hot he's going to be drooling." The minute those words were out of my mouth, I said a silent prayer that he did not have a plus one who was a date.

"Are you wearing that silver beaded gown?" Scarlett had a conspiratorial smile.

"I sure am." I smiled back.

Throwing her head back with laughter, "He's like literally so screwed, Mom. You are so right. He will be drooling. Dude's not gonna know what hit him."

"Good," I laughed and fist-bumped my daughter.

"Love it." She nodded her head and I could see her mind racing.

"This is like literally so cool, bro." Scarlett said to Laynie in the back of our stretch limo.

"It's impossible to drive in gowns. This is the only way to travel." She sipped from her champagne flute, looking elegant in a sheer and beaded crimson dress that left very little to the imagination.

"Will my videos be shown tonight?" Jill asked. She had been involved in two of the videos: one PSA and then her personal story for their website profiles.

Shaking my head, "I have no idea what's on the program for tonight. I'm assuming we'll see all the PSAs throughout the evening, but I don't know about the website videos. Once my part was done, I handed it off to Jamie and I don't think even he was involved with any of the planning for tonight."

As we pulled up in the long line of limos in front of the Waldorf-Astoria, waiting to drop guests off, Laynie commented, "A white-tie gala at the Waldorf. This has got to be costing Wes a pretty penny."

"I'm sure it is. But they will raise a lot of money tonight and if our PSAs do the job I hope they'll do, they will touch people enough to reach deep into their wallets." I said, as our limo inched up to the entrance and I could feel my heart begin to beat quicker.

*What if…*

The ride up in the Ballroom Elevators had me taking deep breaths in through my nose and slowly exhaling through my mouth in an effort to calm my nerves. Standing tall next to me, I could tell my beautiful daughter was feeling very adult-like in her gown attending this chic New York City event. The elevator's carved nickel doors opened to the third floor's ornate Silver Corridor. This was it. The event for which we'd been hired to create the PSAs, C-Kickers' *Kick Breast Cancer to the Curb* Gala.

"Oh my God," Jill's hand flew to her mouth. Three steps out of the elevator we were greeted by a life-sized cut-out of Jill wearing brightly colored C-Kicker workout gear and the quote, "I may be little, but I'm fierce and I've made it my mission to kick cancer's butt." And then there were instructions to watch Jill's video and make a donation via the touchscreen computer monitor set-up on a table next to Cardboard Jill.

Immediately, we rushed over to check it out.

"In your case a life-sized cut-out is actually taller than you are," Laynie kidded, laughing.

"Not with these on." Jill lifted her dress a smidge to show off her skyscraper Louboutin's.

"I love this." Scarlett was whizzing through the screens of the touchscreen. "You can see and hear everyone's story and there's a button to donate on each page." Finally, she came back to Jill's video. I felt tremendous pride as we viewed it. It was real and touching and it spoke directly to the person watching it as Jill shared the devastating blows and kick ass triumphs of her journey.

As we walked toward the reception desk, the corridor was lined with cutouts and touch screens for all the video stories and people were stopping at each one, spending time, hearing the stories and making online donations. It was a brilliant introduction to the evening and I felt a part of the joy in knowing that my work had contributed to the success of the cause.

"We're at Table 36," Scarlett announced, handing all of us our personalized place cards.

"I need a drink," I muttered loud enough for only Laynie to hear as we entered the famed four-story ballroom. As if magically hearing my wish, a waiter appeared with a tray of champagne flutes and we each grabbed one. "Let's find you something else bubbly," I said to my daughter as her hand approached the tray.

Negotiating our way through the room, we found Table 36. Jonathan was already seated with his newest paramour, Andrew.

"Hello, handsome and handsome," I greeted the two of them.

"Don't you ladies look gorgeous," Jonathan rose to greet us all with kisses.

"We do clean up nice," I agreed. "Are Jamie and Shelby here yet?"

"I haven't seen them. But Chris and his contingent are at Table 41."

"Okay, let me go find them and say hello." Putting my purse down on my chair, I turned to Scarlett, Laynie and Jill. "I'll be right back. I need to go say hello to Chris."

Making my way across the ballroom, the pink tulle and ribbon décor for the evening's event gave the room a very ethereal feel and I started singing Train's *Drops of Jupiter* in my head.

"You're a smiley one tonight." My boss greeted me with a kiss on the cheek. Then holding me at arm's length, "You look fabulous."

"Thank you. It's fun to dress up sometimes."

"Have you seen Wes?" he asked.

Shaking my head, "Not yet. We just got here a few minutes ago."

"I think he's like two or three tables away from you."

"Well, I'm sure I'll see Renata because she'll certainly be in something eye-catching tonight. And speaking of eye-catching, how much did you love the life-sized cutouts and displays with the videos we did for their website?"

Chris' green eyes twinkled. "I loved it a lot." He tapped the program sitting on his plate, "And I also loved the visibility they're giving our work throughout the evening."

"Oh, I haven't looked yet. I'll check it out when I get back to my seat. It appears that this thing is about to start. I'll see you in a little bit." As I made my way back to my table, I tried to casually scan the room for Wes, but didn't spot him anywhere.

A moment after I sat down, salads were delivered to our table and the Executive Director of the Breast Cancer International Research & Support Fund welcomed us all to their annual event, promising an evening that would be as uplifting as it was educational. Thanking the evening's host and main sponsor, C-Kicker Athletic Wear, all eyes turned toward Wes' table and that was my first glimpse of him.

I couldn't help but smile just seeing him there in his black tux and white bowtie, looking so freaking handsome that I could feel my body react at just the sight of him. He stood and did a brief wave.

Laynie's arm snaked around the back of Scarlett's chair and grabbed my bare shoulder, squeezing it. Leaning toward her, she whispered in my ear, "Now I understand."

It was the first time she'd seen Wes in person. I knew she could see in my eyes that my heart was breaking all over again just being in the same room as him. There had been no closure and the gaping wound I hid under the sparkly gown threatened to publicly expose itself in a hideous manner.

"Who's the handsome guy two seats away?" she asked.

"The devil incarnate," I hissed, actually sneering.

"Oh, that's him? I am totally going to fuck with him tonight."

My eyes popped open wide.

"Not fuck him. Fuck with him. The douche needs to be tortured." And she sat up straighter and shifted in her chair pointing her high-beam nipples at him like lures.

"Have at it and do lots of damage." She certainly had my blessing.

As the waiters removed our empty salad plates, Wes made his way to the stage and took his place behind the podium. Before he even uttered hello, the room burst into applause and the staff at the C-Kicker table stood, giving their boss a standing ovation. The rest of the ballroom followed suit and I could tell by the smile on Wes' face that he was both humbled and touched by the crowd's response.

Again, reaching behind Scarlett's chair to get to me, Laynie pinched my upper arm hard.

"Ouch." I turned to give her a *what the fuck* look.

"He is so charismatic."

I laughed, "He hasn't even spoken yet."

Holding up his hand, with a smile, to still the crowd. "Thank you." His hand went to his heart, "I'm humbled, truly." He waited for the crowd to quiet, before continuing.

"Survivors, Supporters, Friends – Thank you all for coming out tonight to the C-Kicker Kick Breast Cancer to the Curb Annual Gala. As many of you are aware breast cancer struck my family for the second time recently, and in late August, I lost my only sibling to complications from the disease. Unfortunately, I don't have a unique or rare story, because there is no one in this room whose life has been unscathed when it comes to breast cancer.

"I'm not going to stand up here and spout statistics. I don't need to. This epidemic has become everyone's personal tragedy. Tonight you'll be hearing from doctors working on groundbreaking treatment, which is very exciting and you'll also be seeing the premiere of a series of hard-hitting and very poignant Public Service Announcements. After tonight you will be seeing these PSAs all over your TV and in digital advertising.

"This year C-Kicker teamed up with O'Donnell & Associates to create this signature campaign. You know the old saying 'A picture tells a thousand words,' well, I think a video gives us an intimate glance into a chapter of a person's life. They allow us into their world and together we experience a journey. A very human journey. Throughout the evening, we'll be spotlighting personal stories of some very courageous individuals, their families, their doctors and their support teams.

"It is my hope that three things will come from this. First, as we all know, early detection is the key to a successful outcome and I hope these stories will motivate women and men to make screening a priority. Second, for everyone in this room, I ask that you take to heart the stories you will hear tonight and then dig deep in your pockets to support the Breast Cancer International Research & Support Fund. There are manned stations throughout the room for donations as well as online touchscreens located in the Silver Corridor. And last but not least, it is my hope that this evening will leave you with hope. Hope that as a community we can come together and support patients and their families throughout their challenge and that we can support the research necessary to develop effective treatment that is not worse for the patient than the actual disease.

"I have hope. Tremendous hope. That in my lifetime we will make the necessary strides to ensure that this heinous disease will no longer be claiming lives and destroying families. I have hope that together we can raise the funds critical for the brightest research minds to have the resources they need to find cures for the multiple forms of breast cancer." He paused for a long moment, but didn't move from the podium.

"I have hope."

I squeezed my eyes shut at the emotion in his voice.

And then the stage lights went out. We all sat in total darkness for a mere second before the room erupted into applause and then the screen behind where Wes had been standing lit up and one of our PSAs began to run. By the time the lights came back on, women were digging in their evening bags for tissues and men were trying to discreetly dab their eyes with their napkins. Patrons began to make their way over to the manned donation stations and out into the Silver Corridor.

"Mom," Scarlett turned to me, "you made that?" She was in awe.

"Well, this handsome guy wrote it." I rubbed Jonathan's shoulder. "And that handsome guy is the one that makes everything we do look good." I nodded toward Jamie.

Jill was overcome with emotion. Dabbing at her eyes, "I'm so proud you invited me to be part of this whole process."

My heart was glowing with pride and momentarily the *What Ifs* faded into the background. Tonight, I felt blessed. Blessed that not only did my career allow me to express my creative passion, but with projects like this, it impacted both individuals and the world in a very positive way.

As we ate our soup course, a researcher walked us through his work on detecting circulating cancer cells in the bloodstream. His presentation was followed by another one of our videos and I was pleased to see even more people head to the donation stations. The PSAs were resonating deeply with the crowd.

"Oh my God, our song," I heard my daughter gasp.

Turning to her, I followed her gaze. Standing on the dance floor, a few feet from our table was Wes, first pointing at Scarlett, and then crooking his finger for her to come to him. Practically knocking over the chair in her haste to get up, she ran out onto the dance floor and with huge smiles the two began to dance and sing along to Walk the Moon's *Shut Up and Dance.*

"Well, that's quite the love affair." Laynie looked surprised.

"I'm glad." I watched the two of them cutting up on the dance floor. "Frank has been so inconsistent with her that I'm glad Wes is showing her that no matter what or what not his relationship is with me, that he still values her."

"He is one attractive man," Jill threw in her two cents.

The song came to an end and Meghan Trainor's duet with John Legend *Like I'm Going to Lose You* began and my daughter drifted effortlessly into Wes' arms for the slow ballad. I watched as they chatted like two long lost friends catching up with one another. My heart was melting and aching at the same time and I could feel the lump forming at the back of my throat. I was angry. Angry at myself for not pushing Wes to listen to me that night on the boat and let me tell him about my tryst with Julien before he and I became lovers; angry at Wes for pushing me away the way he did, but, at the same time, happy he had the maturity and character not to take that out on my child.

Giving her a big hug at the end of the song, he then took her face in his hands and kissed her forehead. Then with the Wes smile, I could see his lips form the words, "Thank you, Princess."

Scarlett floated back to the table just as the main course was being served.

"That was so great. *Shut Up and Dance* was our song at the father/daughter dance." She was beaming.

"It looked like you two had fun."

With a little smile, she said, "Well, maybe for the first dance. I'm not so sure he had much fun during the second song."

"Why do you say that?" They were now playing soft jazz music while we ate.

"'Cause I think I kinda like literally blew his mind, Mom," She paused. "He was asking about you and I told him the truth."

My fork was suspended mid-air, halfway to my mouth. *Oh God.*

"Oh shit," Laynie muttered. "What truth?"

"He asked how you were and I told him that you were sad. He also wanted to know if you were seeing anyone and I said, 'Bro, you like literally broke her heart, of course she's not seeing anyone.' And he was like really, I didn't want to hurt your mom and I told him, 'Well, you did. She really cares about you.' He needed to know, Mom."

"How naked do you feel?" Laynie laughed.

Putting down my fork and picking up my wineglass, I twirled it for a moment, looking at the color of the claret liquid through the light, before taking a hearty sip. "Very. Like I'm having the naked dream and trying to pretend I look normal. Please tell me I look good."

"You look fabulous," Jonathan interjected.

I laughed, "Thank you, because I know if I looked like shit, you would tell me. That is precisely why every straight woman on this planet needs gay male BFFs." Leaning over, I kissed his cheek.

"Are you mad at me, Mom?"

Shaking my head no, I smiled at Scarlett. "No sweetie, not at all. The truth is the truth. And here's a saying from *my day* that applies, *put that in your pipe and smoke it, Wes.*"

Laynie and Jill cracked up and my daughter looked at me like, *what the heck are you talking about?*

After the waiters cleared our entrée plates, the lights

dimmed again and another one of our PSAs played.

"I love this one," Jonathan whispered in my ear.

"Me too," I whispered back.

When the lights came back up, a very prominent local news anchor was standing behind the podium. She had never hidden her battle with breast cancer and brought her viewers with her throughout the journey. All of New York attended her doctors' appointments, her diagnostic tests and her surgeries. We cheered at the good news and cried with her on discouraging days.

The room was on its feet, cheering. Not just because she was still with us, a valiant warrior who battled her way into remission, but because she led us all into battle with the heart of a General. She educated us, pulled us along when we didn't want to go any further, and taught us to humbly accept the wins, and cope with the losses with grace.

Sitting back and listening to her wise words as I gently stroked my daughter's hair , I was so glad that Scarlett was getting to experience the power of strong women, who like Jill and Stacy, had fought back with every last ounce of courage and strength when the odds were stacked against them. My heart pinged, wishing Stacy were here to be a part of this event – as a survivor. As that thought filled my head, a pink glint from the chandelier above flashed before my eyes and I knew Stacy Bergman had just told me that she was sure as hell not missing out on this event.

At the end of the newscaster's speech, the room was once again on its feet for a standing ovation and throngs of attendees headed toward the donation tables. Once again, the dance floor filled. A few measures into the song, I realized it was Spandau Ballet's *True,* the last song Wes and I had danced to on *Second Wind's* deck that night after dancing on the neighboring boat and my heart cracked just a little more.

"May I have this dance?" Wes was standing next to my chair.

"Umm, I don't think," I began.

Leaning over Scarlett and practically pushing me out of my chair, Laynie took over. "Of course she will."

Stumbling, Wes took my hand to steady me, and with his other hand on my lower back, led me to the dance floor.

Once in his arms, I could feel the increasing tension in my muscles causing them to twitch at his touch.

"Hey relax," he whispered in my ear.

Looking up to face him, "Easier said than done."

"I don't like that I make you tense."

I didn't answer him and he continued. "I don't know where to begin to apologize, Tara. I'm just sorry that I hurt you and made you sad."

With my eyes locked on his, "I thought we had something special, Wes. I thought we were the real thing."

As the song ended, I went to move from his arms, but he embraced me tighter. The first strains of Roxy Music's version of the John Lennon classic, *Jealous Guy*, began to play.

Smiling down at me, Wes said, "This could be my theme song."

"Jealous Guy?"

He nodded.

"Please tell me you are not jealous of what happened between me and Julien."

Wes just raised his eyebrows and tilted his head.

Blowing out a sigh, I closed my eyes. "It's what I wanted to tell you about the first night we made love. It happened when you were a fifteen-year old memory. It only happened once and frankly was a debacle, and if I could take one day back and make it not happen, I would. But I can't. And as far as you being jealous – of what? A bad memory?"

"He and I have a complicated history."

"Yeah, I know. Bros before hoes." I just wanted to get off the dance floor and away from him.

Wes threw his head back in laughter. I'm not sure what

he found funny about my statement, but I certainly wasn't amused, which he could now see on my face.

Still chuckling, he said, "You know what Julien said to me right after I punched him in the face? He said, 'Hoes before bros'."

"Fucker called me a Hoe?" I was irrationally incensed.

"Yeah. And I punched him again."

"Thank you." I tried to hide my smile.

"T, that weekend nearly broke me. Between Julien blindsiding me with what he told me and the cancer being discovered in Stacy's lung, I got sucker punched twice. Was it right to take it out on you and not listen to you? No. That was a huge freaking mistake. I was already at a low and flipping out about you when I learned that the cancer had metastasized. It was like the two women I loved most were just ripped from me and I couldn't control the spiral. I was mad at you for being with him. And yes, I know it's irrational to be mad at you for something that happened before I was in your life. But there was nothing rational in my emotions that weekend and I knew I had to gather up my strength to help Stacy with this new leg of her fight and I just didn't have the strength to deal with the emotions I was feeling about us. I needed to channel them for Stacy. I thought I'd have her for a while longer and I'd be the one cheering her along, providing hope. Her death so soon was like the last punch down. Except this time, I didn't get back up. I lost hope."

"I'm sorry that you had to go through all that." The song was changing again, but after that baring of his soul, I didn't feel like I could pull away and my first gut reaction was to soothe him. "Did you put in requests with the DJ?" I smiled at Crowded House's *Don't Dream It's Over.*

"I did." He smiled back. "And you have one more song you have to dance with me to after this one."

"*True, Jealous Guy, Don't Dream It's Over* – I can't even imagine what you've got up next."

Pulling me in tight, I just put my head against his chest as we danced in silence. I was being internally drawn and quartered by my own emotions and I wished I could quiet them enough so that I could just enjoy the sublime sensation of being held in his arms again. Part of me wanted to turn back the clock to before the weekend that everything fell apart, and yet overriding that was the fear that this man could once again cast me aside and kick me to the curb. And I knew, that if I were emotionally in deeper, that pain would be unbearable.

When the Gin Blossoms' *Till I Hear It From You* began playing, Wes whispered in my ear, "I want a do-over."

Pulling my head from his chest, I searched his face. It wasn't so simple. Just as he needed to be there for Stacy. I needed to be there and strong for Scarlett. She needed a mother who protected her and the first line of defense for that was protecting myself, so that I could be there for her. "I'm not going to respond to you with the mean thing you said to me when I told you that. Excuse me." I broke free of his arms and walked off the dance floor, headed out into the Silver Corridor in search of the Ladies' Room.

Leaving the ballroom, I took a deep breath before approaching two women behind a table setting up gift bags and asked them where I could find the bathrooms. Wishing I had no make-up on, I was fantasizing about splashing cold water on my cheeks or maybe just dumping my whole face directly into a sink full of cold water and then walking out with streaks of mascara running down my face.

I felt numb. Positively numb. Wes wanted me back. He'd even said something about the two women he loved most and one of them was me. So then why the hell would he have treated someone he loves the way he treated me?

As I washed my hands, I hoped that dessert was served soon. I'd had about enough of this evening. I wanted to settle back into the cushy seats of the limo and kick off my beautiful, yet ridiculously painful, shoes.

Walking out of the Ladies' Room I was shocked to feel the pressure of strong fingers digging into my upper arm. The déjà vu was not a pleasant memory.

"Julien, get your hands off me." I shook my arm hard to rid his grasp. "Don't you touch me."

"What? Not rough enough for you, Tara?"

I wanted to smack the sneer off his face.

"Get out of my way." I unsuccessfully tried to sidestep around him.

"You need to stay away from Wes." The man loomed over me.

That seemed to have been the prevailing sentiment from the time I first met Mr. Bergman. First Stacy and now Julien. Except I didn't think I'd ever become friends with Julien.

"Get out of my way," I repeated.

His finger was now in my face and I had taken the protective posture of crossing my arms over my chest.

"You go near him, Tara, and I will destroy you."

"Number one, get your effing finger out of my face and number two, if you screw with me any further, I will bring you down and the gravy train you have been living off will quickly dry up. Wes has been so good to you and all you do is look for ways to hurt him."

"You know nothing."

I smiled. "If you say so." My answer incensed him.

"You have nothing on me."

"If you say so." I continued to smile.

"Don't push me, Tara."

"No Julien, don't you push me. I know all about April 22, 1994 and even if Wes doesn't know what kind of scum you really are, I've got the whole picture. So, it might be in your best interest to stop threatening me."

"What happened on April 22, 1994?" We had been so engrossed in our argument that neither Julien nor I had seen Wes approach. How much he had heard before my last comments, I had no clue.

Turning to Wes, I put my hand on his upper arm and calmly said, "That's a conversation you need to have with Julien. Though, at least from me, I know you'd get the truth." I took a moment to glare at Julien before turning on my heel and walking away from the two old friends as I headed back into the ballroom.

Returning to my table, a slice of flourless chocolate torte drizzled with raspberry coulis waited for me.

"So, that looked pretty intense with Wes on the dance floor." Laynie remarked, giving me the eyebrow raise that was code for I want all the details.

"Ugh. That was the least of it. I was just accosted by Julien walking out of the Ladies' Room."

"Accosted?" Jonathan laughed. "Ooo, Tara's pissed. She's using big words."

"The man is such a douche." I was still riled up from what had happened in the corridor.

"D word. Tara's cursing. She's mega-pissed," laughed Jamie.

"You need chocolate." Jonathan pointed at my uneaten dessert. It was then that I noticed that all the other dessert plates at the table looked like a dog had licked them clean.

"No, I've lost my appetite." Which I had. But I was also fearful my hands were still shaking from anger and I wouldn't be able to successfully maneuver the cake from the plate to my mouth without making a huge mess.

Jonathan picked up my fork and cut the tip of the torte slice. I was just about to bust on him about a second dessert ruining his boyish figure when the fork approached me.

"Open up, doll face. This will make you happy."

The minute my mouth opened to respond, the chocolate was in there. And divine it was. The smooth ganache melted in my mouth and I instantly felt better.

"Wow, that is delicious."

"Mmm-hmm." Jonathan had the next bite already to my mouth, this time the torte was dripping of raspberry sauce.

"Mmm." I savored the second bite. "If I finish my dessert, can I leave?"

Everyone laughed.

"I think we've all made a good showing tonight and we're at the point where it's no longer rude to disappear," was Jamie's assessment.

"Mom, I want to say goodbye to Wes." Scarlett started to look around the room.

"Okay, go find him and say goodbye and then we're leaving."

As soon as Scarlett left the table, Laynie leaned over. "It looks like you've got a lot to tell me."

"It has been an eventful evening," was all I said.

"I can't find him. I like literally looked everywhere." Scarlett was pouting when she returned to the table.

"Okay then, let me buzz the limo driver and let's get out of here." I was on overload. Wes. Julien. April 22nd. My hurting feet. I just needed to freaking leave, go home, crawl into my bed and process the evening.

Exiting the ballroom, tables were set up on each side of the door with giftbags. Usually you just grabbed one and left, but these all had individual name tags on them.

"That's odd," Jill commented.

"Maybe it gives them a count of the no-shows tonight?" I conjectured, but wasn't really sure.

As we walked the length of the Silver Corridor, I could see Julien up ahead, a roadblock strategically located between us and the safety of the elevator. Just the sight of him again made my stomach knot. I was so done with our confrontations.

"Oh fuck," I muttered under my breath. I just wanted

out.

"I'll handle this." And Laynie was immediately four strides ahead of us, strutting elegantly in her sparkly skyscraper shoes.

Watching her spine straighten to full height and shoulders fall back, I knew immediately what my best friend was doing and there was no doubt Julien would succumb to the siren's call of her barely sheathed breasts. And as if right on cue, enchanted, she began to lure him in. With his eyes focused on the prize(s) and his signature sneer brightening by the second, he was so entranced by the perfection of this exotic creature's breasts, that even he was surprised to be yelling 'Shit!' as his chest met a cart full of dinner dishes filled with leftover prime rib, mashed potatoes and gravy.

As she passed by him, Laynie leaned down and gave him a spectacular view of what was under the crimson silk chiffon. With her lips just grazing his earlobe, she whispered to Julien, "You've got egg on your face."

He looked at her, perplexed.

There was not an egg on the cart.

My lips were twitching, dying to break out in a smile as I reached where he stood, now brushing himself off. Taking joy in his food stained, white shirt, I managed to look straight ahead, maintaining my composure as the ornate elevator doors opened. Although close, I had escaped without another Julien run-in, so I was beginning to breathe easier and when we reached the lobby and immediately saw our limo driver waiting by the hotel's entrance, I felt the thousand-pound weight lift off my heart. Home free. Finally.

"That was fun," Laynie whispered in my ear. "Score one for the hoes."

Settling into the back of the limo, the first order of business was shoe removal. With my legs straight out in front of me, I said to my feet, "Go ahead and swell. You deserve it after what I did to you tonight. But I do want you to know one thing, you looked fabulous."

Laynie was perusing the bar. "Can I interest either of you?" She looked at me and Jill.

Nodding, "My feet want cognac, if they have any."

"My feet want what she's having," Jill piped in as she kicked off her shoes and started to go through her giftbag. "Look how cute this is." She pulled out a bright pink C-Kicker shirt that said, *C Me Kick Cancer to the Curb.*

Laynie had handed us our drinks and began digging through her bag. "I got that shirt too, except mine is in green. Which is good, that goes better with my hair. And oh look, Bluetooth headphones. These are really nice."

Jill pulled out her headphones, "These are nice. I can't wait to use them on the treadmill."

Scarlett pulled a big square box out of her bag. It was wrapped in pale blue metallic paper with silver ribbon.

"What's that?" Jill asked. "I don't have that in mine."

"Neither do I," said Laynie. "I've just got the shirt and headphones, donation information and a box of handmade truffles."

"Me too," Jill corroborated.

Pulling the ribbon and the paper from the box, an excited Scarlett said, "It's from Swarovski." Opening the box, she gasped, staring fondly at its contents before looking up at us. "It's a tiara."

She pulled the silver and crystal headpiece from its box and it was all our turns to gasp.

"Mom, put it on me." Scarlett was shaking with excitement.

The moment it was situated on her head, she pulled out her cell to take a selfie.

"Oh my God, I like literally can't believe he did this. I have to send him a picture."

"Who?" Jill asked.

"Wes. He calls me Princess. This has to be from him."

She snapped another photo of herself with her head tilted, then began to type. Immediately, her phone buzzed back. "Oh, he's bummed we left and didn't get a chance to say goodbye."

"Make sure you thank him."

"I did," and she typed something else. "I can't believe he got me this."

"Tara, why don't you take a look in your giftbag and see if there is anything special in yours," urged Laynie.

I laughed, "I think not." Digging in the bag, I pulled out the shirt, then the headphones, a bunch of papers, and then the truffles. Reaching back down in the bag, my fingers wrapped around a small box wrapped in silver paper with a silver ribbon.

"That matches your dress," Jill commented.

With shaking hands, I removed the ribbon and paper. The box said *Michou*. My heart felt like a stopper in my throat.

"Michou," I said softly.

"Did he know you love her designs?" Laynie was waiting for me to open the box.

"He's seen me wear Michou pieces, but we'd never talked about it." I was shocked at how observant he'd been.

"Mom, open it. I'm like literally dying."

Opening the box, its contents were as perfect and as personal as Scarlett's tiara had been. Opening my purse, I grabbed a tissue to dab at my eyes. This was us.

"What is it, Mom?"

I lifted the round matte silver pin from its box.

"That is gorgeous." Jill leaned in for a closer look.

The pin was made of silver and gold with a mélange of stones in an array of blue hues. The gold laid on the silver was in the shape of moons, stars, shooting stars and planets. It was a gorgeous depiction of the cosmos, the night sky. It was us and had been from the first night we met.

Laynie reached out her hand and I gave her the pin. "It's really magnificent. And you know he purchased this prior to his conversation with our little princess tonight."

I nodded, letting that sink in and wondered if Wes and I would ever get to the same side of the bridge or would Julien Matthews always be taking the toll?

# Chapter 24

As we waited in the conference room for Chris to arrive for the Monday morning staff meeting, the giftbags and Flourless Chocolate Torte dominated the conversation. I had opted not to mention the extra little box in my gift bag which I had thanked Wes for via text over the weekend.

**Thank you for that special Michou surprise.**
**It was perfect for you. I hope you liked it.**
**Very much. Again, TY.**
**YW**

And that had been the extent of our communications.

At 10:15, Donna popped her head into the conference room. "Chris is on a call, he said to tell you it will be about another five minutes.

"I used the headphones yesterday when I was running. They are sweet," commented Jamie.

"The whole event was first class." Jonathan checked his phone as he spoke.

"Sorry I'm late." Chris burst through the door a few minutes later and took his spot at the head of the conference room table. Donna settled into the chair next to him. "So, did everyone have a good time on Saturday night? That was some event."

Everyone agreed and he went on. "So, I just got off the phone with Wes Bergman. The response to the PSAs was phenomenal. He was tracking the data over the weekend from the touchscreens and looking at the donation surges that came in after each of the videos played. They also had the people taking donations at the tables timestamping so that they could track back to the effectiveness of which video had spurred the donation and he's going to use that data for his ad buys."

"Did they hit their target fundraising goal for the evening?" I asked.

"He said they exceeded the goal by 36% and increased donations by nearly $1.5 million over last year's event."

I started to clap and the rest of the team followed suit. Yes! We were part of what made the evening a success and the pride I felt swept away the negative feelings that had encroached on the project. In my little way, I was able to honor Stacy and Jill and countless other women and men, and their families who had all been given that heart wrenching diagnosis. This was a day where I wanted to shout out my office window, *I love what I do.* I felt like a soldier fighting for the cause. I knew Chris had not charged C-Kicker corporate client rates for our work and I was happy he had made that decision, in addition to our corporate and individual donations.

"That's right, a round of applause for this team is well deserved. I can't tell you how proud I am of all of you and of your work. Sitting in that ballroom watching the crowd the other night, seeing how moved everyone was, was the most incredible feeling in the world. Everyone really stepped up to the plate on this one."

"It was pretty awesome," Kim agreed.

"So Wes would like to thank us all, and he's invited the team to a party on his boat in two weeks on Saturday night."

My heart stopped beating with Chris' announcement. No. I couldn't do it. I couldn't be on the *Second Wind* again. Not with him. And definitely not with Julien. I just couldn't do it.

"Oh and Tara, Wes asked specifically for you to make a jug of some special rum drink you make. He said you'd know what it was."

I couldn't respond. I had to get Chris alone in his office after the meeting and tell him that I couldn't attend. There was not a shot in hell I was going to subject myself to being caught in the confines of a boat with Julien Matthews.

And Wes Bergman.

That boat held so many memories for me. It was a vessel of dreams that descended into lies. In my head, I knew that I had to deal with him through the gala, that was a professional commitment I had to honor. But this? This was pure torture. And to act like nothing was wrong with his staff and my colleagues there. I could already feel my stress level elevating.

After lunch I knocked on Chris' office door.

"Hey, can I talk to you about something?"

"Sure, what's up?"

"I'd like to bow out of the boat party in two weeks. It's my weekend with Scarlett and," I never finished my sentence.

"I'd really appreciate if you attended."

It was not the response I expected from Chris.

"And I'd really appreciate a pass on this one." I was trying to remain calm and professional externally, but my anxiety was starting to skyrocket.

"Tara, you need to attend." The look on his face told me not to push anymore. "Please close my door on the way out."

Sitting back down behind my desk, I shook my head. That may have been the single strangest conversation I'd had with Chris O'Donnell in all the years I'd known him. He'd never dismissed me like that before.

Without saying the words *suck it up and be professional*, Chris had just told me in no uncertain terms to *suck it up and be professional.*

Great. Now I had two weeks to stress out about this when I finally thought I was getting a break from it all, that my professional commitment was over and I could put it behind me.

**Hey, can you do me a favor?** I texted Laynie. **Saturday night, 2 weeks from now, can Scarlett stay with you. I just got this work thing sprung on me.**

**Sure. No problem**

**TY.** At least I'd gotten that taken care of.

With Tux Paint loaded on the students' laptops as well as the ones for instructors, we started by showing the kids how to use the different stamps to create designs. With the holidays approaching, we talked about how much fun it is to receive cards and how great it would be to give cards that we made. With Halloween rapidly approaching, our first digital design project was going to be to create a design that we would print out as both a card to give away and a poster to keep.

"Mom, this is so much neater than paint. There's gonna be no clean up." Tech-savvy Scarlett was in her comfort zone.

"Any time we can get the kids to use computers we're enhancing not only their communications, but their work readiness skills, too. I can't wait to see what they create over the next few weeks."

As we were printing out the projects, Camille dropped by the room.

"The students did these?" she was astounded.

"Yes and this was only their first time working with the program."

"Mind if I take some pictures of them?" she asked, whipping her cell phone out before I could respond. "I think the benefactor will be very pleased to see their donation is already at work enhancing the program."

"Please give them a huge thank you from me." I hoped she would pass that along.

"I will," she promised. "Stacy would have been so pleased to see this."

Her comment hit my heart harder than I could have imagined. Was it because it was my deepest wish for Stacy to love what I was doing in her honor or was it because my emotions were heightened because I was seeing her brother tonight? Or was it a combination of the two? Regardless, I couldn't speak, so I just nodded my head.

"I'm really not worried about Wes," I told Laynie. "He will be professional and not do anything to make me feel uncomfortable. It's Julien I'm worried about. The man is a wildcard and has no respect for boundaries and for some reason he hates me."

"Of course he hates you, Tara." She stated as if the answer was clear as day. "You caught onto his game and cut him off really quickly. He's not used to that. Because of his looks, he expects women to keep coming back for his sick form of abuse. And it is abuse. You never even tried to contact him. Plus, you get in the way of his bromance. You know what a fraud he is, so he wants to keep you as far away from Wes as possible."

Pouring my rum whatever from the blender into an

insulated travel jug, I'd already lived up to one commitment for the evening. "So, what are you and Scarlett up to tonight?" I asked.

"Oh, we're going to go into the city, have dinner at Le Cirque and then go downtown to a sex club."

Laughing, "You two have all the fun. Not fair."

"Actually we're doing pizza and a movie. And I promised Scarlett she could wear her tiara."

"Like literally wear it, bro?" I did an impression of my daughter and we both laughed. "She is so in love with Wes." I shook my head, smiling.

"Like mother, like daughter." My friend Laynie pulled no punches. "Now stop hanging out with me and go get dressed or you will be late for this shindig."

"It's going to be freaking freezing on that boat," I muttered as I left the kitchen.

Laynie and Scarlett were on the couch watching *Say Yes to the Dress* when I emerged.

"Not sexy, but very cute," was Laynie's assessment of my outfit, an oversized dark cranberry, funnel neck cashmere sweater, worn jeans and UGG boots.

"I was going for warmth."

"Let Wes keep you warm." Laynie had an answer for everything.

"Let me remind you, this is a business function. And I will attempt to conduct myself with the utmost decorum."

Laynie turned to Scarlett, shaking her head. "Your mother is no fun anymore. I think we need to ditch her."

And the little traitor laughed.

"Don't forget to say hi to Wes from me, Mom." She touched the tiara on top of her head and smiled.

"Wish me luck."

"Oh my God, I can't believe she chose that dress. That is like literally the ugliest thing on the planet. I would like literally not be caught dead in that really," Scarlett said to

Laynie.

And I quietly slipped out with my jug of rum whatevers while the two of them freaked out over some bride's bad dress choice.

My anxiety rose the closer I got to the harbor. I was so conflicted about seeing Wes. Part of me was dying to be in his presence and the other part of me wanted to run – fast and far. He said he wanted a do-over. And that is what my heart wanted. I loved him. There was no doubt in my mind about that. But I just kept thinking, *Screw me over once, shame on you. Screw me over twice, shame on me.* What if this was his M.O. when shit got tough? And that really scared me, both for me and for Scarlett. She had already been through a divorce and a father who put his child bride before his daughter. She'd hit it off with Wes the same way I had. We meshed. We got each other. But I feared for her. If this actually was not an anomaly for him brought on by way too much hitting at once, then it wasn't just my heart that would be broken, my daughter's would as well. I didn't know if I could let that happen.

The fall sky had already darkened as I walked with trepidation along the dock toward where the *Second Wind* was berthed. I just wanted the evening to pass without incident, to successfully avoid confrontation with Julien and to peacefully co-exist with Wes and not incur any further fissures in my already fracking heart.

Wes was on deck stringing lights as I approached. He was a man who could pull off a cream cable-knit sweater and make it look sexy. There were not many who could do that, but he was pulling it off. I took a moment, before he realized

I was there, to enjoy his fine ass in faded out jeans. God, I missed him.

"Tara," he greeted me with a smile.

"Am I early?" I appeared to be the first to arrive.

Wes came and took the heavy bag with the rum jug from me and extended a hand to help me down onto the boat.

"Hey, would you give me a hand with these lights?"

"Sure." I grabbed the strand and held them as high as I could while he attached small clear suction cups with hooks and placed the strand of lights into the hooks. His body grazing against mine was just destroying me and even though he seemed to be engrossed in the task at hand, I thought this has got to be messing with him, too.

"So, is everyone else late?" I asked, my throat suddenly dry.

His face was just inches from mine as he turned to me and shook his head no, his lips twitching as he failed to hide a smile.

"What do you mean?" I was now totally confused.

"Everyone's here."

What was going on? Were they below deck and just being very quiet?

"Where are they?" I asked.

"Right here."

I looked around. "I just see me and you."

"Yeah." Wes could no longer contain his smile.

"Where is everyone else?" Chris? Jonathan? Renata? The dreaded Julien?

"There is no one else. Just me and you." He laughed and I knew he was reacting to the shocked look on my face.

"Just me and you?" I repeated. "Do the others know that?"

"They do."

Nodding, the smirk on his face told me he was pretty

proud of himself.

"So, you're telling me Chris knew?" My voice rose a few decibels by the end of my question.

"Well, not every detail, but he knew." Wes took the end of the strand of lights and slid them into the last hook. "Okay, that's done. Thank you for your help. I think it's time for that rum stuff you brought."

"I think you're right," I readily agreed.

Lifting a wooden bench seat, Wes pulled out two plastic cups and I poured both to the brim. Just me and Wes? I was scared. Nervous. And very relieved. No Julien. Whatever Wes and I had to say to one another, even if it ended up positively heartbreaking, it wouldn't be ugly and hurtful like encounters with Julien.

We clinked glasses and I asked, "So, are you going to explain?"

"Sure," he smiled. "The only way I knew I could get you here 100% was if you thought it was business and you couldn't get out of it."

I laughed. It was true.

"See, I know you. So, I had to concoct this fake business party to get you here."

"Well, you've got me here." A sip of my frozen drink made me shiver in the cold autumn air.

"I do. And I'd like to propose something."

I remained silent and he continued.

"I'd like you to spend the night talking to me under the stars. When the sun breaks the horizon, you can choose to stay or leave. If you leave, I won't bother you again. I will let you get on with your life. I won't pull the business from O'Donnell and Associates, unless that is what you want. And if we do remain just business colleagues, I promise I will not make it uncomfortable in any way for you." Wes paused and took a sip of his drink. His next words were very measured and I could hear the tension in his voice. "If you choose to stay, just know you are mine and I am not letting you go again, Tara."

"Do you think it's that easy?" It was a gut reaction and it was out of my mouth before I could finesse it.

Shaking his head, "No. I don't think it's easy at all. I think we're going to have to work our asses off. And I don't mean that in a bad way, like a relationship with you is a lot of work, because it's actually just the opposite. You are so easy to be with. We fit. We always have. I fit with Scarlett. But we've both been married before, so we understand the work and the compromise and the selflessness needed to make a family unit work. And as we both know, we have some shit we need to talk through."

I just stood there. I wanted to speak, but nothing came out.

Putting up a finger, Wes said, "Hold that thought," and disappeared below deck. Looking up at the stars, I took a deep breath of the cold, night air and held it in my lungs for a moment before releasing it. A few minutes later, Wes emerged balancing large Tupperware containers in one hand and two blankets tucked under his other arm.

Placing them on the table, Wes pulled out the navy reclining seat cushions, our chairs, and set them up on the deck. The memories flooding in were making my heart pound maniacally in my chest. He grabbed the jug and the Tupperware and then brought the blankets over. I settled into *my* chair. I always sat in the one on the left and Wes covered our legs with a down blanket first and then a red plaid wool blanket on top of that.

"Wanna see what's on the menu?" He grabbed the first Tupperware and pulled off the top revealing Deviled Eggs.

"Yum. Love 'em. But we're going to have stinky egg breath," I commented.

Smiling, "No worries, I'd kiss you even if you had tuna breath."

I laughed, choking on a sip of the rum drink.

Opening the second Tupperware, "And for our main course, the health-conscious delicacies of wings and loaded potato skins."

"Yum." He even had blue cheese dressing and celery for the wings and sour cream for the potato skins. "And where's dessert?"

"Dessert," he flashed a smile, "is below deck."

Shaking my head, "Pass the eggs, please." Refilling our glasses, I suggested, "How about we eat first, then talk."

"Good plan. So, has Scarlett taken her tiara off yet?"

"Oh God, no. She's obsessed with it. Please tell me she didn't send you a selfie of wearing her crown on the throne aka the toilet." I knew she took the photo and I was praying he said no.

Laughing, "No, that one she hasn't sent. But that's actually really funny."

"She is really funny. She's a good kid. So, I have something to tell you." I shifted under the blanket so that I was now facing him. "Scarlett and I and her BFF Emmy have been teaching the Saturday morning art class over at Special Friends Organization. I wanted to carry on Stacy's work and I didn't want the kids to lose something so valuable."

Nodding, his smile was a sad one. "I know. Camille was very excited when you showed up on her doorstep. She said you were Stacy's gift from heaven."

I had to look away. It was too early in the evening to shed tears, so I reached for my drink and grabbed a chicken wing.

"You knew?"

"Yes. The cards they made today were amazing."

Shocked, I looked at Wes, half-eaten wing still in my mouth. It had never dawned on me. Quickly swallowing, I had to ask the question. "Wes, did you donate the laptops?"

Looking down in his lap, I could see his smile.

"Wes?" I asked again.

"It was the least I could do. You stepped in where you were needed to make a difference in those families' lives and I wanted to make sure you had the tools to take the kids' skills to the next level."

I should have guessed it. "Well, thank you. I have to tell you that the highlight of my week is Saturday morning. That has been the one bright spot in a really tough time."

"Thank you for not letting my sister's legacy die."

"Honestly, I was shocked when I learned that she taught art there. But Stacy really surprised me a lot. I miss her."

"I do, too."

There was no mistaking the pain in his eyes. I wanted to lean over and hug him, but we needed to let this conversation continue.

"So, I have something big to tell you, too." Wes began.

My stomach knotted. I was definitely in glass half empty mode and had been since the weekend everything blew up.

"Okay," I said, trepidation clearly in my voice.

"Actually, it's something I think you'll like," he paused. "I fired Julien."

"What?" The word came out louder than I anticipated. "What happened?" I implored, modulating my tone.

"Everything happened and had been happening for a long time. The situation with you just brought it to a head."

I bit my tongue because I knew that pun was totally unintended and I needed to let it pass.

"Go on," I urged and grabbed the jug, refilling both our glasses.

"After the fundraiser I confronted him about his conversation with you. And I knew he was lying to me. I've known the guy practically my entire life, he should know that I know when he's bullshitting me. I've always treated him like family, but I'm not stupid." He was very serious as he gazed into my eyes.

"So, what did he tell you?"

"He told me April 22, 1994 was the first time he met you."

"Me?" I choked again on my drink. That was the last thing I was expecting.

"Yeah, he told me that he met you and a group of your friends at a movie theater in Manhattan and that you had sex with him in one of the back rows and then stalked him until you went away to college."

I actually started to laugh at the absurdity of his lie. "Oh my God, Wes. The man is a sociopath."

"Tara, I don't know what the real story is, but I knew enough to know he was lying and it was at the expense of damaging you and he doesn't give a rat's ass about my happiness. It was all about protecting himself."

"Julien is missing a central thing that makes humans' human – empathy and the ability to love others. I don't know if it stems from his childhood trauma or if it is inherent. I'm not a professional. But what I do know is he's dangerous in that he will hurt others intentionally with no remorse. No remorse at all."

"So, what happened on April 22, 1994, Tara?"

Letting out a sigh, my heart was breaking having to tell him this. But Wes needed the truth. Getting up, I walked over to the bench where my purse was and took out my wallet. From the bill compartment, I pulled out a folded piece of paper.

"She was certain this would never see the light of day," I began. "And the reason she never told you," I paused, exhaling deeply, "was because she didn't want you to look at her differently. She never wanted to let you down," my voice cracked. "But this belongs to you." I handed Wes Stacy's letter.

With a surprised look on his face, he took the note from me and unfolded it. I watched his face as he read his sister's words, the pain surfacing both quickly and deeply. He wiped his eyes with the back of his fingers and said, "Excuse me," in a hoarse voice, got up and went below deck.

I didn't follow, as that was a moment he needed to himself.

Wes was composed when he returned a few minutes later. "Thank you for sharing that with me." He shook his head, "That fucking son of a bitch."

"I'm in total agreement with you on that one. Are you okay?"

"Yeah. Just processing that and feeling guilty that Stacy had to put up with him her whole life because of me."

"You can't beat yourself up over stuff you didn't know. The only thing you can do is if you were feeling the least bit guilty about severing ties with him, now you know you totally did the right thing." I grabbed a potato skin and dipped it in the sour cream. I was nervous eating now. "I can't believe he made up that story about me. What a douche."

Leaning toward me, Wes wiped a dab of sour cream from the corner of my lip and then licked it off his finger. "I think it was actually some underlying jealousy and hatred toward me, rather than at you. When we were younger, we'd walk into a club or a party together and all the girls wanted him. If he knew I liked a girl, he would go after her."

Laughing, "I am sure you were not hard up for women. You have always been a chick magnet. I know this firsthand. The women he got were probably as shallow as he was. The man is a shell."

"A good-looking shell. The guy looks like Rob Lowe."

"He's a handsome guy, there's no doubt about that. Until you get to know him and you find out that he's a really ugly person. He was jealous of you, Wes. Jealous that you had a good marriage, jealous that you built a really respected and successful company. And everyone who knows you, loves you. You've achieved everything he is not capable of."

I was now back to the wings and drowning them in blue cheese. I was glad the food was here to keep my nervous hands busy.

"I hated finding out about the two of you. It just resurrected a lifetime of old feelings of him stealing what was mine." He reached for a wing. "I'm sorry you got caught up in my insecurity and jealousy, Tara."

As I finished my wing, I laughed, "So much for eating, then talking." Looking around, I asked, "Do you have napkins?"

He smiled, "I have better. Be right back." He disappeared below deck again and returned a moment later with a handful of packets of Wet Naps.

"Oh excellent." I reached for a packet. "You really are prepared."

"Yeah, but I was thinking this might not be such a good idea to bring them out."

"Why?" I laughed. "Wet Naps are the best."

"Nope. I totally disagree. This is much better." Reaching over, he grabbed my right hand and sucked my index finger into his mouth, licking off the Buffalo sauce.

"Oh, dirty pool, Bergman," I protested.

"I'm on a mission." He smiled, sucking another finger into his mouth.

"You don't know where that finger's been."

"It's been in your mouth. A place I like being." He licked my ring finger.

"This is going to be some conversation. We have a long way until dawn."

"So, as I was saying before you interrupted with your sticky fingers." He smiled, but it quickly faded. "Finding out about the two of you destroyed me." He picked up his cup and drained it, then held it out for me to refill.

"That is why I tried to tell you about it that night. And with the way you responded, I thought Julien had already told you and that you knew."

Wes laughed and sat back with his drink. "You had sex in my shower. That is what I was referring to."

Nodding, "I did. I had sex in your shower. I thought it was his cabin and I went in to pee. I was mortified later when I saw you walk in there. It was like *oh fuck, what are the chances?*"

"See look, you just totally 'fessed up to that. You didn't make up a lie about it."

"Of course not," I countered. "I'm not a psychopath and that is why I wanted to tell you about Julien that night, because I never wanted it to come between us. I knew it wasn't going to be easy for me to tell you, but I thought you had a right to know before we became lovers."

Turning to me, he put a hand on my cheek. The warmth of his skin in the cold night air was like a salve formulated to repair the network of cracks in my heart.

"It was my fault for not letting you tell me. And then I took it out on you, when, in fact, the onus is on me for that miscommunication."

His hand was still on my cheek when I began to speak. "As I said that night in the hospital, from the moment you stepped back into my life, Wes, there's been no one else."

Leaning forward, he laid a soft kiss on my lips. "I'm also sorry that I laid so much on you on the dance floor at the fundraiser. After having no contact, I kinda blindsided you. I realized that afterwards."

"Here's the thing. I know you were going through an unimaginable amount of grief. I totally get that and I can sympathize. But what I don't know is, is this typically how you'd react? Or was this an anomaly because of the extenuating circumstances?"

Taking his hand from my cheek, Wes sat back in his chair and looked up at the night sky. "Tara, I'd like to tell you that this is not how I treat people. But it *was* how I treated you. And I'm not proud of it. I wasn't listening to you that night at the hospital because I needed someplace to put all my pain. And I dumped it on you." Shaking his head, "That was so wrong. You were the last person I should have dumped it on."

"You're right," I agreed. "But Julien had just trashed me to you after you thought what you and I had was real."

"It was real." As was the pain on Wes' face.

Reaching over to grab his hand, I squeezed it tightly. "Yes Wes, it was very real. Which is why this has been so painful."

It was a moment before he squeezed my hand back. "Tara, all I can do is try to show you through my actions that I will not put anyone before you and Scarlett ever again. That this was the exception and not the standard for how I conduct myself and treat those I love." Turning to me, "Please believe me, T."

I smiled at the use of his nickname for me. Pulling the blanket up around my neck, I shifted closer to him and put my head on his shoulder. "It's cold out here, keep me warm."

Wrapping his arms around me, we sat silently for a while.

"Are you sleeping?" he asked.

Lifting my head to look up at him, I smiled. "No. I'm still awake."

Leaning me back in his arms, Wes' lips came down on mine as my fingers got lost in his curls. It was in that moment that I let myself realize the extent of the pain I'd been in and ended the kiss, because much to my chagrin, a deluge of tears began to flow. What kind of tears were they? Anger? Sadness? Depression? Happiness? All of the above? I had no clue. All I knew was that they were drowning me.

"Hey, talk to me, T." He brushed the hair back from my face.

"I don't know, Wes. I think it's just all the emotions of

everything we've gone through surfacing." I wiped my tears away with my sweater sleeve.

"Please tell me what that means," he implored, looking alarmed.

"It means I have been so miserable. I've been grieving the loss of both you and Stacy and trying to stay strong. I thought once I got through the fundraiser, I could move on. That wouldn't be hanging over me anymore and I could work on healing without the scab getting ripped off. And then I've spent the last two weeks really stressed out about tonight. Not stressed so much about seeing you, but more fearful of what Julien was going to pull on me to intentionally rattle me and make me look bad in front of you and my colleagues."

Hitting himself in the forehead with the heel of his palm, "Oh God, Tara, I didn't even think about the strain this would put on you. I really didn't understand the extent of the psychological warfare he had waged on you. I just kept thinking about how fun I could make this night for the two of us and that we'd finally get the chance to lay all our cards on the table. I'm so sorry." His arms went around me in a tight hug. "Jeez, have I been fucking with your head or what? What a dumbass I've been. I am so, so sorry."

Taking a deep breath, I tried to pull myself together, immediately angry that I'd allowed myself to fall apart.

As if sensing my thoughts, Wes whispered in my ear, "You don't always have to be so strong, you know."

I nodded against his chest, "Yeah Wes, I do."

"Tara, look at me."

I pulled my face from his chest. Tilting his head to the side, I could see how upset he was with himself for all the pain he had caused me.

"Tara, I love you." The sincerity in his words was unmistakable.

"I love you, too, Wes." We had both finally said the words.

His smile immediately brought me back to the night we met and the blood rush I felt the first time I saw it.

"Is it time for dessert yet?" I asked. "It's cold as Hell up here."

"Almost."

"What do you mean almost?" I laughed.

Grabbing his phone, I could tell from the look on his face that Mr. Bergman had something up his sleeve.

Standing, he reached for my hand to pull me up. "One dance before dessert."

The first strains of Boston's *More Than a Feeling* began and my arms went around his waist. With my head buried in his soft cable knit sweater, I felt the darkness that had been following me since late summer begin to dissipate and I held onto Wes a little bit tighter.

"I love you, Tara. I've always loved you."

It certainly was more than a feeling.

The smell of strong coffee was an enticing alarm clock. Rolling over, the bed next to me was empty and the sheets were cool. Grabbing my phone from the nightstand, it was 7:15 a.m. I was drawn into the salon by the coffee's fragrant scent and I could see Wes already on deck, cup in hand, watching as the sky lightened.

Quickly pulling on my clothes, I climbed the stairs, steaming mug in hand, to join him topside to watch the sun break the horizon.

"Well, we didn't quite make it talking until dawn." I sat down on the bench next to him, watching the sky continue to lighten and enjoy the colorful show on the clouds that awaited the sun's arrival. I had missed the deep rose colors as the sunrise was entering its pink into deep orange phase.

Smiling, he kissed my temple. "We did pretty good considering we're no longer twenty-somethings."

"We did very good," I agreed.

Lovemaking had been very emotional and claiming. We started fast and rough and primal and ended clingy and touchy. Wordlessly, we each communicated the sadness and angst of the recent past attempting to fuck it into hope and solidarity.

The top curve of the sun broke the Long Island Sound's waters on the eastern horizon. With a smile, I savored my dark roast and stole a glance at the man sitting next to me.

"What?" he asked, as a smile tugged at the corners of his mouth and he lifted his coffee cup to meet it.

"It's sunrise."

He turned to me, this time with a full smile. "I feel like I should go get you my Clash tee-shirt."

I laughed and began to sing, "Should I stay or should I go?"

"So, what's it gonna be, T?"

"You really have to ask?" The morning air was cold and beautiful and very refreshing. I watched the sun light up the world as it totally severed from the horizon.

"I do. I don't want there to be any miscommunications or assumptions between us."

"I love you, Wes."

"What?"

"I love you, Wes," I said a little louder.

"What was that?" That smile was making my heart melt.

"I love you, Wes," I screamed.

"So, does that mean you're staying?" He pushed my hair behind my ear.

"Do you want me to stay?" I looked at him wide-eyed.

"Do you really have to ask?" He could barely contain his smile.

"I do. I don't want there to be any miscommunications or assumptions between us." I kept a straight face as I parroted back his words at him.

"T, you heard what I said yesterday, if you stay, you are mine. This is real. Me, you and Scarlett."

"Me, you and Scarlett." I smiled back at him. "Maybe Laynie, too," I joked.

Wes laughed. "That one's more than I can handle. But me, you and Scarlett, that's perfection."

Standing, I faced him and wrapped my arms around his neck. Wes Bergman was mine. And it was right. I knew that to the depths of my soul. No man had ever been so attuned to me as this one.

"What are you thinking?" he asked.

"Three things. First, how freaking happy I am. Second, how freaking cold I am. And last, but not least, if I'm going to get you back to bed with me to warm me up under the covers."

"Come," he grabbed my hand and pulled me towards the companionway steps, "let's go finish dessert."

"Okay, I texted Scarlett and Laynie and gave them directions on how to get here. Scarlett's so excited to see you and that we're going to be sailing someplace to get lunch." I laughed, "I woke them up. I guess not everyone gets up to watch the sunrise."

"I was receiving an important message at sunrise." Wes cradled my head on his chest.

I pulled the blanket up over me. "I know I should shower, but I don't want to get out from under these warm blankets."

"Is that the only reason you don't want to get out of bed?"

Climbing on top of him, "Mmm, your body is so nice and warm. We do have a little time before they get here."

Flipping me onto my back, "I can keep you even warmer this way." He nudged my thighs apart.

"I think I'm going to love winter," I quipped, reveling in his body heat as he entered me for the second time since dawn.

I was topside waiting for them when Scarlett and Laynie came down the dock. I waved, "Hey Girls, over here."

"Thank God you were on deck," Laynie rolled her eyes at me. "Or we never would have found you."

"Why? I gave good directions."

"Yeah and you also told me that the boat was named *Second Wind*. I'd be walking these piers in search of the non-existent *Second Wind*."

"What are you talking about?" I was thoroughly confused.

"Tara, this boat is not named *Second Wind*."

Leaning over the stern of the boat, I read the name upside down and saw for the first time what I had not seen when I arrived in the darkness the night before. Wes had renamed the boat.

We had pledged our commitment to one another this morning on *The Do-Over*. Amazing.

Wes came up from below deck, "You made it."

Scarlett, decked out in tiara and UGG boots, ran to him.

"Princess, I like the head gear." He slung an arm over

her shoulder and made his way over to greet Laynie. "We finally formally meet." He leaned over and kissed her cheek.

"Well, it's about time." She was sizing him up. "I like this one, Tara."

Wes laughed, "So where do you ladies want to sail to for lunch?"

"Virgin Gorda," Scarlett was the first to respond.

"I think that may be a little far for lunch, but if you have a few weeks off at Christmas…"

"I do. We should go."

"Where's Virgin Gorda?" Laynie asked. "It sounds like a place for pirate sacrifices."

"It's down in the Caribbean, in the British Virgin Islands," Wes explained.

"Oyster Bay?" I threw out a realistic suggestion that was doable before we all starved to death.

"Sure, we can do Oyster Bay," Wes agreed. "You good with that, Princess?"

She nodded, "Can I drive?"

Wes saw the alarmed look on my face. "Well, let me get the boat out of the marina, then you can help me with the sails and assist me in the cockpit. Want a tour first?" he said to her and they disappeared below deck.

"I guess it was a good party," Laynie said to me as soon as Wes and Scarlett were out of earshot.

"Best ever. It had the perfect guest list."

"Who came?" she asked.

"Me. Three times," I confided. "Oh yeah, and so did he."

*Jullie A. Richman*

Epilogue
40 ... and it
Rocks

*Jullie A. Richman*

# Bitter End Yacht Club
# Virgin Gorda, BVI
# Christmas Break

It took a little over five days from Miami, where Wes had his boat transported, for us to sail to Virgin Gorda. We were beyond excited to be back on land, eating food prepared by chefs and enjoying being pampered Bitter End Yacht Club-style.

"We need to win this," my competitive daughter said to Wes.

"We need more duct tape and ornament hooks," he responded as he wrapped garland around the boat's rail.

"Mom, can you go to the gift shop for us and see if they have any."

Grabbing my purse, "I'll be back in a little bit." As I walked along the dock toward the red-roofed resort, I couldn't help but smile. Scarlett and Wes were totally caught up in decorating the boat for the Annual Holiday Boat Parade Competition. Scarlett had read about it before the trip and the two of them had been picking up kitschy holiday items ever since.

With so many guests arriving by boat, their gift shop,

The Emporium, was more like a small town's general store, stocked with so much more than sundry items, as many of the mooring clientele had repairs to make to their vessels upon arrival or before departure and enjoyed many meals on their own accommodations.

Immediately finding the duct tape and ornament hooks, I started to browse the store looking for small souvenirs to bring home to Laynie, Jill, Jonathan and Chris. They had the usual assortment of key chains, shot glasses and glass ornaments with shells and sand inside. I loaded several cute ornaments into my basket and moved on. Seeing the shelves lined with packaged cupcakes and donuts as well as single servings of Chef Winston's famous Key lime pie, spurred a great idea. I would go to the restaurant and see if I could buy a whole pie to take back to the boat for dessert tonight.

Turning toward the checkout counter, I was shocked as I looked into her familiar, smiling face. The painful jolt in my chest made me gasp out loud and drop my basket, causing one of the glass ornaments to shatter. *How could it be? Was I just imagining this?*

Looking down for a moment to grab the basket at my feet, I realized I was practically hyperventilating. When I straightened up, no one was there. The checkout girl was looking at me, "Don't worry. I'll clean that up. Go pick out another one."

"The woman who was here, where did she go?" I asked, totally bugging out.

"I don't know. I guess I didn't see her." The girl shrugged.

"She was standing right there." I pointed to right in front of the checkout counter.

Shaking her head, the cashier said, "Sorry."

Going back down the aisle to replace the broken ornament, I stopped for a moment, leaned against a shelving unit and took a deep breath.

*It couldn't have been her. She would probably be dead by*

*now. She was an old woman when I met her. And Dominica must be hundreds of miles from here. It's in the Windward Islands' chain and this is the British Virgin Islands. But that smile, that toothless smile. And the way she looked at me. Like she knew me. It was her. It was definitely her.*

Realizing that I was shaking, I put my basket down. Maybe I was just dehydrated or something, I wondered, because I would have sworn the old woman who gave me the poppets had just been standing a few feet away from me, smiling her toothless smile. I needed to get out of there. Picking up the basket, I quickly chose another ornament and paid for my purchases.

Greeted by a hostess at the restaurant, I asked if I could possibly purchase a whole Key lime pie. While she left me to go into the kitchen and check, I dug out a water bottle from my purse and took two healthy swigs before putting it back in my bag. When I looked up, coming toward me in his crisp, white chef's jacket, the pastry chef extraordinaire greeted me with a warm, wide smile.

"How are you today?" he asked.

"I'm wonderful. I was hoping to purchase one of your delicious pies so that we could enjoy it on our boat tonight after the Boat Parade," I explained.

"Absolutely, you can. But there is something else I'd like to show you that you may want even more." He piqued my curiosity.

"Even more than your famous Key lime pie?" I couldn't help but smile at him.

"Yes, it is very special and I only make it for Christmas. Follow me."

Joining him as he walked back to the kitchen, the scent was like following my nose to Heaven. The air was heavy with the aromas of butter, cinnamon and cloves and I thought I might never want to leave. Pastry Chef in the Caribbean might be the perfect career move.

Baking sheets lined with parchment covered the countertops. Rolls, croissants, and pies cooled, while warm fragrant air wafted from the ovens. Winston led me to the far end of the kitchen, where a countertop was lined with round cakes heavily dusted with powdered sugar. Their fragrance was intoxicating. Literally.

"How much rum went into these babies?" I smiled at the Pastry Chef.

"You are in the British Virgin Islands," he laughed.

"And these are real English Christmas Cakes, aren't they?"

"Yes, they are."

"You know I can't leave without one," I sighed.

"I thought you might feel that way." He then directed a member of his staff to wrap one up for me.

"What took you so long?" Scarlett asked as I boarded The Do-Over.

"I was getting us a proper dessert for later this evening."

With high hopes, we turned in our ballots for the boat competition before our dinner at The Grille Restaurant.

"I hope we win something." Scarlett had put her all into it and she and Wes had created a North Pole wonderland.

"We'll know in a little bit. They'll be announcing in about two hours," Wes explained as we were seated at our table.

"Some people really went all out." I was amazed at the intricacies of what people did.

"Well, I definitely worked up an appetite decorating ours today. That was a load of work." Wes looked at the menu.

"No dessert," I mentioned. "We're going to have it later,

on the boat."

"Buzzkill." My daughter looked at me with a smile.

I turned to Wes, shaking my head, "What happened to my sweet kid? I swear I raised her with better manners than this."

Emerging from the restaurant, sated and relaxed, the temperature had dropped significantly in the past few hours, the night air taking on a seasonal chill under clear, dark skies adding to the ambiance created by the holiday lit boats.

"Wow. That's invigorating." I leaned into Wes for warmth.

Scarlett ran ahead to the information board, to see if the results were posted. "We got an honorable mention!" she called out.

"No kidding," Wes was excited as we read the results. "Pretty darn good for a couple of first-timers, don't you think, Princess?"

"Really good. There were a lot of boats entered and after first, second and third there were only two honorable mentions and we're one of them." She was clearly proud of the award.

"Let's go take a look at the winning boats and see if we can figure out what all the people voting liked," Wes suggested.

"Great idea." Scarlett was all in.

As we went from boat to boat, Wes and Scarlett dissected each one's decorations.

"Okay, here's what I'm seeing." Wes pointed to one of the boats. "All of the winners lit their mast to the top. So, that is a must for next year. And look how good the lighted garland looks wrapped around the rails. So, we're going to need to pick up some of that. I think by adding those lighted effects, we'll have our basics."

"Yeah, I think so, too," she agreed. "And it really does look better that way."

"Well a lot of these people have been doing this a long time. So, I think we really kicked butt for a couple of newbies, Princess."

"Yeah, we were like literally one of the top five." She smiled up at him.

"I'm so proud of you guys. I think The Do-Over looks beautiful," I said, as we climbed on board our winter wonderland themed boat. "I'm going to go make some hot tea for all of us. I'm freezing."

While they stood on deck and talked to passersby about the decorations, I went below, grabbed a sweater and then started to make the tea. Pulling out the plates and utensils, I set the cake in the middle of the table and stood back and smiled. Grabbing some of the ornaments I had purchased earlier, I placed them around the cake plate to give our dessert a festive look.

*Had I really seen that old lady smiling at me today? What had she told me so long ago – that I needed to communicate and forgive to lighten my aura?* Well, I had certainly done that in my relationship with Wes, so I wondered what colors she saw today. Maybe lighter ones and that's why she was smiling at me.

"Hey you two, dessert's ready," I called up to them.

They were still discussing boat decorations as they came down the companionway.

"That cake looks great," Wes commented as I handed him a slice.

"It's Chef Winston's famous Christmas Cake," I explained. "I went to get a Key lime pie, but he convinced me that I needed to get this instead."

"Good choice." Wes was enjoying it.

"Am I legally allowed to eat this?" Scarlett was smiling and shoveling the cake down fast, before I could reconsider and take it away.

"You can eat rum, just not drink it," I assured her as she

reached for a second slice.

"This stuff is killer. They were definitely not stingy with the rum," she commented.

"I think the proper way to make this, which is probably what they did, is to actually bake the cake in the fall and then feed it alcohol like every two weeks, kind of like watering a plant." I had read that in a magazine.

Wes was helping himself to a second slice. "This is amazing, T. Perfect end to a great evening."

"So, why did some of the boats have Bitter End Yacht Club flags?" Scarlett asked.

"From what I understand, if a family comes back for a second year, they get a flag. So, next year we'll have a flag," Wes explained.

"Oh, that's cool. We need to come up with like literally the most badass theme for next year. And then with the lights, we'll totally have a winner."

Sipping my tea, I sat back and listened to the two of them toss around ideas for next year's competition. The irony didn't escape me, that if we were sitting here with Frank, my stress level would be catapulting off the charts, already fearing that whatever plans he was making with Scarlett would never come to pass. And that she would once again be heartbroken and made to feel marginalized. But with Wes, I could just enjoy the excitement and energy at the table, because I knew, with my entire being, that one year from now, we'd be sitting right here and the two of them would be bouncing off the cabin walls celebrating their first, second or third place victory. And that throughout the year, he would be surprising her with accessories he found for their project.

There was no doubt in my mind that Wes Bergman would not be disappointing my little girl.

I knocked on the door to Scarlett's cabin shortly after she went to bed.

"Come in."

"Shove over." I got in next to her. "Well, this has been pretty exciting."

"This trip has been so much fun. I wish we would have won though."

"Oh baby, we did win." I rolled onto my back and fluffed the pillow beneath my head. "We're healthy and happy and on a boat in the Caribbean with one of the greatest guys in the world who cares about the both of us deeply. I think we won big time."

"You know what? I think you're right, Mom." She snuggled closer to me.

I laughed, "Wow, was that your Christmas gift to me? Teenage daughter tells mother she is right."

We both giggled.

"You guys did a really great job, sweetie. Be proud of it, because I'm really proud of you."

Wes was up on deck enjoying the night sky when I emerged from Scarlett's cabin. I took a moment to watch him, enjoying the realization that here we were beneath the Caribbean night sky again, and the man I once thought was the best friend I was meeting for the first time, was, in fact, my best friend, my love and my lover. I let that sink in before grabbing his cable knit sweater and heading up the companionway.

"Hey," I came up behind him, rubbing his back. "Thought you might need this," handing him his sweater.

Leaning down to kiss me. "You take such good care of me."

"I'm glad that you let me." I smiled.

Stepping behind me with his hands on my shoulders, silently, we watched the night sky.

*Tara, take care of my brother.* The very last words Stacy spoke to me flashed through my mind just as the sky lit up, as if synchronized with my thoughts.

"Whoa," Wes grabbed my shoulders tight.

"What was that?" We watched the bright light arc across the sky, leaving a dimly lit trail in its wake, before disappearing into the sea.

"Wow, we have not seen anything like that in the sky before," Wes finally let up on his grip.

"What do you think it was? A shooting star? Meteor?"

"I don't know. I've never seen anything that bright before." He wrapped his arms around me and rested his chin on the top of my head.

Putting my hands over his, I slipped my fingers into his warm palms.

*Tara, take care of my brother.*

*I got this, Stace.*

I got this.

*Jullie A. Richman*

# Authors Note

B reast cancer is an epidemic. I cannot imagine anyone reading these words has not been touched by it – a friend, a family member, you. In the U.S. alone, one in eight women will develop invasive breast cancer in her lifetime. 1 in 8. And the U.S. ranks 9th in world standings, so it is even more prevalent than 1 in 8 in eight other countries. That is just wrong.

Additionally, 85% of breast cancers occur in women that have no family history of the disease. And the two most significant risk factors – two things you can't do shit about – gender and age. So, if you are a woman, getting older (which sucks, but is preferable to the alternative) – you are at risk to develop breast cancer.

As with any cancer, early detection generally has the best outcome. Take care of yourself and get screened. Don't forget your self-exams.

If you have questions, need information or want to aid in the fight, there are many wonderful organizations ready to help you and that always need a helping hand.

American Cancer Society – **http://www.cancer.org/cancer/breastcancer/**

Susan G. Komen – **ww5.komen.org**

These are just two of many fine organizations providing information and support and conducting research.

Wishing you good health and good reading …

Till we meet again…
~Julie

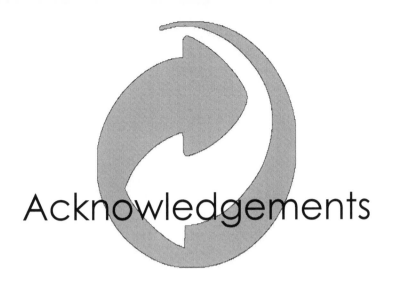

# Acknowledgements

I don't even know where to begin with this. During the writing of The Do-Over, I experienced a health speedbump that I didn't see coming and it totally took me out for several months. When I picked up the half-finished manuscript again, I was absolutely riddled with anxiety that I would no longer be able to pursue my lifelong passion of writing. But when my energy level returned enough, I began adding to my Excel Word Count spreadsheet on a daily basis with decent numbers, and Tara and Wes' story began to share itself once again.

I have a lot to be thankful for and a lot of people to thank.

First and foremost my family, who I put through Hell this year. The lingering effects of this summer surface at turns we don't expect, but I have to believe the worst is already behind us. I just won't accept anything else. Mark, Max and Mom, thank you for everything, every day. Shelly, nice to have you back. I love you.

Mindy, Robin, Eve, Mary, Judy and Linda… Thank you for surrounding me near and far when I needed you most.

Vi and Penelope – You two are my safe place in this

crazy land. Thank you for repositioning me when I jumped the tracks or this manuscript would still be sitting on my computer.

Kristen and Cleida – Always my sunshine. Always my reason to smile. So glad to have you two by my side.

Thank you to Kristin Nelson for believing in my writing, even when it doesn't fit neatly into a box.

To all the Rogue BBCs for the continual support – even when I don't release a book for a year. That group has been my "go-to" place and all of you make it so special. Your cards and notes this past year propelled me to keep swimming hard on days when the riptide was sending up red flags.

Kim Kimball – Thank you for lending your expertise and experience to a subject I wanted to make sure I portrayed correctly – it was important to me to get it right. I appreciate your input tremendously as well as your friendship.

Jena - You outdid yourself with this beautiful cover design. I smile every time I look at it. Thank you!

Deena – Thank you for pulling this all together and getting it ready for readers.

Wander Aguiar, Andrey Bahia and Forrest Harrison – Thank you for this awesome image.

Jennifer Pon – I so appreciate your help in Houston and for making me laugh my ass off. That day made my face hurt and is one of my favorite memories from this past year. You heard a very early rendition of Wes and Tara's story that night.

Donna Salzano – Thank you for your help in Ft. Lauderdale and for your friendship. You are a true gem.

Jenn Watson and Stephanie Ferguson for your help in getting this manuscript out of my hands and into the world.

Denise Tung and Ahren Sanders for checking in on me as much as you both did. Means more to me than you can even imagine.

Trish Kuper for knowing what I needed, when I needed

it.

Michele Sonner - your designs are inspiring and the Cosmos pin was the most perfect gift for Wes to let Tara know he couldn't get her out of his heart. Thank you for allowing me to use it.

**With deep love, appreciation and gratitude to all the readers, bloggers and fellow authors that make it possible for me to do what I love best. I certainly could not be doing this if it wasn't for all of you. I greatly appreciate your support, friendship and love. Thank you for embracing me in this community, reading my stories and sharing them with fellow book lovers.**

Humbly
~Julie

*Jullie A. Richman*

# About Julie

Author Julie A. Richman is a native New Yorker living deep in the heart of Texas. A creative writing major in college, reading and writing fiction has always been a passion. Julie began her corporate career in publishing in NYC and writing played a major role throughout her career as she created and wrote marketing, advertising, direct mail and fundraising materials for Fortune 500 corporations, advertising agencies and non-profit organizations. She is an award winning nature photographer plagued with insatiable wanderlust. Julie and her husband have one son and a white German Shepherd named Juneau.

## Contact Julie

Join the mailing list to find out about upcoming releases and appearances.
http://eepurl.com/RYac1
or

Facebook www.facebook.com/AuthorJulieARichman

or

Twitter @JulieARichman

or

Instagram: AuthorJulieARichman

or

Website www.juliearichman.com

or

Facebook www.facebook.com/AuthorJulieARichman


My website has my signing schedule, links for signed paperbacks, character profiles and more.
www.juliearichman.com

# Books By Julie

## Searching For Moore

I lost the love of my life when she disappeared without even a goodbye.

It was the 80's – there was no internet, no Google, no cell phones.

If you wanted to disappear, you could.

And she did.

She crushed my soul.

A friend just told me he saw her on Facebook.

And now I'm a keystroke away from asking her the question that's haunted me for two decades.

"Why did you leave me?"

Two decades after she broke his heart, sexy entrepreneur Schooner Moore uncovers the truth and betrayal his life has been built on when he Facebook friend requests college love, Mia Silver. Determined to win Mia's love once again, Schooner embarks on a life-altering journey that could cost him everything.

This is the first book of the Needing Moore Series trilogy and is not meant to be read as a stand-alone.

*Jullie A. Richman*

# Moore To Lose

Continuing the fight for their happily ever after that began in Searching for Moore, Schooner Moore and Mia Silver struggle to overcome the ghosts and baggage they accumulated during their time apart.

Exploring the missing 24 years when they were separated, Moore to Lose follows Mia's journey from heartbroken teen to kickass businesswoman to her emotional reunion with Schooner and the exploration of the love that was ripped from them.

But is their love really strong enough to overcome the damage of those missing 24 years or will they continue to be ripped apart by pasts that can't be changed?

# Moore Than Forever

"You have no idea of what you do to me, Baby Girl."

"It's smoochal."

Is the love they always dreamed of enough?

Continuing the emotional journey of love and betrayal that began on a college campus in Searching for Moore and turned their worlds upside down in Moore to Lose, handsome, California entrepreneur Schooner Moore and sharp and sassy, New York advertising agency owner Mia Silver continue to be confronted with the harsh reality of the remnants from the lives they lived apart for 24 years.

Now, Schooner Moore and Mia Silver face the ultimate challenge — were they really meant to be together or will their pasts continue to tear them apart?

On the heels of the birth of their newborn son, Nathaniel, Schooner and Mia must decide if their love and loyalty to one another is strong enough to learn to grow together as a couple or if the life they always dreamed of sharing was better left as a teenage fantasy.

This is the third and final book in the Needing Moore Series and is not meant to be read as a stand alone. Book 1 — Searching for Moore and Book 2 — Moore to Lose should be read prior to reading Moore than Forever.

# Needing Moore Series Box Set

All three Bestselling, Top-Rated Books from The Needing Moore Series by USA Today Bestseller Julie A. Richman, **PLUS** never before seen **BONUS CHAPTERS** for each book.

"I have read well over 125 books since I received my kindle last February (2013). That being said, this first book in this series is the BEST book I have read. I am so sorry to say but it has to be said that E L James, Sylvia Day, etc. have nothing on Julie Richman."

"I loved this story. I could not put it down. Every girl wants a man like Schooner."

"Did I mention how insanely HOT these two are together? Scorching, fanning myself, hot!!"

"I think this is one of the best series out there, Hookers! It is an amazing story, it is full of emotion, and it is real. The relationships are complex and the characters are unpredictable. Julie will wring you out emotionally and leave you craving Moore!"

"I just finished this book and my heart is pounding! I too am a Facebook friend request away from a past love. This book has you hooked from the first pages! I cried, I laughed and I cheered! Such real characters and a love story that every girl dreams of having."

"OMG need "moore" Schooner now!!!!!! … I cannot get enough of this story. Every once in a while a book or series comes out that has me salivating at every word and this fits that bill to the tee!"

"This is just writing at its best. It's so witty and the characters are so well written. I could not put this book down!"

"This series is awesome. It just sucks you in and doesn't let you go."

# Bad Son Rising

People think I'm a douche.
>And maybe I am.
>I use most people.
>It's what I know.
>But if I love you,
>I'd die for you.
>I just don't know that I'm worth loving.

Handsome, privileged bad boy Zac Moore has always played by his own rules - at school, in business, with women. He's rewritten the rules to suit his own needs and his needs are all that matter.

Serious and focused family friend Liliana Castillo has one goal. Leave the pre-Med program at Yale to help people in developing nations.

As their paths cross and uncross, a tale of love, agony, betrayal and growth is woven, transforming two people who've hidden from relationships and love.

This is a stand-alone novel.

# Henry's End

Dreams.
>I used to have them—before the nightmares started.
>I dreamed of nice guys, love...normalcy.

Things like reading the Sunday paper in bed with my lover.

But who needs dreams when your reality is filled with a string of faceless dominating men in uniform? Men that pack a thick bulge and are only too happy to satisfy my deviant sexual cravings.

Me. That's who.

And then HE walked through the door and shared with me, a total stranger, his intimate dream of love. Damn him for verbalizing every single detail of the dream I buried long ago.

And now I don't know how I'm going to live without that dream.

Or him.

# Slave To Love

## IF A MAN HAS AN AFFAIR AT WORK, HE'S A STUD.

He was a royal prick.

The night we met, he ignored me.

Then Mr. Big Shot CEO grabbed my ass in a business meeting.

My boss just loaned me out to this guy.

Now, we're working on a major project together.

And our chemistry is dangerous.

Combustible.

If I allow it to ignite, I'll risk losing that promotion.

Worse, what if I lose myself in him?

## IF A WOMAN HAS AN AFFAIR AT WORK, SHE'S A SLUT.

From the moment I saw her I knew she was trouble.

It was the combination of her fresh face, smart mouth and nipples that seemed to know my name.

This woman could satisfy my needs both in the boardroom and the bedroom.

But there was more to it than that.

I wanted her.

Really wanted her.

And I was in the position to change the course of her life.

But I've got secrets, secrets that could destroy her.
And either make her mine or drive her away forever.

44947868R00177

Made in the USA
San Bernardino, CA
27 January 2017